Daughters of Hunger

DAUGHTERS
OF
HUNGER

by

Frances Sands

CLOVER
PRESS

Copyright © Frances Sands 2008
First published in 2009 by Clover Press
18 Paynes Court, High Street, Buckingham, MK18 1NQ

www.amolibros.com

Distributed by Gardners Books
1 Whittle Drive, Eastbourne, East Sussex, BN23 6QH
Tel: +44(0)1323 521555 | Fax: +44(0)1323 521666

British Library Cataloguing in Publication Data
A catalogue record for this book is available from the British Library

ISBN 978-0-9560924-0-3

Typeset by Amolibros, Milverton, Somerset
This book production has been managed by Amolibros
Printed and bound by T J International Ltd, Padstow, Cornwall, UK

In memory of Sarah and Joseph

Helen

Best

wishes

Frances

MAGGIE

Chapter One

Three days before her ninth birthday Margaret O'Donnell saw God walking on the waters of the lough. After a week of deluge the rain had stopped and a few shafts of sulphurous yellow were pushing their way through the breaks in the clouds. When it was reasonably fine Maggie liked to venture out, putting each time a greater distance between herself and her mother. It was a relief to get away from her nagging questions.

"What are you thinking about?"

"Nothing."

"You're giving nothing a lot of consideration."

She walked quickly and for a time did not notice that the going was getting harder and her feet beginning to squelch in the muddy undergrowth. A frog thrust its head out of the dampness croaking a warning. She paused for a moment, smiled at it and continued on her way. The muddy water had come up over the banks of the lough flooding the surrounding fields and spreading like a great sea concealing familiar landmarks. Not realising the perimeters were obscured, she moved ahead until a downward pull made her stagger. She took a few sucking steps forward and put out a hand to seize a lump of vegetation but it bent limply in her grasp, providing no support. In a flash she realised she was in the lough itself. With each movement she made she was getting more and more out of her depth and further ensnared in a tangle of mud and weeds.

Fear began to rise in her as she looked despairingly around for a way of escape but the cold rippling waste about her suggested no means of salvation. She called out but heard only the lonely sound of her voice echoing and re-echoing as if in mockery. Like a jagged lump of ice, terror scratched its way upwards inside her body. She began to pray, first to her Guardian Angel and then the Hail Mary, but panic got in the way and she could not remember the ending. Devil's Needles skimmed across the surface of the water, flashing blue, gold and red. She thought of the sins she had committed, the lies told to her mother, the sneaking from the classroom to play by the river and the time she stole a handful of aniseed balls from the big glass jar in Kate Black's shop. Only last Sunday she was in trouble with the parish priest for laughing out loud in church. It was at a christening and the baby howled when the baptism water was poured on its head. The little screwed-up face, looking indignant and comic at the same time, was too much for Maggie's self-control.

Leaving home that morning, she had slipped a piece of oatcake into her pocket in case she should feel hungry before she returned. Now she watched as it escaped the confines of her pinafore to float and bob on the choppy waves. A large gull swooped down and scooped it up in its beak. As it rose in the air, Maggie closed her eyes when the cruel talons passed before her face. In despair she prayed again, the act of contrition followed by the Lord's Prayer coming hoarsely from her throat. It was then she saw the figure moving towards her across the water. God had come to rescue her.

"Oh please hurry," she sobbed.

"Stay still," a voice commanded. He was elongated, walking with a stiff gait and making strange swooshing sounds as he approached. She tried to make herself as motionless as the statue of Saint Patrick in the church porch but the waves were now lapping under her chin and her body kept swaying to and fro.

"Take hold of my jacket and don't let go on any account." The voice was authoritative. She heard a sharp screaming coming from the top of a nearby tree and she wondered, was a cuckoo robbing a nest?

"Shut up," God shouted rudely and she realised with a shock that it was herself doing the screaming. She grabbed her saviour's coat and at last found herself being hauled upwards. Clumsily, tortoise slow, they laboured their way out of danger. At the edge of the lough she stood swaying as though she was still in the power of the waves. Then in a wide sweeping gesture, God threw his stilts away and gathered her up in his arms as if she were a hen for the pot.

"What kind of an eejit are you at all? Don't you know the lough is dangerous even when there is no flooding?"

She nodded dumbly, guiltily aware that her mother had forbidden her to go near it.

"You are lucky I was down this way, even luckier that I had my stilts with me." His blue eyes stared down at her sternly. Then, seeing she was just a child, he took her by the hand and steadied her. She tried to think of an appropriate prayer of thanksgiving.

"Thank you, God," she began, her arms outstretched towards him.

"Come on," he laughed. "I'm not God, I'm Paddy O'Neill and I live over there." Her eyes followed his pointing finger to where she could see smoke rising from a chimney.

"We'll soon be home. Who are you anyway?"

"I'm Maggie," she answered and like the time she had screamed, she seemed to have no control over the words that came out of her mouth. She had never used this short version of her name before, nor had she heard it at school or at home. Liking the sound of it, she made up her mind to be Maggie from now on. The decision gave her a tentative awareness of her own identity.

"Maggie, I'm Maggie," she kept repeating in an undertone, astonishing herself with the unfamiliarity of it. They passed the rest of the journey without talking to each other but it was a comfortable silence in spite of her wet clothes and chattering teeth.

Inside Paddy's cottage, an elderly black clad woman was sitting on a stool peeling potatoes and dropping them one by one into a pan of water that sat beside her on the floor. Her hair hung down to her shoulders in a descending grey fog. "Jesus, Mary and Joseph," she exclaimed on seeing them. "In God's name what have you got there?"

"Just a little fish I caught in the lough," he laughed.

Maggie recognised her as a widow who sold vegetables on the outskirts of the town. She rose, twisted her hair into a tight knot on top of her head and stuck a long pin through it to hold it in place. Then she handed a bowl to her son. "Fetch me some water and the lye soap and bring me the old towel hanging on the back of that door. Then get yourself out of here until we've finished. You can clean yourself up in the yard outside."

Paddy grinned and quickly obeyed. His mother gently stripped off Maggie's clothes and washed her body all over with a soft rag, asking no questions. When her task was completed she wrapped her in a clean towel and called out "You can come in now."

Paddy entered. "Are you feeling better, Fish?" he asked.

Maggie nodded dumbly and gratefully accepted the bowl of hot milk the widow handed to her. Pulling out a settle bed from the wall oppose the fireplace, Paddy's mother invited her to lie down while her clothes dried before the fire. Covering her with a blanket, the old woman murmured, "Rest a while now, child. It will do you good to sleep while the heat returns to you bones."

Maggie didn't want to sleep. For a time she lay looking around her. In spite of poverty she could see that there was an air of comfort here that was missing in her own home. The soft rush matting underfoot was warmer than the caked mud in her mother's cabin. Two worn but comfortable armchairs stood, one on each side of the hearth. A dresser held a few brightly coloured mugs and a jug with a big pink tulip on its side. She found she was unable to drag her eyes away from the small flickering light placed in front of a picture of the Sacred Heart which was hypnotic and euphoric at the same time. At last no longer able to stay awake, she fell asleep convinced she had drowned and gone to heaven.

CHAPTER TWO

L ike a small nesting bird, the thought that she belonged
to Paddy O'Neill came to rest in her mind and settled
there. Had he not fished her out of the lough, a useless catch,
but instead of throwing her back into the water decided to
keep her for himself? Now began for her days that were long
and lovely. She though of him constantly, dreaming of the
future they would share. When she had the opportunity, she
would go off in the direction of the widow's cottage,
following the small stream that ran into the lough. In late
summer its banks were scattered with down from the willows
which grew along the side and she would scoop up handfuls
of the soft fleecy stuff and press it to her cheeks. Often, at
first, she would not see Paddy but soon she became
accustomed to his work patterns and learned where to find
him.

"By the hokey," he would greet her, "it's yourself, Fish,"
and he would hand her a light fork, hoe or other tool. She
would smile up at him as they worked away in almost
complete silence. Soon a deep undemanding friendship grew
up between them, of which Cliona knew nothing.

★

Maggie remembered her early years with affection. She thought of the many times she had sat on Cliona's knee and tried to straighten out what she called her 'bendy red hair'. Once when she was confined to bed with some childish illness she watched her mother stitch a rag doll for her after she complained that she was lonely with only Pangur the cat for company. The toy was constructed from scraps of disused material and had two unmatched buttons for eyes. The body was stuffed with straw and the hair consisted of brown curling wool from a pair of worn out, unravelled gloves. A strip of lace from Cliona's best calico petticoat completed the finery. Maggie named it Mena, hugged it to her and covered it with kisses. It was her little sister, she said. At another time Cliona put together an assortment of rags and bits of straw and tied them as securely as she could with string to make a ball. When it became undone she patiently remade it. Maggie loved her mother dearly but as she grew older the respect she had for her diminished. This began when Tim McConville, one of their few friends, let slip that Cliona was unmarried. At first she did not believe him, although all along she had been moidered by the taunts of her classmates. She thought these insults had been engendered by the ragged clothes and the ill-fitting boots in which she shuffled around the classroom like some wounded animal, or the crackle of the brown paper which her mother had placed under her clothes to keep out the cold. She could put up with all this, knowing that Cliona did her best to provide, often going without herself. Most days she managed to ignore the jeers in the playground, but now and then she would retaliate.

"Sticks and stones will break my bones but names will

never hurt me. And when I'm dead and in my grave, you'll suffer for the names you've called me," and she would stare back defiantly at her torturers. All the same 'tatty rag bag' and 'skinny malink malodeon legs, big banana feet' echoed in her ears as she lay down to sleep.

This was all bad enough but the realisation that her mother was capable of deceiving her hurt deeply. In spite of being told about Daddy drowning in a storm at sea, Maggie kept a small hope that somehow it was a mistake. He had escaped to a far-flung island and would turn up again in time. She looked forward to hearing from him that she was his pretty daughter and he was proud of her. Now she was forced to come to terms with the knowledge that she would never see him, not even in a picture. Nor did she want to discover the truth. She despised him, she told herself and Cliona too. She thought bitterly how her mother always insisted that Maggie tell the truth when she herself told lies. Cliona was her best friend and only confidante. She was no longer to be trusted. Maggie felt bereft.

Soon she was finding fault with almost everything her mother said or did. Cliona took any amount of blame as long as her daughter colluded in hiding her shame from the outside world. Maggie too soon learned to conceal things, but this seemed to her to place an unrelenting weight on her shoulders which threatened to crush her. She also resented her mother's expectation that she would become a nurse or a teacher, lifting them out of their poverty. She had no such ambitions although she was tired of wearing rags and being despised by everyone except Paddy O'Neill. She was not like her mother who accepted all that happened without making a protest, saying it was the will of heaven. If Maggie made the slightest complaint about their circumstances, she was told to offer her pain up to God as penance. But Maggie had long ago decided that she did not believe in collecting bonuses for the next world.

One morning she woke to a great stillness. Hurriedly pulling on some clothes, she opened the door and saw that there was a thick carpet of snow covering the ground. Flakes were falling from the sky as though drawn down by a magnet. Pangur darted about, slapping them with a paw and then opening her mouth to catch some as they whirled around her. Maggie wondered if the animal was puzzled by the lack of substance in the thin watery wafers on his tongue. She lifted the cat in her arms and stood staring at the landscape in front of her. It too seemed to have become unsubstantial. Well known landmarks were covered in drifts, making strange humps and hollows she could not easily recognise. The boundaries of the hedges had almost disappeared and a glittering brightness lay over everything. Suddenly she felt lost and a familiar fear that sometimes came to her in nightmares overwhelmed her. It was with relief that she saw her mother coming towards her. Cliona's head was bent against the wind, her tired feet shuffling noiselessly in the snow. Shame filled the watching girl, and, stroking the cat's head, she whispered into its ear a resolve to find a means of escape for both of them some day. A handful of snow rushed through the open door on a gust of wind. When Cliona reached it, she strongly reprimanded her daughter for standing idly by and letting out the little bit of heat that their cabin provided. At her mother's harsh words, Maggie's focus slipped and the pulse of pity she had felt faded away leaving nothing but a dull ache inside her.

CHAPTER THREE

With the passing of the years, Maggie grew tall with a promise of beauty emerging in her face. At school everything was learned by rote, and, as she had a good memory, lessons came easy to her. She was able to answer the questions in the penny catechism without stumbling, knew the times tables and the poetry the children chanted, parrot wise, from behind their desks. The only two subjects in which she took the slightest interest were sewing and poetry. When she took home one of her completed samplers, Cliona, proud of her, commented on the straightness of the seams and the neatness of the stitches. Sometimes when she was with Paddy O'Neill she would astonish him by breaking the silence between them, and chanting a verse by William Allingham.

> "Four ducks on a pond, a grass bank beyond.
> A blue sky in spring with birds on the wing.
> What a little thing to remember for years.
> To remember with tears."

All the same she longed to be able to leave school.

Her only friend, Mary Conlon, had left a year ago and was working in the town's dressmaking establishment. Her appliquéd cotton blouses looked soft as silk and the swish of her taffeta skirt caused heads to turn as she walked up the aisle in church on Sundays. Maggie decided that she too would like to sew fine clothes for herself. Wearing beautiful creations, she could hold her head high and win a name and respect for herself. In the meantime she kept her hopes concealed from her mother and tried to have patience when she related stories from her childhood in the workhouse. Why, Maggie asked herself, could she not forget about the past, it was all so long ago? There were crazy tales, one about a man with frogspawn eyes, and another which recounted conversations with a talking scarecrow. Often she found herself obliged to close her ears and escape to a place inside her head to make up her own stories.

At first Mary Conlon would not agree to try to persuade the supervisor to interview Maggie. The workers she said, were in awe of her and she might be considered too forward. After all she did not want to risk losing her job. Why, she asked her friend, would Cliona not undertake this mission as her mother had on her behalf some months ago? Maggie was forced to admit shamefacedly, that Cliona's abject manner and her ragged appearance could well make such a bad impression that the daughter of such a person would be refused consideration. The pity she felt for her friend after this forced confession finally overcame Mary's timidity and she approached Mrs Moffatt after two girls had left to get married. She carried the news to Maggie at last that she had secured the desired appointment.

Cliona's suspicions were aroused two weeks later when

she came in one evening and found her daughter with each of her elbows cupped in half of a cut lemon. She watched Maggie rub some of the juice on her face and afterwards rinse her hair in what was left. At last she enquired what all the preparations were for, and was pleased when Maggie told her that she wanted to look good the next day as there was prize-giving in school. She thought she might be first in her sewing class and if she was, she would have to stand in front of the whole school. Cliona smiled, nodded her head and proceeded to help her polish her boots and brush her hair until it shone like a blackbird's wing. Then she produced a ribbon which she had been hiding, meant as a present for Christmas. Maggie was touched and was tempted to confide in her mother but then had second thoughts – better to keep the news until she knew the result of her interview with Mrs Moffatt. It was only one more day.

When lessons and the prize-giving were over, Maggie descended to the school basement. Among the dusty pipes, heaps of old exercise books were piled up in a corner and she slipped her sewing prize – a copy of *The Imitation of Christ* that had been donated by the parish priest – deep inside the discarded books. Then stealthily she made her way to the cloakroom which was for teachers' use only. She looked at herself in the cracked mirror that hung over an enamel basin, pinched her cheeks until they glowed and smoothed back a few stray strands of hair. She straightened her stockings and, making sure there was no one about, darted quickly outside. She still had fifteen minutes to go before facing the ordeal of the crucial interview with Mrs Moffatt. Her hands shook and she could hear the beating of her heart. Taking a deep breath, she reminded herself that she was taking the first steps from present limitations, she was breaking free from the chains that her mother had woven around her and she was moving towards new and exciting horizons.

Her timid knock was answered by the superintendent herself who stood looking down with a severe expression at the diminutive creature standing on the doorstep. "What do you want?"

"Please," Maggie stammered, "I have come to see Mrs Moffatt about a job."

The face looking down on her was cold but the grey eyes were not without a spark of warmth. A measuring tape hung about her neck, falling over two brocaded breasts that melded into one broad shelf. She used her cuffs for pin cushions and kept repeatedly pushing the sharp end of one in and out as though she suffered from a nervous tic. This somehow was reassuring and Maggie smiled up at her nervously. There was a long pause before she said, "You must be Miss O'Donnell," and, opening the door, admitted her to a room full of the loud sounds of whirling and clattering machines. She was asked to wait and offered a chair. She sat on the edge of it and found herself shaking, vainly trying to compose herself. She looked around for her friend Mary but she was nowhere to be seen. The girls were silent, bent over their work, unable to talk to each other because of the din created by the machines. Her head began to ache. She found the place deeply dispiriting until her eyes fell on roll after roll of sumptuous material piled against a wall, stacked rainbows of colours; greens, red, blues and golds. Unable to look away she hardly heard her name being called out.

"This way please, Miss O'Donnell."

Mrs Moffatt's eyes ran over Maggie's figure, taking in all the details of her clean but ragged clothes. She was clearly not impressed. However, she set her to sew a fine seam and was forced to admit to herself that it was executed with precision and neatness. With as much tact as she could muster, she explained that she had her reputation to think about and hinted that Maggie's tattered appearance would not enhance the standing of her establishment. When she held out a hand in dismissal the hand placed in it was soft and supple. It would leave no snags in the expensive silks and satins which were handled daily in the sewing room. For a few seconds Maggie stood still, struggling with tears which threatened to spill down her face. Then, straightening her shoulders, she walked towards the door holding her head high. Mrs Moffatt noticed that her figure was trim and her carriage good; dresses could be displayed to advantage on such a figure.

"Wait," she called after her. "We need someone to sweep the floors, pick up pins and do other small jobs around the workshop." She paused: "It wouldn't be much money but if you made yourself useful you might progress to better things." Then severely, "But you would have to dress better. The ladies who come here expect the girls to look not only neat and tidy but also a little bit fashionable."

Maggie nodded, her eyes shining, she heard the magic words, "You can start next Monday," and, fearing Mrs Moffatt might change her mind, she rushed to the door. Outside she ran until she reached home and, darting in, she danced a little hornpipe of triumph.

Cliona wept and implored Maggie to change her mind, but she would not listen. Her mother pointed out once again the many advantages that further education would bring. Her daughter had made her decision and would be glad she said to throw away all of her books.

"You should be grateful," she said, "that I will be starting to earn and contribute to the cost of our food. Not much at first, but it will be a beginning." There was no point, she thought, in explaining to Cliona that the magic transforming garments that she was going to make for both of them was a quicker road to riches than sitting all day in a stuffy old classroom. As usual their arguments ended in stalemate and bitterness, and Maggie was too proud to ask for help in the purchasing of the requisite new dress that was the minimum she needed to satisfy her future employer. She knew that the handleless cup, half hidden in the chimney nook, contained a little money for emergencies and she had no compunction in extracting the contents, promising herself that she would replace them out of her first earnings. She suspected her mother knew of her action but it was not mentioned. A silence grew up between them. Maggie still loved her mother and knew it was reciprocal. But somehow the vehicle for carrying their mutual goodwill had broken down. It stood dumb and motionless and beyond either of their powers to get it started up again.

CHAPTER FOUR

When she thought there was no one looking, Maggie would stroke the sensuous velvets and satins that she promised herself she would wear some day. Mrs Moffatt's eagle eye missed nothing and noticed the girl's love of beautiful things. She was also impressed by her willingness to learn and the diligence with which she performed even the most menial task. It was not long before she was put in charge of the more demanding processes of cutting and finishing. She was given work to do for ladies who were hard to please and learned to be non-critical of their patrons' preferences and foibles. Soon she was in great demand with customers and colleagues alike, the latter grateful for her unstinted help with their less successful efforts.

Now and then pieces of fabric were left over after a garment was finished. These remnants were available to the workers for a few pennies. Maggie amassed a considerable quantity and stored them away from Cliona's curious eyes in her locker in the cloakroom. In spite of her miserable home life, she was able to look back on this time as one of unusual happiness. She enjoyed her work and meeting with colleagues in Mrs Brown's tea shop on their days off, when they giggled and gossiped and admired the invention with which they trimmed their old hats. Her life she felt had a sense of purpose and expectation. As she walked by the river on her way to meet Paddy, she would pause to watch butterflies flitting from shrub to shrub and the long-legged flies hanging poised on the reeds; they too were waiting.

In a short time Maggie was transformed from an insecure girl into a confident young woman, slender and dark eyed. When she gradually became aware of the admiring glances bestowed on her by the young men in church or those she encountered on her way to deliver a completed dress, she developed an easy assurance in her manner with people. Now elegantly clothed, graceful in movement, she was, however, never quite beautiful but eye-catching in a quiet way and this air of modesty remained with her all her life.

After some years, when her apprenticeship was completed, Maggie was given a rise in pay and several privileges hitherto denied to her. She was allowed to remain in the workshop after hours and use the machines to sew for herself. She stitched curtains and coverings for her home, thereby gaining the merest nod of approval from her mother. Undaunted, she sewed a dress for her in fine blue silk, trimmed the waist with navy and put tiny pin tucks down the front from shoulder to waist. She caught the sleeves in a wide cuff and edged them with cream lace. She gave the merest hint that it would be suitable for a wedding. She watched her mother's face anxiously and noted that at first it shone with pleasure. The fitting, Cliona said was just perfect and it was beautifully made throughout. She stroked it lovingly before taking it off, declaring that is was far too grand for her to be seen in.

"What would people say," she exclaimed. "And anyhow I wouldn't be comfortable wearing such finery." She covered it carefully with an old sheet and hung it out of sight.

Maggie tried again with something less ambitious, a black taffeta skirt and a long-sleeved green silk blouse without any ornamentation. She said the colour of the top would compliment her mother's auburn hair, which as yet had only a few grey streaks in it. Cliona refused to be flattered and, having admired her daughter's hard work, stowed them away with the dress, hanging the garments at the back of the bedroom door. Meanwhile she continued to wear her shabby old bombazine skirt. Maggie hid her disappointment and continued to sew during her lunch breaks. She made several shirts for Paddy which he wore with pride to mass on Sundays, and now and then she stitched a few delicate undergarments for herself with picot edging and feather stitching around the hems.

One summer evening, when the midges were gathering by the water's edge, Maggie and Paddy had their first quarrel. They had been strolling arm in arm by the river and Maggie began to tell her companion how Tim McConville, in Cliona's presence, kept referring obliquely to their meetings. He chanted, Maggie said, silly little ditties like the one they used to keep time to when they were skipping as children.

"Jump to the east, jump to the west, tell me the name of the one you love best," and he would tease, "Go on, Maggie, tell us, tell us."

She could see that her mother was not amused by her frown and the tightening of her lips.

"Well," Paddy observed, "it's not really funny when you think about it. Why don't you just tell her we are walking out?"

"Why should I? She doesn't tell me any of her secrets."

"Even so she must guess and I'm sure she is hurt when you keep things from her."

At first Maggie refused to listen, tossing her head and informing him that, as far as her mother was concerned, she was the best one to judge what should be said or left unsaid. Paddy would not accept her arguments and she strode off home without saying goodbye to him. Next day, however, having thought it over she went to their usual meeting place and finding him waiting there, reluctantly agreed they should take her mother into their confidence. He would have to come to their place for tea some Sunday and tell Cliona himself.

A few weeks later Paddy came to visit and nervously informed Cliona that he loved her daughter and wanted to marry her. There was a stony silence and then he was informed that Maggie was too young to know her own mind. Maggie protested, saying that she had been meeting Paddy for several years.

Stung, Cliona retaliated, "And of course this was all going on behind my back. You see," turning to Paddy, "she is not to be trusted. Someone who would keep secrets from her own mother is dishonest. I think you should be warned."

"You're a one to talk..." Maggie burst out but stopped when Paddy gave her a warning look. They drank their tea quickly and in silence and as the visitor got up to go he offered, "My mother died in the spring, God rest her. We hoped you would agree to come and live with us on the farm."

When Cliona shook her head firmly, Maggie burst out again impatiently, "Would you not like to leave this miserable hovel with its mud floors, damp walls and draughts that nearly blow the fire out on a stormy night?"

Her mother straightened up and answered quietly, "It was the best I could do for us, daughter, and, besides, I have always treasured my independence. I am not yet ready to give that up in spite of the comforts you offer me."

Paddy said he was sorry he had upset her and trusted in time she would change her mind. He held out a hand but she turned away from him and began to tidy up the tea things.

Tight-lipped, Cliona later pointed out to Maggie that Paddy's mother had sold their vegetables at high prices to even the poorest of the local women and never gave credit in any circumstances.

Have you considered that he might be just as tight-fisted as she was?"

Maggie denied this slur on the dead woman's character, although she suspected there could be some truth in it.

"He will change when he is married. I'll see to that."

For several days they continued to argue until nothing could be added to either of their persuasions and from then onwards Maggie went silently on her angry way while Cliona learned to keep her own council.

CHAPTER FIVE

Maggie spent many happy hours with Mary Conlon in the workshop during lunch breaks. They cut out a wedding dress from patterns made from silver paper. They basted, sewed, trimmed and stitched together the pieces of precious silk with the greatest care. A bench was used as a turntable, Mary ordering her friend to gyrate slowly, lift her arms, stand still, stop laughing. When they contorted their lips in an effort to stop, pins fell from their mouths in showers, where they had been held for convenience. Maggie could not be persuaded to wear a crinoline which Mary thought would look romantic. The bride-to-be preferred, she said, the new bustle style but in a modified form, to allow her to climb the church steps in a measure of comfort. She found it difficult to curb Mary's exuberant taste when it came to the making of the bridesmaid's frock, which ended up more lavishly decorated than the bride's, a pink concoction of lace, frills and flounces. Maggie insisted on tacking loose removable pleats to the bottom of both dresses, to act as fenders against rain and mud. She purchased a fur tippet for each of them, made of rabbit, to wear against the cold, and warned Mary that if the day turned out to be wet they would have to cover up their finery on their way to church with their old surtouts. Mary protested, saying that they should be showing off the results of their hard work instead of hiding it, and was only placated when Maggie assured her they would be able to discard their outer coverings in the church porch. She decorated the hats herself, her own with small flowers covering the brim and Mary's less ostentatiously with a feather which swept down one side of her face.

As Maggie was spending most of her free time away from home, she guessed that her mother would realise she was making wedding plans. Guilt assailed her now and then when she looked at Cliona's set face. She relented enough to ask her to put on the new clothes that hung in readiness behind the bedroom door, and accompany her to the church, but Cliona shook her head stubbornly and went on with the ironing of a pile of dry washing that lay on a heap on the table. Maggie did not try again. She pushed her anger deep inside her, determined to press on with her own life.

On a cold January morning she rose early, and, before her mother was awake, drank a cup of hot milk, left a note to say that she would not be returning that evening and giving the reasons for the break in her routine. Paddy was waiting for her at the end of the lane and they drove off in his pony and trap to the church where Mary was waiting with Tim McConville, their only witnesses. When the short ceremony was over, the bride and bridesmaid, glorying in winter sunshine, walked the few steps to the dressmakers to show themselves off to the girls and Mrs Moffatt, while the groom and his best man waited outside. Maggie was presented with a half dozen silver spoons and a bunch of flowers, the first bouquet she had ever received. Amid shouts of "good luck" and showers of rice, the wedding party set off to the nearest town of Newry. There they had a festive meal of baked ham followed by apple dumplings and Tim and Mary toasted the couple with schooners of sherry.

It was late afternoon when they reached Paddy's cottage. Maggie looked around remembering the first time she had been here. She could see no change from the way she had pictured it and she was drawn immediately to the small winking candle burning before the Sacred Heart. Carefully arranging her flowers in a container, she placed them nearby. Paddy kissed her lightly, removed his good clothes and donned a pair of working trousers and his worn-out boots. Then saying he would not be long, he hurried outside to lock up the hens for the night. While he was away, Maggie slowly removed her hat and wedding dress, hanging both up carefully, while wondering if she would ever have the opportunity to wear them again. Then she knelt before the votive candle and prayed that she would learn to become a better wife than she had been a daughter.

CHAPTER SIX

It was not long until Maggie learned that Paddy's few rented acres were just not viable. He was forced into taking back-breaking jobs on the roads in the winter months to make ends meet. In spite of the most stringent economies, she knew that unless she discovered some means of earning herself, they would never have the standards of comfort to which she had begun to aspire. One day she removed most of the artificial flowers from her wedding hat, donned her best dress and set off for town while Paddy was sowing the seed potatoes in a field some distance from the house. When she arrived at Mrs Moffatt's domain, she hesitated, fixed her hat at a jaunty angle and holding her head high, walked in unannounced. She was welcomed by her former employer and treated to tea in the parlour. After many compliments were paid to her appearance and to her past contribution to the workshop, Maggie felt confident enough to ask if there were any vacancies? Mrs Moffatt informed her that several of the customers had made enquiries as to where she could be found. It was clear that her former employer was enough of a business woman to realise that custom would be lost if the new Mrs O'Neil took it into her head to work privately.

She said 'yes' but with the condition that she would accept a lower wage than that she had previously earned. Shortly after they had reached this agreement, Maggie was able to inform her delighted friend Mary that she would join her again in two weeks time. Although he expected his wife to help with most of the jobs on the farm, Paddy was against the idea of her going outside the home to work. He had, however, already learned that she was a woman not easily persuaded against something on which she had set her mind.

Each morning Maggie rose early, drank a cup of tea and went outside to collect the eggs. Then she fed the chickens and released them from the hen house. Indoors she brushed the floor, shook out the mats and prepared the porridge for Paddy's breakfast. If it was wet she put rubber galoshes over boots and pinned a fender to the bottom of her skirt. Her morning's work accomplished, she set off to walk the two miles to town. At first she found it difficult to adjust but before long she was enjoying the walk, especially on fine mornings. She saw the blossom on the wild plum in the hedgerow, snow white at first and then darkening to deepest crimson. The cows, released from their winter quarters in Nesbitts' sheds, came running down the pasture to meet her, galloping wildly until there was only the hedge between herself and the animals. They mooed softly in greeting and seemed to expect an answer, following her through the fields until they reached the entrance. Here they waited until she manoeuvred the stepping stone to avoid mud and manure. At the gate she would put an arm through the bars and let the calves such her fingers, laughing at the sensation of their rough tickling tongues. Then wiping her hands on the rough grass by the roadside, she would resume her journey.

In autumn, when the workmen were cutting the hay the smell of it, new mown, came to her carried on the wind. She grew familiar with each tree she passed and gave some of them a special greeting, an oak or an ash here and there, smiling and nodding in their direction as if they were her friends, a sentiment she sometimes convinced herself they returned.

It was easy to fit in to the old routine in the sewing shop and soon she was enjoying once again the sense of importance both the employment and the wages brought to her. She no longer socialised with her friends on her day off, finding that washing, ironing, cleaning and cooking all had to be caught up with, leaving no time for frivolity as she now thought of her former pursuits. She saved her wages, putting them into an account of her own and Paddy never enquired how much it contained.

It was with mixed feelings she found, after a little over two years of marriage, that she was to have a child. The prospect delighted her in one way but she knew she would have to give up her dressmaking. For some time she was able to conceal the pregnancy but Mrs Moffatt called her aside one day and told her that the sight of her protruding belly had been noticed by one or two of their best paying customers. It offended their sensibilities when they came to the workshop for fittings she said. Mrs Moffatt would be sorry to lose her and gave her an extra bonus in her last pay packet.

After this setback, having made numerous small garments for the coming child, Maggie looked around for another occupation that would increase her savings. The only things that was available to her was hemstitching. The local linen shops received bundles of handkerchiefs, table and bed linen from the manufacturers with the ends unfinished. These were completed by women in their own homes. The job was poorly paid, monotonous and hard on the eyes. Worst of all it had a deadline which was not always easy to meet. If the sewing was not neat enough or any of the other conditions remained unfulfilled, payment was withheld. She threw herself into this project for a while before realising it was not worth the labour she was putting into it. Then she persuaded Paddy to buy ducks and geese, selling their eggs at better prices than those produced by the hens. She fattened turkeys for Christmas and they were almost swamped by the demand. She started to grow unusual vegetables; chard, spinach and different varieties of broccoli. More and more customers found their way to the holding in search of these specialities. Her workload grew and with it her savings, but still she dreamed of even bigger profit-making ventures.

CHAPTER SEVEN

Their first child Johnnie was born two and a half years after the O'Neills were married. It was an easy birth and Maggie felt well enough to enjoy her first weeks of motherhood. When she touched his little hand he grasped her finger, his gaze widening and an expectant look came into his eyes. She loved his total dependence on her as he sucked greedily at her breasts. Paddy was as much delighted with her as he was with his son. He said little but came in one day with a tiny white kitten which he produced from under his jacket, exclaiming delightedly, "Pangur Two." She smiled as she heard him singing to himself as he went about his tasks. Because of Paddy O'Neill and the son he had given her, she now felt she was secure, more real, her existence grounded in the new life they had made for themselves.

At the same time her pleasure was tinged with guilt. When Mary Conlon came to see her, accompanied by her young brother, Maggie dispatched the lad to her mother with a message announcing the birth of her grandson but did not invite her to visit. When Paddy offered to fetch her she made excuses, saying she would like to wait until she felt a little stronger or when the baby was able to sit up and smile at his grandmother.

"Maybe," she murmured, "when the weather gets a little warmer …"

But spring came and went and the summer too without Cliona having made the acquaintance of her grandson. At last Paddy stopped pressing her on the issue.

Six months later she was pregnant again, but this did not stop her from a frantic round of activities. She rushed from one task to another and refused to listen to her husband's pleas to take things a bit easier. At night the two of them fell into bed exhausted.

It was a time of greatly escalating political discontent which had spread even as far as their remote farm. Maggie tended to think that the stories she heard from the customers who visited them were greatly exaggerated. She slept soundly and was oblivious to the strange shouts and marching feet that could be heard sometimes in the night. At last the time came for Paddy to be dispatched to fetch the midwife and as Maggie waited for his return she became aware of disturbing noises in the darkness. She put out her own candle and the one she had lit in the front window to guide her husband and tried to remain calm. The voices grew louder. There was screaming and she was unable to tell if it was human or animal. Her pains were worsening all the time. When unmistakeable shots were fired Maggie shook with fear. Johnnie woke and began to cry. She hugged him tightly to her but he sensed her fear and sobbed uncontrollably. She had no way of knowing what was happening and dared not look outside. She was trying to console herself with the thought that nobody would want to harm a child and its mother, when there was a shattering of glass and the window panes in the bedroom scattered in small sharp slivers over the bed where she lay. Frantically grabbing Johnnie, she cleared a safe passage for them to creep across the room, her hands now cut and bleeding. With her remaining strength she pushed the baby's cot across the doorway and crouched beside it, Johnnie howling loudly in her arms. Her labour pains were coming faster, more strongly now, and she willed herself to keep from falling into blissful oblivion.

Paddy told her later that he had found his way into the town barred by an angry mob that had earlier maimed cattle on an unpopular landlord's estate. Unable to get through, he was forced to make a detour. When at last he reached the midwife's house, she was too scared to open the door but was finally persuaded to speak to him through an upstairs window. No pleading on his part could coax her to venture out among the rioters. The best she could do for him she said was to instruct him in the help his wife would need. Having done this, she closed the windows and disappeared inside.

When he got home Paddy found Maggie cowering in a corner plucking at her nightdress, babbling incoherently and enduring blazing assaults of pain. Johnnie was asleep on the floor with his thumb in his mouth. Paddy could see that his face was streaked with tears and his little hands and legs caked in blood from the shards of glass that were scattered over the floor. Taking the boy into the kitchen he assured himself that the scratches were superficial before giving the child a cup of hot milk and a piece of toffee to suck before putting him to sleep on the settle bed. Meantime he used a little of the water he had boiled to make raspberry leaf tea, as instructed by the midwife. In the shortest possible time he was at his wife's side again. While she was sipping the drink he shook all the bedding free from broken glass, covered the mattress with layers of brown paper and a clean sheet. Then he lifted Maggie on top. While she dozed between contractions he swept the debris from the floor and when she was awake encouraged her to push until the baby's head appeared. At last he washed and dressed his daughter in clothes once worn by Johnnie.

Maggie was amazed when she thought later of how her usually clumsy husband had coped so competently, cutting the umbilical cord and slapping the child until she took her first breath. She could not bring herself to ask where he had deposited the afterbirth and he never revealed its whereabouts. He had saved her life for a second time. Her admiration for him grew to a deep loving gratitude that remained with her for the rest of her life.

CHAPTER EIGHT

Occasionally Paddy took time off work to be with Maggie after the difficult birth of their daughter, which had left the mother so weak that her legs felt like sticks of rhubarb. As she rested in bed in the afternoons her mind went over the traumatic events of that night. She asked Paddy to explain the cause of all the trouble that was sweeping the country but he was at first reluctant to talk, saying she should not bother her head about such things. But his wife quietly persisted and at last he told her that a new movement had started called the Land League. Its inspiration came from a man called Michael Davitt. Davitt realised the problems of the country centred around the question of land and its ownership.

"You mean," Maggie said, "the absentee landlords?"

"Yes, as you probably know most of these are simply not interested in anything but the collection of their rents. They leave things in the hands of agents who have no pity on anyone who is unable to pay. In a bad season when the crops fail the tenants who are unable to meet the demands of the agent are liable to be evicted. You see, an owner has to pay a tax for each hovel on his land so it is more profitable to clear these people out and pull down their homes. Animals are more valuable and the fewer the tenants the larger area there is for pasture."

"But Paddy, surely all that is no reason for the killing that is going on?"

Paddy was silent for some time and when he spoke it was slowly and carefully, "Having nothing to lose, they turn to violence because they can see no other way."

"But don't you think life is more important than land?"

"I do indeed and in any case violence only breeds more violence."

"I still don't understand why anyone should want to break our windows. We have nothing to do with all of this."

For a while Paddy was silent. "No, but when men have had too much to drink they sometimes want to destroy anything they see in front of them. Breaking our window was not intended as an insult to us."

A little later when she thought of this conversation she said to her husband, "I still don't understand why there is so much bloodshed. I know there are people who are poor and sometimes hungry but surely no one now dies as they did before in the famine? And nobody rebelled then."

"True enough. In those days they had neither the energy nor the leadership. Now the league is trying to make people aware of the reasons they are downtrodden and to convince them things can be changed."

"The whole country seems to be exploding, it's frightening."

"Yes and the boycott sometimes creates trouble when some folks are coerced into leaving their jobs."

"Boycott?"

"Yes. The league decides that if a person continues to work for an unjust landlord, for instance one who demands a rent that is set too high or one who evicts a tenant without good reason, then anyone who remains in his employ will be shunned in his community. No one will communicate with him or any member of his family or sell him anything. This is a hard punishment for people who are as dependent on each other as we are in this country, not only for buying and selling but for the sort of friendship that provides help in times of stress."

Maggie's face cleared. "Ah so that's why Minnie McCann came to me crying the other day, asking if I could give her some work to do. I suppose she got the sack from her kitchen job in the Manor. Poor Minnie. I can't see how all this is doing anything but add to her sufferings."

"Well some small victories have come out of it. There are now fewer evictions and some rents have been reduced. Since the politician Charles Stewart Parnell took up the cause and is arguing for it in parliament, there has been a great deal of public sympathy for the Irish. In fact Gladstone is promising reforms. But enough, you must not bother your head about such things, Maggie, politics is for men."

However, Maggie found that she had begun to be deeply bothered about such things. When she looked at her two sleeping children she wondered what was in store for them? Prosperity she could see, lay in the land. Now and then she asked Paddy had he heard any news when he came home from town and one day he informed her that exciting things were afoot. Mr Gladstone was as good as his word. His response to the agitation was to pass a major Land Act.

"It comes into effect," Paddy reported, "in 1881. That's

only a year away. What's more he is promising further reforms."

She asked Paddy to buy the *Belfast Telegraph* when he was in town in future so that they could have first-hand information about events. Soon they read that several more acts had been passed, called collectively the 'Three Fs', namely, fixity of tenure, free rent and fair sale. At last Maggie began to hope that hunger, to which she had been no stranger in her childhood, might become a thing of the past in her country.

CHAPTER NINE

Maggie stood one mild evening looking out of the cottage door. Earlier in the year she had watched the crows carrying twigs and sticks to use for building their nests in the tall trees that grew behind the farmyard. Listening to the creek of their wings as they returned homewards before dark, she wondered if they were as content as their calm passage seemed to imply. There was still a great deal of unrest in the country, and, without being aware of it, this had begun to affect her, spreading like damp through her bones. She looked around her and realised she had left the interior of her home almost untouched since Paddy had brought her here as a bride, apart from one or two small items – the clock given to her as a wedding present by Mary Conlon and a few odds and ends she had taken from Cliona's hovel.

The window panes that had been broken on the night of Sheila's birth were still unattended to, covered over as a temporary measure with thick brown paper. Now she looked at it with distaste and decided she would dissuade Paddy from merely replacing it as he intended and instead get him to install a greatly enlarged window. This would give more light in the living room and an extensive view over the fields. New chintz curtains, decent coverings on the floor and a couple of new chairs would brighten up the place. When she was a little stronger she decided she would get these improvements under way.

For the next two years, life for Maggie passed fairly uneventfully. Then Paddy was given a tip that the estate adjoining their five rented acres was to be broken up and sold in lots. The owner had long since forsaken the 'big house' – it stood roofless with parts of its walls removed, the stones carried away to build outhouses for cattle or to make improvements to existing dwellings. Maggie woke up to the fact that as a result of the recent reforms, natives were permitted to buy land at reasonable prices. Why should she not manipulate these changes to her family's advantage? If they could manage to buy their own and even a few of the acres next to them, the investment would make their smallholding viable. Access would not be a problem after the removal of one or two hedges. There was plenty of water from the small stream at the bottom of the field they called 'the cloughans' which drained into the lough a little over a mile away.

Maggie had no difficulty in persuading her husband to make a bid after he confirmed that the government would sponsor a loan. With this and Maggie's savings, they succeeded in securing a deal. To repay their debts Paddy had to work harder than ever but soon they had the satisfaction of knowing that the neglected land was productive again. Until this time Maggie had been like her mother, servile when she considered she was in the company of her superiors. Now she saw herself as one of the up and coming landowning families, and she assumed little airs and graces that she thought would help her on the ladder to success.

People could see that the O'Neill family was prospering. Maggie continued to sew shirts for her husband and son and dresses for herself and Sheila. She turned cuffs and collars, lengthened hems and skilfully patched and mended. When the next child Susan was born, Maggie found time to crochet a delicate lace shawl which she draped round the infant on Sundays and special occasions. When they took their places at mass – women to the left, men to the right side of the aisle – she would look across at Paddy and Johnnie and admire her handiwork. They were handsome, a credit to her care and management. She came to believe that there was no such thing as fate, just a correct way of doing things in order to impose a pattern on life. Nobody would ever hear her say, "There's nothing to be done about it."

At home the cream was skimmed from the milk and sold. There was meat on the table on Sundays only; usually one of the scrawniest chickens. Potatoes and other vegetables, oatmeal and buttermilk and occasionally soup from a bone from the butcher constituted their staple diet. No crumb of food was ever wasted. Clothes were adjusted and carefully mended before being handed down from one little one to the next. In the home no idleness was allowed, even the youngest was given a daily light task. The older girls were expected to look after the babies. Johnnie helped to feed the animals which they could now afford, and his father had already begun to teach him the ways of farming.

CHAPTER TEN

When he was a boy of six, Johnnie came into the kitchen one day carrying a rusty old pistol. His father, cap resting on one knee, sat eating his midday meal. When he saw the weapon, his face grew distorted, and, jumping up from the table, he grabbed the gun from the boy's hand, cursing with a loud explosive anger. Maggie was so astonished at this outburst from her usually mild-mannered husband that she dropped the can of buttermilk she was holding, spilling the contents over the floor.

"You must learn to leave things where they are," he bellowed, "and not go bringing trouble into this house."

He aimed a blow at his son who staggered back against his mother and began to cry. Maggie put a protecting arm around the child and for a moment she thought Daddy would do them both a mischief as he stood glowering threateningly above them. After a minute he drew a deep breath that sounded like a sob, lowered his arm and ran out of the house. She was perplexed. The old pistol was eroded and did not give the impression that it could inflict much danger. Johnnie told her he had found it in the hay shed. He had gone there to look for Pangur whom he had not seen all day. When he heard a twittering above his head, he climbed up to find out if there might be a nest of scaldies in the straw. Some of it fell down leaving the gun exposed. He thought there would be no harm, he said, in showing it to his father. Maggie calmed the child, gave him a sweet to suck and set him to help Sheila peel the potatoes for the evening meal. Outside she called for a long time and, getting no reply from Paddy, returned to the house and began her usual task of making the butter, turning the handle of the churn round and round in a continual monotonous movement until the milk and cream separated and formed into globules of butter, floating free.

It was nearly midnight when Paddy returned. Maggie was waiting up for him in front of a good fire and with a bowl of hot soup in readiness. She asked no questions and it was not until they were in bed that he began to talk. He told her he started walking, not caring where his feet carried him.

"I crossed the fields," he said, "and suddenly heard myself naming them as I went, the Clougans, Curlew's Rest, the Field of the Gaberloonie and the Giant's Grave. I was out of breath and sat down for a little on the flat stone that tops the grave. Looking around, I began to think how much these places meant to my forefathers who had personalised each patch of earth and tilled it so carefully to feed their families. At last I got up and when I reached the lough I pulled the gun out of my pocket and flung it as far out into the water as I could."

He stopped speaking for some minutes and then carried on.

"For a long time I just sat there on the bank, my mind blank, until at last the sound of the waves lapping on the stones came to my ears and I grew a bit more calm." He paused again. "Then a kingfisher swooped down just a few yards from me on the bank and rose in the air again with a field mouse clutched in its talons. I watched as it let the animal fall and the creature almost escaped, ducking behind some branches. But the bird, with great ferocity, scrabbled and scratched around the hiding place and eventually rose again into the air with the mouse held, tightly this time, in its cruel claws." Paddy sounded puzzled. "I don't know why, but I was reminded of the day long ago when I witnessed a similar scene, the prey being a fish and the predator a heron. I had fled to this same spot to escape a scene between my mother and my brother Johnnie. She had found him cleaning a gun and he refused to tell her where he acquired it and he would not hand it over to her. She appealed to me to plead with my brother, but I had had enough. I loved them both but could never get used to the way I was expected to take sides in their quarrels. So I simply walked out, deciding to let them get on with their bickering, and sat for a long time by the edge of the lough."

He drew a hand over his eyes and sighed.

"When I got back to the house, I found that Johnnie had left home without saying goodbye to me. He never returned."

For a while she thought he had fallen asleep but he began again.

"You see Maggie, we had a great sorrow in our family when I was seven years old and my brother just two years older than that. My father died mysteriously, coming home from work just at the edge of dark. He was driving the horse up the lane when someone shot him in the back. The horse bolted and galloped up to the door, standing there patiently until Johnnie went out to see why our father was not coming into the house. Poor Johnnie found Daddy lying dead in the cart, blood flowing from his wound and trickling onto the horse's tail. You can imagine the shock it was. My brother never got over it."

Maggie made no comment and Paddy went on.

"Although enquiries were made by the police, no one ever discovered who the murderer was or why this dreadful thing had happened. It was at a time when there was great rivalry for land and many secret societies grew up, all of them sectarian. My mother always believed that someone from a subversive group mistook my father for a member of a rival set-up. Someone around here, you know how people gossip, spread the rumour that he was active in one of these."

"Did you never find out?"

"No, never. My mother maintained that he was not associated with any secret society. She insisted she could not fail to know. He worked all the daylight hours that God gave him and only left home to go to market or attend mass on Sundays. According to her, he spent the dark winter months when there was no outside work to be done, sitting by the fire with herself and their two children. I have no reason to disbelieve her." He was silent for a few minutes. "No one was ever charged with the offence but it had a very bad effect on our whole family."

Maggie reached up and took one of his hands in hers.

"Why didn't you tell me all this before?"

"Ach Maggie—" he turned towards her "—it happened before you were born, and anyway I thought you would never guess that such wickedness existed, as you and Cliona lived in great privacy. Anyway the end result was that Johnnie took to the drink, and when he was less than sober he would vow, wildly, that he was going to find the murderer and bring him to justice. He was warned that this kind of talk would only get him into trouble but he didn't listen to any of us. He rowed constantly with my mother until the day he went away. Down there at the lough I realised that the peace I thought I had found was more fragile than I supposed. I learned that my old fears could still haunt me and remained barely hidden below the surface of my mind. My thoughts, as you have guessed, no doubt, were in turmoil, and I walked to and fro for hours. I came at last to sit by the edge of the lough, and then I saw your face in the water; your dark hair floating like seaweed and your great eyes full of trust, just as you looked that day I pulled you out when you were a child."

He turned to her and for a long time she held him in her arms. At last he said, "I sat back listening to the night sounds all around me; the hoot of an owl, the barking of a prowling fox. I stretched up a hand to pull down my cap in order to protect my eyes from the biting midges that were swarming around me. To my amazement my head was bare. It was time to go home."

She thought he would go to sleep now he was so still, but he murmured quietly, "There is so much hatred in our country, Maggie. I have often wondered if it would not be better to leave altogether. I hope our children will not grow up with such bitterness in their hearts. And you," he continued, "must take things a bit easier. You push yourself too hard."

"Nonsense," she replied, but she knew that he too pushed himself hard until his body was often one great ache from physical fatigue. She understood too, that it was an ache which found release only in her body.

"When the children are a bit older we can both take it a bit easier."

CHAPTER ELEVEN

From behind the fence Paddy was mending, Maggie and he watched the figure trudging up the lane. This was not, they decided, one of their usual customers coming for vegetables or eggs but nevertheless there was something familiar about his gait. Paddy was the first to recognise him and throwing down his billhook he went to meet him, hand outstretched.

"Is it yourself, man?" Maggie heard her husband's greeting, his voice was warm and welcoming. "The wife will be glad to see you."

Maggie thought that Tim McConville, though looking older, was better dressed than she remembered him, sporting now a silver watch chain stretched across his chest. "It's right welcome you are," she hailed him, "but you took your time about coming to see us."

Paddy returned to his hedging and Maggie escorted the visitor into the house. At the sound of an unfamiliar voice the baby woke up and began to cry.

"Wait till I get this one settled again and I'll put the kettle on," she said. "Just give me a minute. And sit here," indicating the most comfortable chair.

Tim picked up the youngster who was crawling around the floor and set the child on his knee.

"How many have you now?"

"Five. Two girls and three boys and another on the way."

"You're not letting the grass grow under you feet. You always said you wanted a big family."

When the infant was settled, Maggie laid him in a cot near the fire and went to the kitchen to make tea. While waiting for the kettle to boil she made guesses as to why he had come. She had not seen him since her wedding day. The visit must surely have something to do with her mother.

She returned to the living room with the teapot and a plate of broken biscuits and while they were eating the talk turned to old times. The 'do you remembers' had them both laughing, in spite of the fact that Maggie felt an unacknowledged tension between them. Impatient for news of her mother, she found it impossible to ask outright and began to build up a resentment against Tim. Why, she asked herself, does he not speak of her? He must know how I long for news. Has she sent him? Tim was struggling, and so was she, to keep a conversation going. The strain between them was palpable. At last the talk dwindled to a silence. Maggie handed one of the boys a piece of biscuit, bending over him as though he might have difficulty in finding his mouth.

"Go outside and find your daddy," she said harshly. "Tell him he should come in and talk to Tim."

As the child ran out, she turned abruptly to her visitor and asked in a strained voice, "Have you seen my mother lately?"

"Yes," he answered slowly.

"And how is she?"

"She is as well as can be expected, I suppose. But I think I should tell you that in my opinion she is getting very frail. Her hands and feet are crooked and she is in much pain with rheumatics. I think all that standing with her hands in water and the dampness in her home has caused most of it. She can't walk far now and pays a youngster from town to pick up and deliver the clothes that she launders."

He paused, and then, looking straight at Maggie, continued, "I think life has become hard for her and she might not be able to go on much longer."

Noticing the look of alarm on Maggie's face, he added, "Of course I may be wrong. The last time I saw her, about two weeks ago, she told me she was feeling grand. But your mother was never one to complain."

Maggie stood up abruptly and gathering the tea things together, went into the kitchen where she rinsed them with a great deal of unnecessary clatter. She opened the window and called out impatiently, "Paddy, are you not coming in to have a word with Tim?"

The conversation became general again. Paddy asked if Tim liked living in such a big town after being used to the country. In a slightly superior tone Tim informed them that Belfast was no longer a town. It had been granted city status in 1888. It was now a busy place with lots of employment. There were ropeworks, soapworks, linen making and, of course, the shipyard which was expanding to build two new great sister ships, ocean liners. Wealthy merchants had grand houses with large gardens on the outskirts of the city and it was in these he was employed. It was open air work and suited him, he said. Maggie listened eagerly, putting thoughts of her mother temporarily out of her mind. She would store away Tim's information. Her family was doing well she thought, but all the same the farm would not provide all of her sons with a living. Some of them would have to leave and earn their bread elsewhere.

Maggie's cure for anxiety was violent action. After the news of her mother's decline, she threw herself into extra work and expected those around her to do the same. Her husband did not guess the plans she was tossing around in her head until one night as they were getting ready for bed she said, "Paddy, would you be able to fix up that old building on our new land? After all, it was a home once. It shouldn't take much improvement to make it more comfortable than Cliona's place."

"I suppose we could do something about it, Fish. Are you thinking of asking her to live over here?"

"I wouldn't want her in the house with us, but it would be nice to know that she was near so that I could go to her if she needed me."

"It would indeed. It would take a bit of time to put on a new thatch and patch up the walls here and there, but I'm sure we could do it. Johnnie is big enough to give me a hand to fetch and carry. We can make a start when the spring sowing is finished."

Maggie knew he was pleased that she was softening in her attitude towards her mother. He had often hinted that he would like to visit Cliona himself but she had never encouraged him. Tentatively he asked, "Do you think it would be a good idea if we sent Johnnie and Sheila over now and again on a Saturday when there is no school? They could take a few vegetables to her. She can't be that well off."

"And a can of fresh buttermilk," she answered eagerly. "They could go once a week. It shouldn't take them long to walk there and back."

CHAPTER TWELVE

The renovations to the old cottage were nearly complete. Maggie covered the floor with rugs she had made from scraps of material for which no other use could be found. She whitewashed the inside walls and hung a picture of the Sacred Heart over the fireplace. Looking around, she decided that an extra fireside chair was needed for the times she, or one of the children, would come to sit with Cliona. And a few flowers would be welcoming. She smiled to herself as she anticipated the look of pleasure on her mother's face when she led her into her new home. How long was it since she had seen her in the back of the church at mass? Several weeks she guessed, and always she had slipped away before the service was finished, no doubt not wanting to be seen in her old rags, in case her daughter found it shameful. Maggie planned to go alone to fetch her mother. She wanted no one to witness their reunion. She hummed to herself as she closed the door and walked back to the farmhouse.

A weak November sun threw a few shining beams through the open window of the kitchen. Dust motes cavorted about in them driving Pangur into a frenzy with their antics. The cat sat on her behind and watched with narrow eyes, intermittently one of her paws darting out in an effort to capture the elusive dancers. She hissed with anger at her failure, making Maggie laugh out loud. Sheila, who had just returned from school, stood in the doorway listening to the unfamiliar sound and watching Maggie watching Pangur.

"Bring a chair over here and sit by me."

Sheila did so and stayed without speaking until her mother enquired about her day at school. Had she enjoyed her English class with Miss O'Dowd, and was she tired after her walk home?

"Get yourself a cup of milk and rest a while. The work can wait for once."

Suddenly Maggie was taken aback to see tears falling on her daughter's pinafore.

"Why, child, what is the matter?"

Sheila jumped up and threw her arms round Maggie.

"You do love me, Mammy, don't you?"

"Of course, child. Why wouldn't I love you?" she answered, giving Sheila a reciprocal hug. Maggie had entered into a period of calmness and optimism. She was at peace with herself and looked forward placidly to the birth of the next child. Unlike other pregnancies, this one gave her a not unpleasant feeling of lassitude, and to Paddy's satisfaction he would sometimes find her sitting in the old rocking chair, her sewing forgotten in her lap.

Towards the end of December Tim came again, this time with devastating news. He told Maggie that when he had visited Cliona that morning he found her sitting in her chair with a smile on her face. At first he thought she was asleep but when she did not respond to his greeting, he realised she was dead. He carried her to her bed, he said, and found she was light as a feather. Then he picked up two small stones from outside the door, washed them, and placed them on her eyes after he had closed them. He had hurried here as fast as he could. Maggie sat still without speaking while Tim talked. Just then Paddy came in having seen Tim rushing up the lane. Hearing the rasp in his throat he asked, "What ails you, man? Take your time. Whatever news you have can wait until you get your breath back."

"She's gone. God rest her."

"I don't believe you." Maggie jumped up and grasped the hapless Tim by the sleeve of his jacket, dragging him outside and across the fields to the renovated cottage. Paddy followed helplessly behind. Once there, Maggie pointed out the evidence of the loving care she had lavished on the place; the easy chairs, the new bed, the rug she had made, all the time talking, her eyes feverish and uncomprehending.

"Margaret," Tim said at last, laying a hand on her arm, "your mother won't need these things any more."

"Margaret, Margaret. Why do you call me by that name?" She gave a harsh gasp before falling at their feet in a faint.

Sheila was left in charge of her mother. Paddy had forced a glass of brandy between her lips and she was put to bed where she lay tossing restlessly and muttering incoherent words between heartfelt sobs. Meantime her husband went to see the parish priest to arrange the purchase of a small plot of land in the local graveyard. He also engaged a carpenter to carve a tiny wooden cross that was to be placed on Cliona's grave. When he got back home Maggie seemed unchanged and it was some time before a sharp scream made him aware that his wife was in labour.

It was a long and difficult birth. Maggie made no effort to help the midwife and gave no sign that she knew what was happening. At last the twin girls were born, sickly babies that were baptised at once. Maggie turned her face away from them and refused to make any decision as to what names they should be given. Paddy asked Sheila to settle the question and she decided on Rose and Lily, the names of her two favourite flowers.

CHAPTER THIRTEEN

After some time Paddy went over to Cliona's place to sort out her belongings. Although Maggie was up and about again she refused to accompany him, instructing that he should burn everything. He told her on his return that mouse and mildew had done their work and in spite of opening up windows an unpleasant smell of decay lingered over everything. Big black spiders with spindly legs scuttled around in an effort to escape his brush. He hauled an old zinc bath he said, from under the sink and filled it with the few chipped mugs that sat on a shelf, several cracked plates and a teapot with the spout missing. He added three jam jars, one containing the remains of what looked like blackberry jam and an aluminium saucepan blackened and dented with use. The light was beginning to fade, he explained, so he hastily threw everything else that was around into the bath and dragged it to a field where he pushed it in a hedge and covered it as best he could with broken branches. Outside the door he piled Cliona's clothing into a heap with other light rubbish, sprinkled paraffin on it and set the whole lot alight. For a long time he stood, watching the remains of Cliona's meagre legacy go up in flames.

After he had told his wife exactly how he had disposed of her mother's possessions, Paddy was silent for a few minutes before starting to speak again slowly.

"I know you asked me to burn everything but I have kept back one item. I found this packet neatly wrapped up and securely tied with string and decided I should open it. Then I saw your name inside and after a quick look at the contents I felt I should carry it home to you." Maggie listened silently to his story without moving and still without comment she held out a hand to accept the package. Then she carried it upstairs to the bedroom and pushed it with the toe of her slipper below the bed where it became entangled in the wire springs of the mattress.

On Sundays after mass Maggie would stand waiting, chatting to neighbours and friends while Paddy and Sheila placed wild spring flowers on Cliona's grave or in winter, berries and sometimes just green leaves. At its head there was a simple wooden cross with the inscription: CLIONA O'DONNELL 1848 – 1907. On the way home Maggie relayed all the gossip she had heard and this was the only occasion in the week that she showed any animation. Otherwise she was silent and unpredictable. She knew the younger children had learned to keep out of her way in order to avoid her sharp tongue, or worse, the smack from an open hand. Usually Sheila was the butt of her ill-temper being less able to avoid it as she was required to spend so much time in the kitchen under her mother's baleful eye. However, Maggie managed to come to terms with some of the anger and disappointment that had built up inside her by engaging in hard physical work. Her apathy then was often replaced by a new energy and she became more and more occupied with ambitious plans for the farm. She insisted that the roof of the house should be raised to give another three bedrooms. Paddy had to agree they could do with more space but said he did not look forward to the additional work that it would necessitate. The bulk of it would have to be undertaken by him with only occasional assistance from neighbours and perhaps a day now and then from Johnnie when he could be kept from school. Nevertheless he agreed to Maggie's proposals and in a short time the farmhouse was two storied. The settle bed was removed from the kitchen. The crook over the open fire with its black iron pot hanging from the hook disappeared in favour of a cast iron stove. The heap of turf that had been piled in a corner of the hearth was no more to be seen. Now only a few sods were kept, placed neatly in a wicker basket. The old stone floor was covered with new linoleum and the place took on a more modern appearance. The cottage intended for Cliona was rented to a newly married couple. The income Maggie said, was to be used to buy more land. She was always on the look out for any few acres that were for sale or conacre. It was easier now to acquire from people who had rushed to buy a few years ago. Those who had no experience of farming, finding there were no quick profits to be made, were willing to get rid of their newly purchased acres at knock-down prices. The O'Neills were always ready to purchase if it was within easy reach of their own place. As they grew richer Maggie grew more tight-fisted every day.

CHAPTER FOURTEEN

Sheila was darning and yawning and trying hard to stay awake. Maggie warned her that she must finish the whole of the work that was piled high in the basket at her feet before she would be allowed to go to bed. The door opened, Johnnie came in and dropped a pair of boots by her side.

"Give them a good cleaning for me," he said. "They are very mucky."

Maggie saw her daughter's shoulders stiffen as Johnnie went out of the room whistling. Sheila continued to darn steadily. Fifteen minutes later, the boots unpolished, Johnnie stood remonstrating with his sister who, stubbornly silent, pushed the needle in and over the threads of a worn sock, creating a mosaic on the dome of a wooden mushroom. Maggie listened to the carping voice of her son for a few minutes, holding her peace, but at last she rose and took the shoe cleaning box from the shelf over the back door. Then she bent and picked up the boots. As she did so she put a hand to her back and a groan escaped her. Sheila did not lift her eyes from her work, continuing to darn calmly, but her mother knew she was aware that she was pregnant and that her victory over her brother was a hollow one, tinged with guilt.

The eighth and last O'Neill child was born at the beginning of the twentieth century. He was named after his father Patrick. For some time his mother's health was precarious and care of the new baby fell mostly on Sheila's shoulders. Maggie watched as she touched the soft cheeks of the twins, stroking them with hands already hardened by rough work. She saw too that the complete dependence of Paddy was a pleasure to her and it was these observations that enabled her to stifle any guilt feeling that rose now and again in her mind.

One evening as Maggie sat with her husband at the kitchen table after a late meal, their talk turned to the future.

"Johnnie," Maggie said, "will have the farm. Martin and Tommy can both be put to a trade when they are old enough, and I pray every night that Paddy will become a priest."

"And the girls?"

"Well Susan is the good-looking one," he smiled across at her. "She will catch a rich husband, no doubt about that. It's too early to plan for those two amadons Rose and Lily, but there are worse jobs than dressmaking. Sheila, of course, will stay on the farm to look after us in our old age."

"But Mammy I want to remain at school." Maggie was startled by the urgency in Sheila's voice. "There are some women who don't get married, like Miss O'Dowd. She says if I work hard I could become a teacher, and I would give you all the money I earned."

"That's enough out of you. Miss O'Dowd has your head turned, telling you how clever you are."

"It's not fair." Sheila was sobbing now. Forgetting that she too had once rebelled against her mother's ambitions, so many years ago, Maggie said sharply, "No. The world is not a fair place and the sooner you learn that the better."

Paddy rose and putting a hand on Sheila's head murmured, "We'll see, mavourneen. That is all far away in the future and we don't know how things will change over the years. Someone though will have to stay on here at the farm to care for your mother and Susan when I am gone."

Sheila dried her tears and smiled up at her father.

For many years Maggie had preferred to see what she believed, rather than believe what she saw, regarding her daughter Susan, but there was something she could not quite put her finger on. It was as though she was in league with another world, the way she'd salute a blackbird or mutter something as she passed a well. She seemed to pay respect to things unseen and unheard by anyone other than herself. Maggie suspected the rest of the family was aware that their sister's mental development lagged behind her physical maturity. They must have noticed, she thought, when they saw her skipping around the garden talking to hens, ducks, birds, frogs, anything that moved. She treated all these creatures with the same affection that she showed to her parents and siblings. In the home, though willing to work, she was more a hindrance than a help. When her teachers said that she was making no progress in school she was allowed to leave. One day just before her thirteenth birthday, Maggie found her with her little brother Paddy in a field some distance from the house. She had removed all her own and the child's clothes and was stepping around him with outstretched arms, chanting in a low monotone. Susan was not taken aback in the least when her mother appeared beside them and began to dress Paddy, indicating that Susan should do the same. She complied happily and chatted engagingly as they made their way to the house. Maggie decided to tell no one about this but from that time onwards kept a close watch on Susan's activities. It was only after this incident that her mother was able to admit to herself that Susan was dancing to a tune of her own and would not be able to achieve any sort of independence or make her own way in the wider world. All the same she hoped that some day she might find a husband who would love and take care of her. She was the favourite in the family, a tall slim girl with an oval face and haunting grey eyes. None of her sisters or brothers seemed to resent the fact that her mother's love for her was so fervent that it seemed to have used up most of her affection, leaving only a very meagre portion for the others.

CHAPTER FIFTEEN

That day Maggie and the baby were the only two in the house. Now and then she raised her head to look through the kitchen window to where the low drumlins rose gently to meet the edge of the high field where the rest of the family were gathering in the potato harvest. On the skyline she could see the old horse toiling backwards and forwards urged on she guessed, by soft words of encouragement from her husband. The children followed, backs bent, lifting the crop and placing it in creels. They emptied these into pits which had already been dug out a few days ago. They would be covered with soil later to exclude air and opened again only when the need arose. It was wearying and monotonous work. Tomorrow the after-effects would be felt in aching backs and stiff knees; the only consolation, if it could be called such, was the assurance that the pain would not last but disappear in a day or two when the joints eased with usage.

It was not time yet for the tea break. The food was ready, neatly packed in a willow basket, mugs, soda bread thickly buttered and today some slices of cheese as a treat. The tea would be made last, sugared strongly, milked and poured into glass bottles, then a twist of newspaper from the *Belfast Telegraph* inserted into the neck to ensure there would be no spillage. Maggie paused and set down the knife with which she was scraping carrots for the evening stew. Why had the horse stopped? The potato gatherers were crowding round its head, Rose was holding the reins. Johnnie was helping his father down from his seat. The three boys carried him over to the nearest hedge and laid him in the grass. Without waiting to untie her apron strings, Maggie rushed to where Sheila was whispering the Act of Contrition into her father's ear.

"Go for Billy Nesbitt," Maggie ordered Johnnie. "And then run for the priest and the doctor. Sheila, hurry to the house and put the good linen sheets on our bed, they are in the top drawer of the tallboy. And tidy the house up. Martin and Tommy, unharness Jasper and put everything away where it belongs." She looked about her: "You two girls," turning to Rose and Lily, "must finish closing the potato bing. Then all of you come back home."

Within less than half an hour everything was organised and the house was a house of mourning.

As long as Maggie was occupied, she was able to contain her grief and shock. It had never crossed her mind that although her husband was twelve years her senior, he might die before her. Without him she felt completely adrift inside, while outwardly calm and competent. At the wake she was generous with whisky, stout, cold ham and home-made cakes when mourners called at the house. She insisted on attending the funeral even though it was not the custom for women to do so and in spite of the pleas of her sons Martin and Tommy. As she walked down the aisle of the church behind the coffin, she noticed in the very last pew an odd-looking figure. His head was bent but as she passed he raised a tear-stained face and gave her a penetrating look before sinking down again. She thought fleetingly that he seemed faintly familiar. Outside she more or less forgot about him as she stood accepting the handshakes and condolences of neighbours. At last she was free to leave and looking around for her family, noted that the children were all beside her with the exception of Johnnie. As they moved off she saw her eldest son by the side gate of the cemetery. He was talking to the stranger she had noticed in the back of the church.

Back home there was much to be done. Borrowed plates, cups and chairs had to be returned to their owners and the place set to rights again. The boys went out as usual to feed, milk and close up the animals for the night before kneeling down to say the 'rosary' for the soul of the departed. Maggie was determined to get back to her old routine and it was some days before she got round to questioning Johnnie about the unknown man who had attended Paddy's funeral. He shrugged his shoulders saying he didn't know the man's name. There was nothing much to tell, he said, and anyway it was not important. He claimed to be his uncle and adamantly refused to meet other members of the family. In answer to his mother's question, he assured her he had tried very hard to get him to come back to the house.

"It seems," Johnnie continued, "he has been out of the country for several years and was in a hurry to get back to Dublin as he hoped to set off from there to Australia the next day."

"Did he say he was married, had any children?" asked a frustrated Maggie.

"No, I didn't ask him too many questions, as he didn't wish to talk to me at all. I'm sure he would have slipped away without making himself known to any of us if I hadn't approached him as he was sneaking out of the side gate of the graveyard."

The lack of information was disconcerting, but Maggie was able to put it to the back of her mind for a time and busy herself with plans for the future.

CHAPTER SIXTEEN

Now the owner of a sizeable farm, under her management the work continued to prosper. Johnnie was only thirteen but he was a strong healthy lad and able to tackle most aspects of the work involved. He left school a year early without regrets on his part, as far as his mother could tell and with the help of a permanent farm hand seemed to be settling into an agricultural career.

The work slowed down in winter and in that first season after Paddy's death, Maggie gradually began to confront her loss. In bed at night regrets and recriminations came to assault her serenity. Memories surfaced of the time she had encouraged him to undertake work beyond his physical capacity. She wondered now if she had taken good enough care of him with regard to diet and warm winter clothing? Had she been kind to him, listened to him carefully when he talked of the running of the farm? At last, however, she realised these thoughts cast out another worry. She would have no peace of mind until she had settled once and for all the question of the existence of Paddy's brother. Her husband, as she understood it, considered that he was dead. Now it seemed there was a possibility that he might return and claim at least part of the farm. She owed it to her fatherless children to do everything in her power to prevent it. Paddy had worked hard as she herself had done to build up the place. Could she now, she asked herself, stand idly by and see them robbed of their inheritance? Her pride would not let her make enquiries of the neighbours and she could not ask Billy Nesbitt nor his brother, both of whom had known Paddy since childhood. No. It would reveal that her husband had not told her everything, in fact did not trust her.

After much thought she decided to see a solicitor. Mr Byrne, an elderly man, was a native of the town. He was not someone she thought of as properly acquainted with her but she had often seen him at mass. Sometimes she would encounter him on the street and he always smiled and raised his top hat to her. His neatly trimmed whiskers and twinkling eyes made her feel she could trust him.

Dressed in her best dark suit and a soft white blouse, Maggie set off one day for town. The trees she had grown to love in the early days of her marriage remained the same but time had seen improvements to the road. It had been widened to make the passage of humans and animals easier. New saplings of oak, ash and beech were making headway in their bid to reach the sky. When she got to the outskirts she saw that sheep, goats and a few horses were tethered and lined up for sale under the trees. She had forgotten it was a fair day; there were lots of people around just when she wished to go unnoticed. She walked past the row of cottages leading to the post office and coming to the Church of Ireland with its beautiful iron-wrought gates, today she failed to admire them. Skirting the railings surrounding the graveyard, she had arrived but she could not bring herself to enter the solicitor's office. Crossing the street, she went into Proctor and Gamble's store and spent some time picking through a box of assorted buttons. When an assistant approached she felt obliged to buy half a dozen tiny mother of pearl discs, persuading herself they would come in useful some day. Then unseeing, she watched her payment being whisked away in a system of tubes to a glass counting office above her head. A few minutes later the shop girl had to speak to her twice to attract her attention when her change was removed from the little bronze cylinder. She could feel the woman's eyes on her back as she walked out.

There was plenty of time she told herself so after leaving the shop she took a walk to the more prosperous end of town where she saw a lady emerge from her house with an iron rod in her hand. Maggie watched as she fitted the crank to the front of a car and gave it a hefty turn. Nothing happened but on the second attempt it spluttered and finally fired off. With a sound like a cannon shot, car and owner rushed down the street with a rattle. She had seen women in cycling shorts and striped blouses wheeling about the countryside, but ladies in motoring veils and stout leather gloves amazed her and gave her something to think about for a few minutes, taking her mind of her anxieties.

At last, after a deep breath and straightening her shoulders, Maggie walked towards the solicitor's office. A quick glance around had satisfied her that there was no one about who might recognise her as she slipped through the door. Mr Byrne shook hands with her and asked her to make herself comfortable. She sat on the edge of the chair with well polished black boots placed tidily on the floor. He offered her a cup of tea and his comments gave her to understand that he knew who she was and she found this comforting as though he was claiming her as a friend. Thoroughly charmed by his old world courtesy, she had no difficulty in pouring out her fears. He listened and at last said that at the time of the incident she referred to he had been away studying in Dublin. He could tell her nothing about it. However, he promised to look up old records and find out all he could. His comments about the ownership of the farm reassured her and she left well pleased with the consultation.

A few weeks later Maggie received a letter which offered another appointment. When she entered the office she noticed at once a pile of files and newspapers heaped up on the floor. Mr Byrne waved his hand towards them and said she was welcome to stay as long as she liked to examine the contents. He had marked the relevant articles; however if she wished he could summarise. Maggie agreed to this last suggestion but insisted that he should tell her the whole truth. Mr Byrne advised her that Johnnie, Paddy's brother, when he was about sixteen, had begun to drink heavily and sometimes became aggressive and quarrelsome, imagining people were trying to insult him. One evening in a pub, two lads taunted him saying his father had been a member of a subversive group and had paid the price for his folly. Johnnie lost his temper, lashed out at them and was only restrained by the intervention of the barman and some of his friends. He was advised to go back to his lodgings, which he did. However, the two who accosted him waited for a few days and then came after him. It was a wet murky afternoon and the light was not good but Johnnie could see well enough to detect the flash of a gun when it was brandished in his face. Somehow he managed to wrest it from his attackers and, grasping it, fired two shots in the air. In court he claimed that he only intended to scare them off and this indeed was the result, but he was not a good shot and one of his assailants was caught in the line of fire. This man was later found to be badly wounded and he died a few days later in Newry hospital. In court there were several people who attested to Johnnie's good character and witnesses came forward to support the defendant's claim that he had been provoked. The judge gave the live attacker three months but Johnnie was found guilty of manslaughter and sentenced to a long jail sentence. Mr Byrne thought that with good behaviour he had been released shortly before Paddy's death.

"No doubt," the solicitor concluded, "he would not want to be recognised in the neighbourhood. His statement to your son Johnnie after the funeral, about leaving the country, in my opinion is likely to be correct, otherwise I think you would have seen him since. News travels fast around here.

A murderer in the family, Maggie thought in horror. She had always believed that her marriage had not only lifted her out of poverty and shame but also placed her in a sphere of inviolable respectability. She kept her shock a secret and revealed to no one what she had learned. At night she prayed that her children might never hear of this traumatic episode. Meantime she decided to hold her head high as though she knew nothing of the shaming events in the past.

CHAPTER SEVENTEEN

Go back to bed, I'll deal with this." Maggie snatched the back door key from Sheila's hand. "I suppose you think the two of you can keep secrets from me in my own house? Go to your room, I said."

Maggie watched Sheila reluctantly climb the stairs. They could both hear Johnnie singing in a tuneless monotone at the other side of the door.

"My Bonnie lies over the ocean, my Bonnie…"

His mother turned the key in the lock and he stumbled inside. Immediately she lifted her hand and gave him two hard slaps, one on each side of his face.

"What's that for, Ma? Sure I've only had a wee drink or two."

His voice was slurred and as he tried to push past her to go upstairs, he staggered against her and she had to save herself from falling by grabbing the banister. Snatching at his jacket she turned him round to face her.

"What kind of behaviour is this, coming in drunk to a respectable house at two o'clock in the morning? Won't this give the neighbours something to gossip about? Won't they think that I have failed lamentably in my task of bringing you up decently? What would your father have said?"

Johnnie muttered something under his breath about respectability being the only thing she cared about, then, louder, she heard him accuse her of making his father's life a misery. Enraged, she lashed out at him with her fists, hissing, "You are turning out just like your namesake. I should have been warned years ago when you brought that gun into the house. Your father had a right to be angry."

The unfairness of the remark, although it seemed to sober the young man, also angered him. He raised a hand to strike his mother, paused and then let his arm fall limply to his side. Silent now, the two stood looking at each other for a second until Johnnie pushed past her and went upstairs to his room.

Both Johnnie and his mother were deeply affected by what had happened. Looking into his face, she had been dismayed and frightened by the depth of anger she had seen there. She wondered if at the time a picture of his younger self had flashed across his mind, when Paddy had stopped himself using violence towards his six-year-old son. She would give anything to be able to undo the misery she had caused that night. Johnnie was deeply offended, she could see. She tried to make amends by cooking his favourite foods, putting herself out to do little jobs that were his responsibility and scolding the younger children when their behaviour displeased him, but she could not bring herself to apologise. He maintained a silence she found hard to bear and avoided her whenever possible. One day she overheard him telling Sheila that he thought he deserved more appreciation from his mother for the hard work he did, day in and day out with never a break since the day he left school. Maggie had to admit that she did indeed make great demands on him and was resentful that she depended as heavily on him as she had on his father. When communication between them did not improve, she began to wonder if her son had more grudges against her than she was aware of? Did he know more about this uncle's history than he admitted? Billy Nesbitt or his brother Joe might have been persuaded to tell the whole sorry tale. Resentment built up in her again. If her surmise were correct, was it not the duty of a son to pass on this sort of information to his widowed mother?

Johnnie grew even more silent in his mother's presence. The only one he seemed to really care for was Susan. When she brought him a magpie with a small wound in its side he helped her nurse it back to health and consoled her when it flew away. He encouraged her to ride on old Jasper's back, a privilege not allowed to his brothers and sisters. He brought her little gifts from the market; a few sweets, a brightly coloured ribbon for her hair or a stick of liquorice. Otherwise he treated his siblings as his mother treated him, expecting them to work hard on the farm when they came home from school and to obey his orders indoors. Maggie could see that he had no time for Rose and Lily, ignoring them whenever possible as if they were beyond his consideration, and although he looked on Sheila and young Paddy with a more indulgent eye, he kept himself fairly aloof from both of them.

CHAPTER EIGHTEEN

Maggie sent Martin and Tommy together to Belfast to begin apprenticeships as soon as they were able to leave school. Dismissing their protests, she assured them that they would be able to return and find work locally when they had good qualifications. Diligently she sewed shirts, got Sheila to help her mend their old clothes and at last packed their bags with no great regret. After their departure the house was even more sombre and Maggie began to look forward to Tommy's homecoming at weekends. She listened to his descriptions of the city and especially the outskirts, the Divis Mountain and Cave Hill with its outline of Napoleon's face on the summit. Quietly sewing, she absorbed all he had to say, enjoying vicariously those places she would only ever visit in her imagination. His brother Martin came home rarely but Maggie gathered from Tommy that he considered himself quite the gentleman now, smoking Wild Woodbines and Sweet Afton cigarettes. He visited the dance halls and was a big success with the girls.

"And do you not go with him?" she asked.

"No," Tommy said. "I'd rather be out seeing the sights. He keeps introducing me to girls whom we meet coming out of mass on Sundays, but none of them are as pretty as our Susan," and he jumped up giving his sister an all-enveloping hug.

For the next few years nothing occurred in Maggie's life of any note. There was a hardness in her now, perhaps partly born of the struggle she had made from dirt floor to comfortable farm. She was fairly calm in her day-to-day living and her word remained law on all matters concerning both the domestic and farm arrangements. On wet days she could be seen, wrapped in Paddy's old thin Holland overcoat, collecting the eggs or closing up the hens in the evening.

She had thought, in 1912, that Belfast was a place that had recovered from past hunger and strife, and was surprised when Tommy told her of the sad feelings of insecurity that followed the launch of the liner *Titanic,* which he and his brother had watched from the quayside. It was the biggest and grandest passenger ship in the world and its construction had given much employment to the city's work force. Now as it sailed away, despair mingled with pride in its achievement could be seen on the faces of those who had a hand in its construction. The city not only faced unemployment on a large scale but a surge of antagonism between Catholic and Protestant which had already manifested itself in the graffiti that was found on the planks on the underside of the ship. All this came as a surprise to Maggie who, absorbed in her own world nowadays, rarely gave a thought to outside considerations.

"But none of this will affect you and Martin?" she enquired of Tommy.

"No," he replied and then, tentatively, "Did you know that Michael Morgan our grocer's son left college and got himself a job on the *Titanic*? When I meet him he always asks after our Sheila."

Maggie ignored this last part of the remark and went on with her sewing.

It was with disbelief at first that the news of the *Titanic's* fate was received. Maggie noticed Sheila's tear-stained face but seemed uninterested in the cause of her distress. She herself had learned to deal with life's problems by ignoring them as far as possible. She had developed a talent for oblivion to what was going on around her and expected her daughter to do the same.

CHAPTER NINETEEN

Afterwards Maggie said that had she known in time, she would have prevented Johnnie from attending the political meetings that took place in the run-up to World War One. Members of the Parliamentary Party led by John Richmond spoke persuasively about joining forces in the fighting that was sure to come. Maggie knew that until that time Johnnie had not been greatly interested in politics. She was convinced he only went to meetings to be with his friends. She could see how easy it was to get caught up in the emotions of the speakers who claimed it would be a just war, fought for the freedom of small nations.

"Are we not a small nation?" she had heard him ask his brother Tommy. "So how can we be refused Home Rule when this is all over?"

Maggie had no strong feelings about living under British rule and had somehow taken it for granted that this also applied to the other members of the family.

He told them one evening at supper he was going to fight for the brave new world they were promised and he would have a hand in making this come about. Nothing his brothers or sisters said made him change his mind. Susan got up from the table and, crying, threw her arms round his neck, pleading with him not to leave her. He tried to console her, promising that if he was sent to Belgium – a great country for chocolates – he would bring back boxes and boxes for her. He kissed his mother coldly on the cheek one morning and for the first time in his life hugged Sheila, asking her to be good to Susan when he was away. Although he whistled 'Pack up your troubles in your old kit bag' as he went through the door, Maggie could hear the note of desolation that came through his gritted teeth.

Herbie the telegraph boy came up the lane. In another year he told Maggie, he hoped that he too would be in uniform. He looked forward to marching with Johnnie and the Nesbitts to that old tune 'It's a long, long way to Tipperary', which, no matter how hard he tried, he could not get out of his mind. He handed the telegram to Maggie but she stood like a statue until Sheila moved forward and took it from the boy's hand who, mounting his bicycle, rode off whistling as he went.

Sheila read it and passed it on to her mother. "Missing. Presumed dead." Suddenly it was as if a wind had entered the room, whipping itself into a turmoil, before, after a lengthy pause, it stole away to create havoc somewhere else. Maggie carefully replaced the buff-coloured sheet of paper inside its orange envelope and put it behind the clock on the mantelpiece. Without speaking, she removed her shawl from the hook on the kitchen door, placed it carefully round her shoulders, and went outside. She crossed the field nearest the house and on to where the whins glowed golden on the mound they called 'the dundery knowes'. Rabbits scurried away at the sight of her, their white tails bobbing and scuffing in the bushes. Today she did not see them and pressed on to 'green acre' where the cattle, fenced in by dry stone ditches enjoyed the lush grass. A cow stood in her path blocking her way and mooing softly. She stroked its brown head and noticed a fly on the animal's neck, rubbing its hands together as if this was a day like any other. Flicking it away, she chased the cow and continued to walk until she came to the lough. Everything here was dark and mournful. She saw that an elm, familiar to her from childhood, was leaning to one side and soon would topple over. In spite of its healthy appearance, Maggie knew that the tree – unlike most other species – was dying from the inside out as though unwilling to declare its suffering to the world.

His letters had been cheerful enough. He told of how he had escaped death at least once but wrote with a bravado and excitement that suggested he was enjoying the life at least to some extent. Maggie had not been fooled. She had read about the meagre rations, lack of sleep, the continual roar of the bombers overhead, the mud and stench of rotting corpses. Had there been anything of value in it? Had the finding of fun and companionship with his fellow soldiers made any of it worthwhile? What were the messages he tried to convey to his family that were eradicated by the blue line of the censor's pen?

She looked at the lough with its small island in the middle. Paddy once told her it was made by sinking stones and logs in the water. A wall constructed of mud and wattle, now mostly disintegrated, ran from the island to the shore. Parts of it could still be seen in very dry weather when the level of the water was low. He explained that the crannog was a defence system. Now she wondered about her ancestors, the people who had built it. Their method of warfare she supposed was ingenious. They must have picked off the enemy one by one as they tried to cross over to the island by the narrow wall which allowed passage to only one person at a time. Did they use bows and arrows or more simply throw stones to knock the oncomers off balance and into the water? Was this a less humane method of killing than had been employed by Johnnie's enemies? Could Paddy have prevented the death of his eldest child? He had saved her from drowning, she had been his fish and without him she was nobody, nothing. She had been floundering all these years since his death. He had given her Johnnie and she had failed to take good enough care of him, letting him travel far away from his roots. Both he and his father had risen early every morning to farm the land, returning home with the smell of the good brown earth clinging to them. Now she would not even have the comfort of laying him to rest beside his father in his native soil.

Daylight was beginning to fade. In the next field a corncrake started up a loud mating cry. The rough cranking sound woke her to present reality. There was a movement in the reeds and, dimly, she discerned the outline of a grey heron. It dipped its beak into the water and speared a fish, flicking it high in the air before swallowing the wriggling creature down. Sympathy for the victim suffused her, and, searching around, she found a stone and lobbed it in the direction of the bird. It flew away, and her eyes following it saw that orange slits were beginning to appear in the sky, denoting the setting sun. The heavens seemed far off as they had when she was a child. She began to pray. It was a song of praise and gratitude.

"Morning Star, Health of the Sick, Tower of Ivory, House of Gold." Suddenly she was filled with an inexplicable lightness and was astonished to realise that the deepest grief could contain a sort of painful thanksgiving. The beautiful flower had faded but it had been beautiful. She walked to the very edge of the lough and looked into the darkening waters, her tears mingling with the rippling waves on its surface.

Returning to the house, she found Sheila preparing soda farls for the evening meal. She sat down on the rocking chair and watched her daughter mash hot potatoes with the handleless mug, add salt, hot milk and melted butter. Next she shaped the mixture into triangles and put them on a floured griddle. After a few minutes she turned them and soon removed them from the heat. Each farl was now stacked neatly against its neighbour and left to cool. Maggie felt she would like to compliment Sheila on the dexterity and skill she showed in making the bread, perhaps even speak of Johnnie but the years had taken away her words.

In the evenings she sat in her rocking chair with Pangur on her knee, giving an impression of resignation. It was not until she received a packet from the War Office that she showed any signs of grief. When she opened it, she found it contained the contents of the jacket Johnnie was wearing when he died; a rabbit's foot, a piece of string and a lock of Susan's hair tied with a ribbon. Moths were flying in through the open window, hurling themselves against the hot glass of the oil lamp. Some found their way over the top, but most ended their life in a hissing shrivel, the self-destruction of creatures who had a hunger for light. For a time she sat motionless watching them and then suddenly she rose, and, seizing the lamp, staggered outside and flung it far out into the back yard, shattering the glass irreparably. Leaving the room in darkness, she made her way upstairs, but as she lay on her bed, no peace came to her as she saw, haunted and harrowed, a picture of her son, his eyes frantically trying to get out of his face.

CHAPTER TWENTY

Before he returned to Belfast after Johnnie's death, Martin told his mother that he had met the girl he intended to marry. Her parents did not approve of the fact that she would be marrying a man of a different religion. After long consideration they decided to go and live in Australia. It was all settled and they would be sailing in less than a week. Maggie received the news with a shrug of her shoulders, and turned to Tommy, begging him to give up his apprenticeship and come home to work on the farm. Tommy agreed and, with some help from his young brother Paddy, he began to take charge. He did so with little interference from his mother, although she made suggestions from time to time about the purchase of more land; suggestions which he acted on – profitably.

Maggie at last woke to the fact that Rose and Lily were causing problems. Rose, tall and gaunt with a shock of red hair, had the face of a friendly potato and was easily led into any mischief her sister suggested. Her appetite was good, but she often dismayed her mother by vomiting after a meal. When the doctor found no cause for this affliction, her mother lost sympathy and lamented the waste of food. Lily was pale and pretty with delicate bones and a quiet voice that belied her stubborn nature. Maggie considered both of them irresponsible, fond of a good time and given to giggling at jokes which they refused to share with others. When Lily became involved with a middle-aged penniless widower, Maggie roused herself to do something about it. She had kept in touch with Mary Conlon, who lived in Dublin, and now she enlisted her help in finding places in dressmaking workshops for the twins. Lily had no regrets, it seemed to her mother, when she left her lover for an exciting life in the city, and Rose refused to be parted from her. Barely concealing their pleasure at the promise of freedom, they left eagerly to find new adventures. At weekends they arrived home with armfuls of material and Butterick patterns. They tried to persuade their mother to buy one of the new Singer sewing machines that had been invented in America some fifty years ago, but her reply was disheartening: "Bad scran to you, do you want to beggar us?"

Nevertheless, the machine was waiting for them in the kitchen one Saturday morning a few months later. Maggie took no interest in it, nor in most of the activity going on around her. She was more silent than she had ever had been. On a wet day she would sit, listlessly, looking out the window and crooning, "Rainy rainy rattle stones don't rain on me, Rain on John O'Groat's house far across the sea." Or if it snowed, "There's the old woman a plucking her geese, And selling the feathers a penny a piece."

Sometimes it seemed she was living in a space between fantasy and reality, but the old critical Maggie would surface now and again. She would rebuke whoever was around, usually Sheila, for not sprinkling enough water on the collars of her brothers' shirts before ironing them, or failing to remove all the blemishes from the potatoes before putting them in the pot to boil.

"That's not the way I taught you to do things, you lazy clart."

After the Great War came the Great Flu. Tommy arrived home early one day from the fields saying he had a pain in his head and his bones were aching. As he was never one to complain, Maggie was alarmed when he took to his bed. The doctor diagnosed 'flu and said there nothing that could be done to save his life. In a few days he was yet another victim of the outbreak that was sweeping the country. Then Susan succumbed. Her death, unlike her brother's, was protracted. Maggie sat by her bed, allowing no one but herself to tend to the invalid. While she slept, her mother took short naps and when she was awake, kept her amused with stories about animals or fairies. Susan was laid to rest beside her brother Tommy. Maggie managed to stay calm throughout the church ceremony, but stood rigid as a statue at the graveside as the soil was thrown on her coffin. She heard her family weep and Sheila, standing beside her, murmured at last that is was time for them to go home.

"How can you talk of walking away and going back to the warmth of our house leaving my child in the cold earth?"

It took Paddy and his sisters some time to persuade her to move.

In the days that followed Maggie, in her loneliness, tried to build up friendships with her four remaining children but they were sunk in their own grief and her efforts met with little success. Although they were dutiful and gentle with her, she felt no comfort, nothing but pain. She continued to eat sleep, breathe but wanted nothing but Susan back, her anguished mind told her. When neighbours came to commiserate, she would retreat into herself like a snail that had been touched on the horns. Even the jobs that had given her satisfaction in their execution failed to please her. She no longer enjoyed making bread, sewing or even churning the butter and sank into gloom that impinged on the rest of the family.

CHAPTER TWENTY-ONE

In spite of her apathy Maggie continued to read the newspapers, even though most of the printed word failed to make an impact on her mind. When she learned about the Irish delegation in London, however, she woke up to the fact that things of importance were happening in her country. She listened to the arguments of Paddy and his farming friends as she sewed quietly and understood that there was now a definitive split between those who were for and those who were against the treaty. One evening she heard Paddy declare that there was now a Free State but not a free country. It was a disaster, he claimed, to get independence for twenty-six countries and alienate Ulster. A new fear was born in Maggie. She realised for the first time that Paddy felt passionately about such things and that many who were of a like mind might easily be persuaded to take up arms in the split between the political parties. Was it possible she asked herself she would lose her last and only son in yet another war?

One night, unable to sleep, she went into Paddy's bedroom and woke him. She sank down on her knees and weeping, implored him not to take up arms, ever. Her son comforted her and promised, he said, that in any case he could never bring himself to kill another countryman. A grateful Maggie dried her tears and said she would leave him all she had; animals, land, the farmhouse. Then she returned to her own bed and said a prayer in thanksgiving.

Soon Maggie's life took an upturn. Paddy told her he was planning to get married. Overjoyed, she sent for Rose and Lily to meet the proposed bride. Sheila was ordered to cook several delicacies, a ham, a tongue, a plum cake, and the house was cleaned meticulously. Paddy suggested they should live in the cottage which was vacant but Maggie wouldn't listen to this proposal. Elizabeth, she told her son, was going to be mistress from now on.

The family was agog to see Paddy's fiancée, and both she and Paddy were pleased with the welcome they were given, neither being aware of the twins' unkindly remarks made to Sheila in whispers when they thought, wrongly, that their mother wasn't listening and Elizabeth was out of earshot. Now skilled dressmakers in the capital, they considered themselves qualified to pronounce on what was elegant and in good taste. That bright blue dress needed to be toned down; her boots were no more fashionable than their mother's old button-ups, and her hat…oh, her hat was a thing to be wondered at, all that fruit and flowers among which the birds vied for the choicest morsels. It was, Lily said, almost choking with laughter, as though some bird of paradise had found its way into the poultry yard. Their mother made no comment on her future daughter-in-law's character or dress, and only said that she would know all about the domestic side as she was a farmer's daughter. When Rose asked Sheila how she would feel about having another woman in the house, she just shrugged and Maggie said something about there being no harm in having extra help. When the excitement at the prospect of the wedding had died down, Rose and Lily turned to talking about themselves, the new plays at The Abbey and The Gate theatres, and dancing in the city's many ballrooms. In a few days there were off to Dublin again.

Perhaps because she was preoccupied with thoughts of Paddy's marriage, or maybe she was less observant than she used to be, one way or another, Maggie failed to notice that Sheila too had a suitor. Joe Sanderson had been coming to the farm for over ten years to buy poultry and was well liked by the O'Neill family. Joe had been proposing marriage to Sheila at approximately six monthly intervals for several years. He was fifteen years older than she was, and had a warm, cheerful personality. Later she told her mother she had hesitated to marry at first because of the promise she had made to her father to stay on the farm. When she had explained to Joe, he had suggested firstly that she had been too young then to understand the implications of this, and secondly she could now hand over the responsibility to Elizabeth and Paddy. An alternative was to ask Maggie to come and live with them. It was this kindly suggestion that had persuaded her, she told her mother, to say 'yes' at last.

Maggie suddenly recovered her old fire and energy when Sheila told her she too was getting married, and greeted the announcement with a storm of rage. "What has come over you? At your age you are not likely to have children so why on earth do you want to get married?" Without waiting for a reply, she went on, "What's got into you? Is this place not good enough?"

"Of course it is, Mother, but I would like to have a home of my own."

"Home of your own? Leave this prosperous farm to live in some small pokey house in a village no one has ever heard of?"

"Please listen. Wouldn't it be better for Elizabeth to have the farm to herself rather than wondering where she will fit in...?"

"Fit in? You, my girl, are the one who must fit in. Patrick and his wife will be the ones who decide everything from now on. And don't think you will get a penny from me, I am giving over the farm, lock, stock and barrel, to your brother." Her face had grown ugly.

"All I need will be a few pounds to tide me over the wedding."

"A few pounds indeed. You won't get a halfpenny from me. And another thing, what about the promise you made your father to look after me in my old age?"

When Maggie heard that Joe was willing to have her to live with them she answered loftily, "I shall never leave the farm Paddy brought me to as a bride."

Although she could see there were tears in her daughter's eyes, as she turned to leave the room Maggie hissed, "May sorrow run a hunting with you."

Afterwards Maggie acted as though no disagreement had taken place and went about things as usual. To Joe's delight, Sheila brought the date of the wedding forward but no pleadings on the part of Paddy, Rose and Lily made their mother agree to attend the ceremony. It took place with only two of Joe's cousins and Sheila's siblings in attendance.

CHAPTER TWENTY-TWO

W elcome, daughter," Maggie greeted Elizabeth on her arrival. She waved her hand vaguely around: "This is yours to do as you please with, I've had my day and now it's your turn."

"How very generous you are," Elizabeth replied, stepping forward to give her mother-in-law a hug but Maggie evaded the overture by deftly turning on her heel and pointing to a door.

"I've made up the bed for the two of you in the best bedroom."

Paddy followed them upstairs struggling with suitcases and hat boxes. He dropped these at the women's feet and went to get the remainder.

"I'll help you with the rest of it," his mother offered.

"No, don't do that." Elizabeth barred her way. "Paddy will see to it himself." The two women stared at each other for what seemed to Maggie a long minute. Finally she took a deep breath, relaxed, and headed for the stairs. Elizabeth followed and stopped when Maggie pointed to the wonderful view from the landing. Waving a hand from side to side she exclaimed, "It all belongs to us, almost as far as the eye can see."

She had prepared a lavish meal for them and waited with some impatience as Paddy continued to carry more bags into the house. She noted that none of them seemed destined for the kitchen. At last the three of them sat round the table. Maggie smiled faintly when Elizabeth complimented her on her cooking and begged to be instructed so that she too might attain such perfection. For most of the meal Paddy remained silent.

★

When she received Sheila's letter announcing that Joe and she had a daughter, Maggie remembered the birth of her own first child. She told herself she would not let the past repeat itself and made preparations to accept Sheila's invitation to visit. She was pleased that Joe came to fetch her in a well sprung trap drawn by a shiny chestnut-coated pony, and she found it impossible not to warm to his genial personality. Having admired the baby Patricia, she launched into a glowing account of Elizabeth's competence and good sense, and gave the impression that the three of them were as happy as sandbirds.

"Paddy and Elizabeth will do well together," she said. While she was talking her eyes roamed around the small sitting room with a distaste she could not conceal. "And when they have children, they will have plenty of space to run about. So important not to have them under your feet all the time." Sheila saw the twinkle in Joe's eye and refrained from comment.

A year later the relationship between Maggie and her daughter-in-law was strained. When Paddy said he enjoyed a dish his wife had cooked, she would leave most of it untouched on her plate. Elizabeth asked if she could move some furniture around, and, though the answer was in the affirmative, Maggie complained that she was beginning to feel a stranger in her own house. One day she found that in her absence her rocking chair was moved from its place in front of the fireplace. When she asked why, Elizabeth replied reasonably that it made access to the oven much easier. Maggie insisted it should be returned to its former place. Elizabeth agreed, saying that Paddy would replace it when he came in from the fields. With some asperity in her voice, Maggie demanded, "Now."

Elizabeth protested that the chair was too heavy for her in her advanced state of pregnancy.

"Anyone would think," Maggie spat out spitefully, "that you are the first woman in the world to get pregnant. Wait until you've had as many as I've had, and although the two of you now own this place, I would remind you that I still have some rights."

Taken aback, Elizabeth burst into tears and ran outside to find her husband.

The youngest in the family, Paddy was an amiable and peace-loving man, indulged by his sisters and mother who rarely turned her anger on him. Faced with two strong-willed women and pushed to taking sides in their disputes, he was Maggie knew, sometimes vexed beyond measure. On such occasions he tended to maintain a sullen silence that left both of them exasperated. An underlying current of discontent simmered below the surface to which none of them would admit. The women used conciliatory phrases to try to achieve some sort of equilibrium but neither was able to forgive the other for real or imagined wrongs.

A few weeks after the disagreement over the chair, Maggie found that Elizabeth had, in sorting out the wardrobe, thrown away some of her dead father-in-law's clothes, jerseys, shirts, all of which were worn threadbare. Maggie's rage knew no bounds. It simmered inside her until the end of the day when Paddy returned from work, tired and hungry. Then in his presence she accused his wife of having no feelings of respect for the dead or for the grief of the widow.

"You could have asked me what I wished to do with my own husband's belongings instead of acting as though these things were of no importance. I have made little objection to your turning the place upside down but this time you have gone too far."

She would not listen to anything that her son or his wife had to say, not even when Paddy offered to retrieve the things Elizabeth had discarded. She would not be talked into any state of serenity.

"I'm leaving this house. No one could share it with you, Elizabeth. It was a peaceful home until you came. Sheila never complained or took it on herself to alter my arrangements. I will go to the cottage I prepared for my mother. Luckily it is vacant just now. My wants are few and it will suit me very well.

No amount of persuasion on Paddy's part had any effect.

"It's so cold and wet just now. Why don't you leave it until the spring?" he begged. "That would give me a little time to do a few repairs and make the place comfortable for you."

But Maggie was determined to have her own way – instantly. She stormed upstairs and began to pack, filling a large tin truck with linens and several pieces of glass and chinaware that she had treasured over the years. She stripped the bed and noticed the packet which she had so unceremoniously pushed under it many years ago. Gingerly she opened one end, wrinkling her nose at the strong smell of camphor that came from it. She went to throw it on top of a pile of articles she had heaped on the floor, deeming them to be useless when it burst open revealing her old rag doll. Recognising it instantly, she bent down and picked it up but it disintegrated and underneath she could see there was something that appeared to be in a better state of preservation. This was covered in oiled paper and had the scarcely legible name 'Margaret' written on the outside. She shook off the remnants of dust that had fallen from the doll and placed the packet on top of the items in the trunk. Closing the lid, she went downstairs. She left instructions with Elizabeth to get Paddy to bring her dress-making mirror, her rocking chair and her trunk to the cottage when he had finished milking the cows. Then taking one last long look round the kitchen, she donned her hat and coat and left the farmhouse.

Paddy had lighted a fire in the cottage. She found him sweeping and clearing the place up but ordered him to leave things as they were and to go back and fetch her belongings. When he returned he helped her to place the heavier articles of furniture around the two small rooms. Shaking his head sadly he left, closing the door softly behind him.

Maggie opened the trunk and removed her mother's journals. For a time she stood still, undecided, holding them in her hands for a long while before putting them on the dresser beside the clock which Mary Conlon had given her for a wedding present. She made herself a cup of tea and sat sipping it, looking into the flames of the fire. She had never been alone before and now she was feeling uneasy in the silence that was broken only by the tick of the clock and an occasional hiss from a damp log. At last she got up and took the package from the dresser. She lighted a candle, carefully opening the writings, and began to read, starting with the letter "Dear daughter Margaret". The unfamiliar form of address scarcely registered the fact in her mind that the letter was meant for her and she continued to read until she came to the end of the third notebook.

FIRST NOTEBOOK

November 1906

Dear Daughter Margaret,

I know you have never wanted to hear about your forebears. You have always turned away when I have tried to talk to you of the old ways. I have sung the song of sorrow all my days because I could not get you to understand what shaped my early life and that of my father and mother. Even if you are ashamed of me and you make it plain that this is so, you should not shun the grandparents you have never known. You are part of their flesh as well as mine. Their story is more tragic than ours and I hope you will pray for their souls and in time maybe include me.

For many years things have not been right atween us. I am not, now that I am old, trying to be a butter mouth and make excuses for myself, for indeed I have done wrong and will carry the guilt of my sin to my grave. In the end I hope you will forgive me, although I am sometimes not clear what I should be forgiven for. I had few choices in my life.

Thank God you are settled and married to a good man. Paddy told me two days ago that you are expecting your first bairn and since then I have tossed back and forard in my bed at night before deciding to write down all I can remember of our family before my eyes and my memory fail me. Even if you do turn away from these writings, your children (please God you will not rear an only child as I have done) might like to read about their ancestors. I shall leave the whole spiel and my few belonging for you to do as you like with them when I am gone.

May God hold you in the palm of his hand, Alanna. You have been everything to me. Where I have failed in my duty, I pray the Almighty and you too will forgive me.

Cliona O'Donnell
Your mother

All of this was told to me by Mrs Moore, the warden of the Newry workhouse. She sent for me just before she died and the story may be a bit mixed up as she was far through by that time. I was then working for the Fosters who allowed me to go to see her on Sunday afternoons when I was free from household duties. She made me sit by her bed and sometimes she would fall asleep in the telling. I have no way of knowing how near the exact truth it all is, but I have no reason to disbelieve her. Her memory may have played tricks on her for all I know and at times I think mine does too. When I start to think back I get confused. Still, I will try to write down everything as I understand it.

Sheila Mary O'Donnell was my mother's name. She was born in Donegal and married Declan, an itinerant weaver. He was an orphan, reared by an aunt in the county of Down. At first they lived in Dunfanaghy, near to Sheila's parents. This was during the worst of the famine. After the failure of the potato crop for three years running, Declan could no longer find work. There was no money now to pay for weaving the oiled bainin yarn into trousers for farmers or fishermen. Orders stopped for the making of shawls and stockings for women. All around, people were dying from hunger and disease. Souperism was common and a few did indeed turn away from their faith for the bowl of soup offered by those who would have them deny their religion. Some went to the Protestant church on Sundays and returned well fed and well clad, and sure, could you blame them? Anyway they could always go to confession afterwards. But most stood firm, even if it meant leaving the country to begin new lives in Liverpool, Canada or America. In general, those who remained were old or infirm and a few who stayed behind to look after them.

Sheila's father, encouraged by his landlord, gave up his few acres so that the owner could avoid paying taxes on their miserable shanty. With his wife and son, he set sail from Sligo, bound for Quebec. Mrs Moore said that the cost of the passage to Canada was cheaper than that to America and with good reason. American ships had some rules about safety and overcrowding but the regulations for Canadian vessels were few and far between. Before 1848 steamships were rare and in any case well beyond what Sheila's family could afford. They were therefore forced to travel in one of the overcrowded and disease-ridden sailing ships which later became known as 'coffin ships'. Both Mrs Moore and myself made such enquiries as we could but nobody from whom we sought information could find any trace of them in the registers of ships – landings or embarkations. I was forced to come to the conclusion that the likelihood is they caught fever and were buried at sea, like so many other unfortunates.

My mother's parents were not pleased when their only daughter refused to sail with them. Declan had persuaded her to go with him to County Down where he heard the famine was less severe. He hoped there was still work to be had, even the government-sponsored building of walls round demesnes or the breaking of stones for road-making for a penny a day. It would be laborious he knew but he was young, and willing to do anything to provide for his wife and his coming child. He did not believe in running off, he told the warden, as it always involved coming back. Sheila realised he would never be happy for long away from his native place. Her father complained that he was not of the land, not one of us, he said. She would not be comfortable living among strangers. He was none too pleased when Sheila pointed out to him that the land, at the best of times only provided them with the barest of livings and now had let them down completely. He wept as he listened to her. She knew he had an obsessive love for his native soil and she almost gave in but at the last moment told her father that she loved Declan and would follow him to the ends of the earth.

There was only one place they must avoid, she told Declan and that was Belfast. She had heard a story of how, just over thirty years ago, two weavers were hanged publicly on Peter's Hill for setting fire to a cotton manager's house. This was in protest against the new industry which was squeezing out the demand for traditional wool. She did, however, look forward to living among the low drumlins that her husband said dominated the landscape of County Down and the gentle Mournes he loved so dearly.

It took them nearly a week to reach their destination. At first they made good progress in one of the new Bianconi carriages which was fast and well sprung. Carlo Bianconi was an immigrant peddler who, in 1815, started a one-horse, two-wheeled passenger goods service. It radiated out from Dublin, the forerunner of the stage coach and was a popular means of travel. On the third morning of the journey however, at first light, a tragedy struck. It was found that a mother was concealing the death of her child by wrapping her in a shawl. There was panic. The occupants of the carriage knew that fever was contagious. The driver refused to go any further and abandoned his passengers in the town of Omagh.

The place, Declan said, was eerily quiet. No sound of horses' hooves came clattering over the cobbles. When an occasional carriage was abroad, those inside could be seen holding bunches of herbs to their noses to ward off fever. People were afraid to touch and if a sick person fell or stumbled, the unfortunate wretch might lie there for hours until some Good Samaritan chanced to pass that way. The instinct for self-preservation, Mrs Moore said, is very strong. Who would want to catch their death in such a painful way? Our travellers had no choice but to continue their journey on foot. Declan said that Sheila gave him a wry smile, when she realised she had no alternative, and ordered her legs to carry her forward.

The last days were difficult. Sheila was nearing the time when she would become bedfast. No complaint escaped her, when at the end of the day she lowered her aching feet into a stream and the sting of the water hit her blisters. Soon all the food they had left was one salt herring and a few small barley cakes. They were, however, looking forward to resting in Declan's old home on the outskirts of Newry. They were not prepared for the sight that stood fornenst them. The cottage was in ruins. Its bare walls rose starkly towards the sky. Masonry bees hummed as they darted in and out of the gaps in the lurching walls. Sheila turned away and let her eyes wander to the deserted garden. A wren made no sound as it hopped down a fallen branch looking for insects. She heard the soft bounce of a twig somewhere behind her as a bird ascended and began to sing. Turning toward Declan, she saw that tears were streeling down his face. She told him afterwards that it was at that very moment she felt her present life begin to float away. Her senses remained acute and she saw everything in the sharpest colours. A deep silence rose in her and she thought she had glimpsed paradise. Minutes later she became aware of the first pains of childbirth.

Declan said I was born in a tumble-down shed and even there the sweet sickly smell of decaying potato stalks invaded the building. My mother's labour lasted all through the night and most of the next day. He talked to her, holding her hand and murmuring words of encouragement in her ear. Once in the night, when they heard the raucous call of a corncrake, he made her laugh, in spite of her pain with a story he heard from his aunt. "When God was giving song to the birds," she said, "he called them all together to share out the sweetest melodies. The corncrake, however, dallied in the meadows and when at last he showed up only two notes were left and one of them was flat."

He sang her a song that he thought was called 'The Blackbird by Belfast Lough'. "What little throat has framed that note? What gold beak shot it far away, A blackbird on his leafy throne tossed it across the bay."

He told her about his boyhood, brought up with all-female cousins who taught him girls' games. Skipping, he said, was his favourite. Sheila said she could not imagine him bobbing over and under the ropes to the tune of "In and out goes Nancy Bluebell" or "Down in the kitchen, doing a bit of stitchin'". She loved to hear him talk of his childhood with its rhymes and sayings so different from those in Donegal.

It seems a few days after I was born my mother grew weak and couldn't manage to feed me herself and in spite of the help of several kindly women and many prayers she died. My father was distraught. He was dismayed to find that the Relief Act had been rigorously put into effect. This meant that all public works ceased and he and his child would be forced to depend on soup kitchens run by charitable Quakers. Sorrow moidered his brain; he felt defeated and for a time was unable to make any plans for the future. At last he was persuaded that there was only one way to keep me alive – something that until then he had refused to contemplate.

I was seven days old when Declan came stumbling into the workhouse holding me in his arms. At first he was refused admittance. His wife was from Donegal, didn't he know the law? Each county was required to look after its own destitute. In any case they were full up and overworked as it was, without taking an able-bodied man and a sickly looking child into their care. He promised to leave in a day or two, he just wanted to see me settled in, he said. He continued to plead until at last Mrs Moore held out her arms. Maybe it was because of an earlier acquaintance she had with my father or because she herself was childless. Something made her change her mind; the reason I shall never know.

"What will we call her?"

"Cliona Mary," he answered promptly, "that is what her mother wished."

He handed Mrs Moore my mother's wedding ring; the one you've seen me wear all my life, which you said was a hypocritical thing to do as I was never married.

The workhouse was originally built to hold about one thousand people, but when I arrived it had twice that number. I could write pages about my life there but will stick to a few details that will give you some idea of what things were like. Mrs Moore was kind to me and although this was consoling, it brought troubles down on my head. Because of my relationship with her, some of the others were jealous. They said I told tales, which wasn't true. There was a lot of bullying and stealing food from younger children who could not defend themselves. I was lucky that an older girl, Annie Sweeney, befriended me and protected me from the worst of the bullying. We were very great. Annie and I shared everything. Poor girl, she died just before her fourteenth birthday – a rickle of bones at the end. Nobody seemed to know what was wrong with her. She was tall and Mrs Moore said she had outgrown her strength. May she rest in peace.

Life was regimented. We rose at six-thirty, winter and summer, and washed in cold water. Sometimes on a frosty morning we had to break the ice first. Then we said morning prayers and ate breakfast which was oatmeal and a cup of buttermilk. On Sundays and Holy days we had champ, mashed potato mixed with shallots and a little milk, for supper. If it was your birthday you might be lucky enough to be given a herring. You can imagine the envious looks you got from others. Some of the older children suffered from scurvy but it was the little ones who were most affected by the poor diet. Many of them became blind.

I was lucky to escape to school for at least part of the time. In 1831 the English government began an experiment in education all over Ireland, partly to eradicate the language. National schools were built to educate all children. Attendance was compulsory although we were allowed days off to help with the harvest. Subjects were taught in English. It was forbidden to use the native tongue. If a child was heard communicating in his own language he was punished. You can imagine the confusion in some of the homes when there was eventually a situation where parents were unable to understand their children. Nevertheless, most youngsters grew up bilingual. The scheme was opposed by many of the Irish and hedge schools were set up to continue the language and Gaelic traditions. I would like to point out to you, daughter, that although a lot of people disagreed with what was happening, it proved to be a great boon in the long run to those who left the country. If you were able to speak and write in English it was much more likely that you would be able to get employment wherever you found yourself. I was glad I had the chance to go to school for many reasons. It gave me an interest in reading, although it was not always easy for me to get hold of books. I greatly enjoyed geography, and in my imagination I was able to travel to far-away countries, smell their exotic flowers, and see so many strange places and animals. I loved poetry although I was not able to understand much of it because mostly it did not relate to anything with which I was familiar. I still, however, remember the poetry of my very earliest days at school,

'Oh to have a little house' and 'I met a little elf man once'. My favourite was 'Pangur Ban'. Come to think of it, if I had not had any teaching, I would not now be filling these copy books for you or your children.

When I was almost fourteen and it was soon time for me to leave school, three gentlemen from the Board of Guardians came to the workhouse to talk to us about where we might find useful employment. One of them was a man called Harold Foster, tall and thin, with piercing grey eyes that I thought could see right through me. He told Mrs Moore that his wife needed another pair of hands in the kitchen. She wanted someone who would do as she was told, who wouldn't sit around all day with her two arms the one length. Mrs Moore assured him I was strong and willing, and she thought I would fulfil all his wife's needs. He made me stand in front of him and for a long time he stared down at me with cold, frogspawn eyes. He turned me round and whispered words to his fellow guardians which I could not hear but they laughed loudly, causing me to go red in the face. At last he informed Mrs Moore that I could start working in his house in two weeks time.

Harold Foster's looks had made me nervous and his long dangling arms, when he reached down to pat my head made me tremble all over. Mrs Moore told me I had no need to be afraid and that this position I was offered was a favourable one. She said I would have time off and be well paid. I must admit I was pleased to be leaving the workhouse but I was sorry to be parting from the warden and even more upset to have to give up my studies. I knew that bright pupils were sometimes awarded scholarships so that they could continue to learn. Mrs Moore, when she spoke to my teachers, was told I was eager and willing. She made exhaustive enquiries on my behalf but my hopes came to nothing.

By this time I had given up the possibility that my father would come back and claim me. When I was very young I dreamed constantly of his return and made elaborate plans for setting up house with him. Oh what a good housekeeper I would be, looking after his every need, cooking his favourite food and cleaning and maintaining our house in perfect order. I talked to Mrs Moore about my hopes before I left her care but she at last persuaded me that they were not likely to be fulfilled. She guessed that some tragedy had befallen him; he was, she knew, a good man who could not abandon his child. She had known him since he was a boy and believed in the sincerity of the promise he had made. Better now to put away all thoughts of him forever, she advised. I tried to take her advice and to fill my mind with other things, with the new life I was about to begin but in my inner heart I blamed him for letting me down. At last I promised myself, I would forget he ever existed and changed my name to my mother's – O'Donnell. It was only after you were born that I was able to let go of my bitterness, but by then I would have been so ashamed to have him find out the trouble I was in.

It was with mixed feelings that I took up my duties in Harold Foster's household. To my surprise and delight, I became as happy as a lark. By degrees I got used to the staff in the kitchen. I was teased at first but in a kindly way. I was taught how to clear out the ashes from the grates, lay paper, sticks and coal in layers to make ready for lighting the fires. I learned how to clean silver, set a table properly and many other duties that were not difficult once I was used to them. There were lashings and leavings of every kind of food. I ate so much boxty bread that I grew plump and pink-cheeked. I even became a few inches taller. The house boys joked with me and to my surprise I found myself laughing often. I tamed my wild red hair under a lace cap and rubbed cream into my hands at night to keep them from becoming red and chapped. Harold Foster's wife gave me some of her old dresses to be made over when cook told her I had grown out of the few things I owned. The seamstress did a good job and the girls said I looked pretty when I was dressed up to go to mass on Sundays. I felt I was a new person.

Most people had a good word of Harold Foster although one or two of the staff were seemingly afraid of him. One girl was vindictive. She said he would charm a bird from the bushes and then crush it in his hand if it suited him. I had no cause for complaint at that time; he did not seem to notice me, in fact he rarely saw any of the kitchen folk as he left all the domestic arrangements to his wife.

I continued happily for about two years until one day Harold Foster was unwell. He stayed in bed and I was sent to make a fire in his room. He told me he felt lonely all by himself and asked if I would stay with him for a while to keep him company. He patted the edge of the bed to indicate where I should sit. After some minutes of silence his long arms reached out and pulled me down beside him. I needn't go into the details of what happened next, you are, after all, a married woman now and will come to your own conclusions. This was the first time he had taken advantage of me but it was not the last. He would waylay me in the outhouse where I went for kindling. He would send me on little errands and I would find him waiting for me in the garden or the coach house. He gave me small gifts; liquorice or Peggy's leg, and once a lace handkerchief. He expected me to repay these kindnesses with the use of my body. I was terrified of him and too young to know the possible result of our actions. Things continued like this until it became clear to everyone that I was pregnant. My life changed overnight. The staff, once my friends, became distant and cold. The kitchen boys sniggered behind their hands when they saw me. One of them tried to be familiar and when I refused him he was quite insulting.

At last Harold Foster sent for me. His wife stood upright beside him at his desk. The room was full of fear. I was told I would have to leave. I was not to speak to anyone, not the staff or Mrs Moore in the workhouse, where I was a regular visitor. I was not to appear in public except after dark. Then I was advised to have the coming child adopted, all the arrangements would be taken care of, and I could have my job back after the birth. All this time his wife said not a word. I shook my head. Something in my own earlier desertion made me decide not to give you up, even though I had no idea what would become of us. If I was to get another job I would need a reference. Mrs Foster had never spoken to me in her life. She knew nothing about me and would defend her husband's good name. The blame would certainly fall on me. Harold was a Justice of the Peace, a landowner with a reputation for giving lavishly to good causes. His wife was well known for her charitable works. Who would listen to me?

When Mrs Foster left the study, without having once looked in my direction, her husband seemed to relent a little.

He said he would arrange a place for me to live in and when my time came he would send a midwife to help me, although he didn't make it clear how this was to be done. He then told me to pack my things and wait in my bedroom until I was called.

Just at the edge of dark, John the coachmen drew up at the back door. He carried my few belongings down the back stairs and put them inside the coach and we set off across town. We seemed to have gone a mile or so when he stopped and asked me to get out. I enquired where we were. John and I had always been friendly but now he did not answer. I will never know if he had been instructed not to speak to me or if he despised me because of my condition. We had drawn up at this cabin, where you and I lived all our lives until Paddy O'Neill came and took you away from me.

End of First Notebook

CHAPTER TWENTY-THREE

Maggie finished reading. She replaced the letter carefully on top of the notebooks and sat motionless until the tears that were welling up inside her broke loose and spattered down on the writing. She shook the letter to obliterate the signs of her grief and held it to the flames until it dried out a little. Then she wrapped the packet up again, adding an extra layer of strong brown paper. She rose and placed it in the trunk and, without undressing, fell into bed. When Paddy came to see her the next morning she was still there and only drank a cup of tea at his insistence. For several days she remained listless and at night experienced the same nightmare, always waking in terror, her body wet and sticky. At first she was only aware of a tiny light in the far distance which emitted a faint, hardly audible hum. Slowly it grew stronger. It approached with an increasing loudness which became unbearable. Just as it was about to explode in her face she would wake with a scream. For about a week she hovered in a sort or twilight, talking to herself, alternately moaning and weeping.

One morning Paddy opened a window. Through it the call of a blackbird came to her, clear and insistent. She lay listening and when the bird flew away she got out of bed and dressed slowly. Lack of food left her mindless and listless but now she told her son that she needed to get out. Refusing to allow him to accompany her, Maggie slowly climbed the small hill behind the cottage. The last of the autumn leaves described a circle in front of her where she sat breathless and suddenly she had the sense of some secret just out of sight, like a half-forgotten piece of music. There was an earthy smell all around her and looking down she saw some tiny pink mushrooms growing at her feet like magic discs. Her mind cleared and she felt that someone had removed a great weight from her shoulders. She was able to function once again. Maggie, who thought that the past did not matter, was astonished to find how much she had erred. Her mind kept returning to her mother's miserable life in the workhouse, her pregnancy and betrayal. She could appreciate how, in spite of this, Cliona had managed to make her child's early years blissful. She realised that she had never recognised her courage and endurance and knew she herself was not blessed with such tolerance for the hardships of life. She was astonished how the memories had reclaimed both her mother's and now her own past.

"Cliona could only have written them to help me to overcome my present sorrows," she told herself.

A strong wind blew up scattering the ripest of the mushrooms into dust. Where, she asked herself, has my happiness gone? What had she achieved with the life Cliona had struggled so hard to give her? A husband and three children dead, another child in Australia whom she was unlikely ever to see again, Rose and Lily in Dublin, too feckless to be bothered making the journey to see her more than once a year. The breeze was blowing with the voices of emptiness. The more feelings Maggie faced, the deeper were her sufferings. It was growing cold and at last the old woman rose and made her way back to the cottage.

She stood in front of her full-length mirror looking at her reflection. She saw a woman who had never been called beautiful but who was still she could see, straight and tall and with a good skin that had surprisingly few wrinkles in spite of her seventy-odd years. A smile crept to the corners of her mouth, softening the lips that were habitually set in a straight line. Slowly she put her hands to her hair and took out the pins that held it in place. She began to undress, uncharacteristically leaving the garments on the floor in an untidy heap. A small gasp made her aware that she was being watched. Ignoring this, she continued to divest herself of her chemise and lastly the whalebone corsets that had imprisoned her for most of her life. She went into the bedroom and when she returned she was wearing a comfortable wide skirt and a soft muslin blouse. Pushing open the door, behind which Elizabeth was skulking, Maggie called her inside. She picked up the corsets, wrapped them in newspaper, handed them to her daughter-in-law and ordered her to put them on the dung heap at the far end of the farmyard. Meekly, Elizabeth obeyed.

Maggie was unable to explain to herself, never mind the curious Elizabeth, the significance of her actions but she realised that the past was where she had been and now she had a need to move on. She had read about the struggles for women's emancipation in the newspapers, finding it ironic that ladies like Mrs Pankhurst would chain herself to a railing or go to prison to endure force feeding; a vote would not fill an empty stomach. Most of it made little sense to her. These ladies had lives that were to be envied, beautiful clothes, money, leisure. Women like herself had to toil simply in order to exist, to feed and clothe their children. Nevertheless, she was vaguely aware at some level of consciousness that she had sympathy with their aspirations and she did admire their pluck. From now on she decided she would resist all corsets and strappings and would step out in at least a measure of freedom. Cliona had lived a constricted life of poverty and shame to ensure that her daughter would find freedom. She had not fulfilled her mother's hopes but from now on she would live as she was and not as she might have been.

CHAPTER TWENTY-FOUR

Some days later Maggie rose early and went to gather the mushrooms she had seen. The walk tired her and having filled a basket she returned home and made herself a cup of tea, sat down by the fire and soon nodded off to sleep. She woke to find Sheila bending over her saying her name softly. Maggie reached out a hand and touched her daughter's face. She saw her head crowned with Cliona's copper coloured hair and whispered, "Mother, Mother."

It was Cliona's features she saw before her, the same auburn hair, the same gentle voice. Suddenly a rush of understanding came to her and she knew that the rejection she had felt for her mother had transferred itself to her own child. Maggie stood up and, ignoring Joe, held out her arms and drew Sheila into a close embrace.

"Elizabeth says we are all to go over to her for lunch."

"Indeed. And what else did Elizabeth have to tell you? Did she say that I had gone completely out of my mind as well as being sick in my body?"

Joe looked at his wife and answered, "Well, she wrote and said that you were really ill and she and Paddy thought you should not be living in this damp cottage. Sheila and I would like you to come to stay with us."

Maggie grinned, "And where would you find room for me?"

Sheila explained that they would not be living in their admittedly cramped house for long. "Joe," she said, "owns another property quite near to us in the village. There have been tenants in it for some time but now they are gone, thank goodness. After a few formalities are cleared up with the solicitor and repairs carried out we can move in."

Sheila broke into the short silence that followed.

"It's quite a sizeable property with an orchard and a walled garden, the house itself is old and quite beautiful."

Until this time Maggie had not been aware that her son-in-law was a man of property. Once, she would have been impressed by this information, but now she shrugged and told them she could live anywhere.

"Places," she said, "are not as important as people."

"Well, shall we go to Elizabeth?" Sheila asked, but Maggie was reluctant.

"If we are not there on the dot of one o'clock she will be over here like a shot. Let's make our meal here. We can sit cosily by the fire instead of venturing out in the rain, and when Elizabeth comes we can share with her."

She cut some bread and handed each of her visitors a toasting fork.

"I was just wondering what I was going to do with all the mushrooms I picked this morning. Would you like me to scramble a few eggs to go with them?"

Maggie relished the look of astonishment on Sheila's face, and immediately felt guilty when she remembered she had not cooked for her daughter since she was a child.

"I'm starving," Joe said, "and there's nothing I like better than mushrooms."

A month later Maggie left the cottage. Joe helped her to pile her few belongings, most of which fitted into her trunk, into the well of the trap. It was a sunny day but all the same he covered her knees and legs with a rug and put another round her shoulders.

"Sheila would make my life a misery I if let you catch a cold," he told her.

Maggie thrived on the attention that was now lavished on her. She played happily with her granddaughter Patricia for hours without tiring. When the foxgloves opened she showed the little girl how to burst them with a crack against the palm of her hand. They could be heard in brisk competition sticking acorn cups to their tongues to see whose could accommodate the most. Maggie placed a flat log on top of a stone and they sat, one at each end, swaying and singing: "See saw Marjorie Daw, Jackie shall have a new master, He shall have but a penny a day because he can't work any faster."

Her caustic tongue was stilled and instead of bitter words from her mouth came a string of doggerel and nonsense verse.

"Hey diddle diddle, my black hen, she lays eggs for gentlemen, Sometimes eight and sometimes ten, Hey diddle diddle my black hen."

She grew more like Susan and would point out to Patricia a frog, a pismire or a many-legged insect that she called a 'Hairy Mary', describing it as 'bimsey brown' in colour. Every minute that passed now held for her an intensity of shades, smells and texture which she had never taken time to notice before, and which gave her a new sense of being alive.

At times she was forgetful, but at others told stories of her early life that intrigued Sheila, who had been starved of such family lore. Direct questions elicited little response but now and then it was as if a latch seemed to loosen in her mind and she would reveal previously unspoken details of the hardships of her childhood. At last Maggie came to realise that her daughter set great store by these revelations, and she was glad that she had this one gift left to give. In her old age she felt she had been uprooted, but was now thriving in the soil into which she had been transplanted.

SHEILA

Chapter Twenty-five

The honeymoon plans had been kept secret. On the evening of her wedding Sheila Sanderson found herself in the Belfast Opera House listening to *Aida*. She was totally unacquainted with the classics. In those days before radio or television, living in the country as she did, the only music familiar to her was the traditional Irish jigs and reels, played mostly for dancing. At school 'Bobby Shafto' and 'Greensleeves' found no resonance in her. Of course, when her sisters Rose and Lily came home from the city at weekends, they sang snatches of popular music hall hits. 'Daisy, Daisy' and 'Oh Mister Porter' they warbled, to their mother's disgust, who said they were vulgar.

Sheila never dreamed that opera, which she'd vaguely heard about, could be so dramatic. Not that she understood much of it. The chorus was loud enough to make her want to stick her fingers in her ears and as for the animals galloping across the stage...what kind of man had she married, she asked herself? He was completely absorbed in the music and only noticed she was there during the intervals.

Yet she had known him for over twenty years. His steady blue eyes had sought her out on his fairly frequent visits to the farm when he came to buy poultry. She was a good-looking woman and had other proposals of marriage, all of which she turned down as acceptance would necessitate her leaving home. And she had promised her now dead father to remain on the farm to look after her mother. Joe Sanderson, unlike her other suitors appeared not to mind her refusals. He continued to smile at her, drawing her into a sort of warm complicity that suggested things could be different some day.

When her brother Paddy, who would inherit the farm, announced one evening that he would be going to marry soon, Sheila saw a bleak future stretching out in front of her. It was not that she minded sharing the home, indeed she would welcome the prospect of some young female company but she realised that in the likely arrival of babies, some at least of the childcare could well be added to her already burdensome workload. When Joe came by again she said, "Yes."

A few days after the wedding she began with great enthusiasm to put an end to the bachelor confusion she saw all around her. The sitting room floor was mosaiced with manuscripts. The piano top supported heavy opera scores and there were sheets of music littered all over the place. She found two sugar sacks and filled them with the dirtiest, most thumbed and best loved pieces, leaving only what she considered to be clean and presentable. Then she dragged the sacks to the bottom of the garden, sprinkled them with paraffin and set them alight. When the fire had done its work she returned to the house to prepare the evening meal.

The supper waited and was wasted that evening. When Joe came back from work and found what she had done, he picked up his violin and without a word, walked upstairs. There he closed himself in a bedroom and nourished only with the 'Food of Love', he stayed until long after midnight.

CHAPTER TWENTY-SIX

Not knowing what else to do with herself, Sheila continued to spring clean. She worked quickly. In the mornings she went over the rooms, scraping, polishing, scrubbing floors and doors, ledges and walls. On a good day she hung rugs on the clothes line and beat them with the handle of a broom to remove the dust. She sprinkled carpets with the damp tea leaves she had collected, before sweeping them up with a hard brush. She cleaned window panes with wet newspaper and scoured pots with ashes. The delicate Belleek china she removed from its cabinet, washing each piece with soapy water and rinsing it in cold before giving it a good polish with a linen cloth. Just before noon she would stop to make a meal for Joe and his helper Jimmy, so generous that they protested they would soon be as fat as Bran, the old Labrador, if she did not reduce the quantities. She bought knitting needles and fashioned so many pairs of socks that they suggested laughingly she should start a shop. She filled the small garden with lettuces and cabbages, but still she had time to spare.

Sheila was now free and unfree. It did not occur to her that she could adjust to a more leisurely way of living. When she tried to, she found that some essence in her life seemed to bleach away, leaving her vaguely guilty. The repetitive patterns of her old life had no sense of novelty, but they had purpose. Now everything in her working day was growing meaningless. Joe's attitude was even more bewildering. She thought he didn't notice her efforts when he arrived home with armfuls of blossom. They would make the place more cheerful for her, he said. Sheila wondered secretly if they were meant to hide some omission on her part, and looked around to see what else she could improve. She had been brought up in a home bereft of flowers, books, plants or ornaments, which were considered extravagant and unnecessary. True, there were a few plaster representatives of the saints and a statue of the Sacred Heart, but these were to encourage holiness, and flowers were to decorate the altar in the church. It took her some time to realise that hard work was not the most important thing in the world, nor was it expected of her. In her mother's home she had learned that a woman's happiness lay in the fulfilling of men's desires and this included keeping his house immaculate. Now, when Joe returned from work, he buzzed around her like a humming bee that had found a rich source of honey. He was proud of her, she knew, and like a thirsty flower she was ready to drink in any praise or compliment that came her way.

He took her walking and explained the existence of several derelict buildings in the village. They were, he said, disused scutch mills. The growing of flax was introduced to Ulster by the Huguenots, sixteenth-century Protestants who had fled from France to avoid Catholic persecution. Eighty per cent of Europe's flax was grown in Ulster. The seeds were imported from Holland, America and as far away as Russia. The land around, Joe pointed out, was ideal for growing the crop. It was pulled by hand, a back-breaking job, and tied into beets or sheaves with bands of rushes. Then it was placed in dams, made by diverting water from the numerous streams that abounded in the district. The flax was now weighted down with stones and left to rot, giving rise to an unpleasant odour in hot weather. After removal from the water, it was spread out to dry before being carted to the mills for a process called scutching. This involved machines which beat the flax, separating out the coarse tow which was called shoughs. Thus the village earned the nickname Shough Town. The mill work was dusty and posed a danger to the lungs. There was, however, a far greater risk. It was not uncommon for an arm or a leg to be lost if a worker was not vigilant when feeding material into the machines. Sheila had seen one-armed Alice round the streets.

"Yes," Joe replied in answer to her question. "Alice was one of the victims and got no compensation from the mill owners, who said she had been negligent." The process of making the linen came to an end when the flax was woven and spread out on bleaching greens to whiten before being sold to the manufacturer to be made into sheets, table cloths and all sorts of wearing apparel. Then the demand for it began to fade, partly because it was overtaken by the popularity of cheaper imported cotton and partly because the crops failed occasionally. The mills closed down one by one and the workers drifted away from Shough Town to find employment elsewhere. As a result the place was now shrunken to village proportions.

Listening to her husband relate the history of his village

she could see that the people who had once laboured in the fields or worked in the mills were still alive to him. Although her own upbringing on the farm was not without an awareness of the past, it had never seemed accessible to her. Did the 'Gaberloonie's field' indicate that a mentally defective person had once lived there? And what about 'the giant's grave'? Sheila did not believe in giants any more than she believed in fairies. Joe's world was more real to her even if she did not feel she fully belonged to it yet.

CHAPTER TWENTY-SEVEN

She liked it when Joe spoke to her of his childhood, a happy time spent with three brothers and two sisters in the rambling old house into which they would one day be moving. Sheila had to be coaxed to tell him of her early life and he was surprised to hear that, in spite of being one of a big family, she had felt left out, lonely. He asked her if there were not lots of men wanting to marry her and she laughed, relating how Billy Nesbitt, their nearest neighbour, came along one day as she sat in the sun drying her freshly washed hair.

"Billy," she said, "laid his hand on my head and suggested, 'Any time you want to marry, I'll be ready and waiting.' This proposal was anything but flattering. Billy could only walk with the help of a stick; it was a nurse he needed, not a wife."

"And how did you answer him?"

"I didn't. I just ducked under his hand and moved away. I had a picture of him in my mind slapping the rump of his dung-splashed cow with the same hand that was stroking my clean hair. His boots and trousers were always splattered with manure, and he stank. No marriage would be worth putting up with that."

"But there must have been others."

Hesitantly then, she began to tell him of the love she once had for Michael Morgan.

"I used to go with my mother every Saturday to do the shopping in town, mostly to buy groceries. The owner of the place we frequented had a son called Michael, and his father hoped to pass on the business to him. At that time," Sheila said, "he was attending college in Belfast but he came home at weekends to give a hand in the shop, weighing out rice, lentils, barley, oats and other dry goods into stiff blue bags."

"Did you mother know about him?"

"No, no. She did not allow any of her girls out on their own, especially in the evenings. We couldn't meet, but Michael was clever and thought up a scheme so that we could communicate."

"Did you never manage to go out walking together? Not even once?"

"No. One day he made a signal to me with his eyes when my mother was at another counter. I watched as he took a note from his pocket and put it in a sack of lentils which always stood in the same place. I saw that he did not push it far down, just covered it over lightly with a handful of grain. I was able to reply by the same method, but I used the barley bag."

"A cereal romance," Joe quipped, and then, apologetically, seeing the sadness in her face, "I didn't mean to make a joke about it. What happened in the end?"

"Well we continued exchanging letters, and eventually began to write things that we would never have the courage to say face to face. We grew very close, and the fact that no one knew made it very exciting for me. The letters were a lifeline, making things bearable in the anticipation of Saturday's communication."

Although she was growing less shy with her husband, Sheila did not reveal what, to her, was an epiphany in her life. At the time it had seemed easy and natural to write of it to Michael, but now she was more careful of what she wished to reveal about herself. She had finished hanging out the washing that day. Her mother was in town on some errand and the sun tempted her to take a few minutes break from work. Wandering across the fields until she reached the grassy sloping bank of the stream where the cattle drank, she stretched out lazily on the soft moss. She pulled a spent dandelion head and blew on it, watching the small umbrellas float and fade. A thin thread of smoke arose from Nesbitts' cottage and made its way towards her, but petered out just short of where she lay. A grasshopper thrummed to her right and she rolled over trying to catch a glimpse of the elusive creature. Her movement must have alarmed it into silence but she stayed quite still and soon she saw again the pale green gossamer wings unfolding from its slender body. Ants bustled about in the undergrowth and suddenly she was aware of all the sounds around her. She heard them together at first and then individually; a dog barking in the distance; a bee buzzing above her head, and again, the chirruping of the grasshopper. Each noise grew louder, clearer, and then they blended, becoming invested with a strange sense of anticipation. She listened intently. They faded, leaving behind a stillness, the purity of which she had no words to describe. It might have been a second, a minute, an hour. She sat up and looked around her. Nothing was changed, but all was different. She had experienced a timeless moment when all the strands of her life seemed to come together and assume some great meaning. She felt she knew who she was. She was the earth, the sun, the air. She no longer struggled to find a meaning in anything. She was part of everything and everyone. She understood little of it but some pulse of longing was born in her that day. Often she tried to recapture the experience and although she could recall every detail of the circumstances, and in spite of the intensity of her wish to do so, she was completely unsuccessful. Michael's reaction to her experience was disappointing. He could not understand any of it. He held to the conclusion that she had fallen asleep and dreamt it all.

Joe often went back to the subject of her early romance.

"I can't believe your mother was not suspicious about this affair with Michael Morgan. Surely she noticed something?"

"No," Sheila answered, giving her head a little shake. "She had nothing to go on except for the smiles we exchanged in the shop. I only left the farm on weekdays if there were October Devotions in the church, or very occasionally Benediction. On Sundays there were always those who where ready to gossip to my mother. I was never allowed out on my own so all we could do was to nod to each other in public."

"I think I'm jealous of this fellow Michael Morgan."

"You have no need to be as you'll find out when I tell you the rest of the story. In his letters he told me he wanted to go to sea in the great liner *Titanic* that was being built in Belfast at that time."

"He was not the only one caught up in the myth of the 'Unsinkable Ship'," Joe broke in. "Lots of people who should have had more sense left their homes and their jobs to sail on her, and I heard that many ladies in Belfast pawned their jewellery in order to pay for the passage. It was as if some madness got into them."

"It got into Michael all right. He would go down to the shipyard with some of the other students from his college. At first his letters described the ship as if it were sacred. The scaffolding, he said was like the nave of a cathedral. It rose above everything in the vicinity, towering up into the heavens as though to rival the mountains surrounding Belfast. Under the 'cathedral' floor, men had to kneel on concrete in order to construct pavements of oak and iron to support the bulk of the vessel when the time would come to slide it into the water. Space for three ships was given up to accommodate this liner, the biggest cruiser in the world, a floating palace. Michael wrote, too, of all of the beautiful fittings and furnishings; crystal chandeliers, polished mahogany staircases, the finest glass and china. No money was spared, and to think it all now lies beneath the sea." She paused in her story and her voice took on a darker tone.

"Michael wrote that towards the end there was a lot of intimidation and violence between the workmen. Insults were traded between Protestant and Catholic, superstitious tales were told, casting forebodings of gloom and evil that would await the ship. None of this prevented Michael from applying for a job on it and, to his delight, and his father's fury, he was accepted as a stoker for a trial period before the launch, and finally made permanent."

"Do you know, Sheila," Joe asked, "that fourteen years before the *Titanic* was built, a man called Morgan Robinson wrote a book of fiction in which he described just such a ship, which would carry three thousand passengers? It too was believed to be unsinkable, and suffered the same fate as the *Titanic*."

"That's a book I should never have the courage to read."

She did not tell her husband that for many years she had kept Michael's memory alive in her heart, hoping that somehow he had escaped, perhaps with his memory gone, but would one day recover it and return to her.

CHAPTER TWENTY-EIGHT

Sheila and Joe had accepted that they would not be able to have a family because of their advanced years. They were therefore surprised and delighted, if somewhat apprehensive, when they learned that Sheila was pregnant. Joe introduced her to an old family friend, Dorothy Maguire who never missed an opportunity to involve her in community activities. Soon the local women who had at first, she thought, been rather unfriendly, began to give her lavish advice on birthing, diets and to which saint she should pray for a speedy delivery. Dorothy, more sparing with advice, gave her the companionship she needed and much practical support.

Patricia was born on 17th March and named in honour of the saint. Sheila thought her life was bliss as she gazed into her baby's eyes and touched the small fingers and toes that reminded her of rows of peas without their pods. She felt she had served out the sentence of her childhood which had extended long after she had put her hair up and let her skirts down. It was over and now she had not only a family of her own but a close woman friend. What more, she asked herself, could anyone want?

Although Sheila was aware of the unrest and gun running that was rife in the countryside in the aftermath of the signing of the Treaty, she followed Joe's example and rarely spoke of the 'troubles'. It was easy to absorb herself in the cares of motherhood and the household. At night however, when she got up to feed or soothe a fretful baby, she sometimes heard alarming noises she took to be gunfire. One evening at the edge of dark, when she and Joe were returning from a visit to a friend, they saw shadowy figures which melted away into the bushes at their approach. Joe slowed the pony down and reached under the rug for her hand. She could feel that he was trembling. It was not until they reached the safety of their home that he was willing to answer her questions about what was going on.

"Not all the men," he said, "who were involved in the rebellion in 1916 laid down their arms. Some had long and bitter memories and are still roving around in groups, marching and improving their shooting skills in the hope that a time will come when they will be needed in another uprising."

"Didn't the treaty give them some independence?"

"Yes, but some would say not enough. For them it's a whole duck or no dinner." He was quiet for a while and then continued.

"And just how free are any of us? I am not free to live in my own house. Just a year before we were married, the police barracks in this village was blown up by a bomb. You know that heap of stones below the school house?" She nodded.

"Well that was where the police once operated from. It was then decided that my home, being central and spacious, was suitable to accommodate them, but I was not asked for permission, never mind given a warning. I returned from work one day and found all my belongings pushed out into the street and I was handed an official document stating that the property was requisitioned by the government."

Joe had related all this calmly and it was not until he came to the end of his tale that she saw his face grow dark as he described what he would like to do to the man or men who had manhandled his piano and broken the back of his precious violin.

Now she could understand why her husband had been apologetic when he brought her to the small cottage after they were married. He did not see that to her it was a paradise, a refuge, bringing her freedom from the demands of her family. She could never explain to him that in the end, it had been easier for her to submit to its tyranny, which could wear her out day after day in petty feuding and cause so much distress to all of them. Joe simply thought she had lived quietly keeping the best of herself for him.

When Patricia was a little over a year old, Joe persuaded Sheila to leave the child with Dorothy for a day. He took her to Belfast where they visited the places she had heard her brothers talk about. After lunch they went shopping, and he persuaded her to buy something for herself, refusing to allow it to be of a practical nature. At last she chose a little saucepan of a hat with a jaunty feather at the side. When she got home, she set it aside, declaring she could not possibly wear it out as it was far too stylish. But at last she was persuaded by Dorothy to change her mind, who said it was time someone brought a bit of fashion into their backward village.

Sheila lived a happy, uneventful life for a further six

months. Then Joe's solicitor told them that after much wrangling over rents and repairs, they were at last free to take possession of Benovent, their large property. Unthinkingly Sheila began to slip back into her old habits of scrubbing and cleaning, and it took quite a few hints from her friend Kathleen to make her see this was not the way to keep her husband and children happy, until at last she was able to relax and enjoy the spaciousness and freedom of the orchard and walled garden that surrounded the old Queen Anne house.

Chapter Twenty-nine

A visit from Paddy and Elizabeth, shortly after the move, disturbed the even tenor of her life. They admired the three-year-old Patricia's shiny hair and her wide smile and when they had consumed large quantities of cake and drunk several cups of tea, a silence descended on them, nobody seemed able to find anything to talk about. Elizabeth fiddled with her teaspoon and Paddy crossed and uncrossed his legs. Gradually the atmosphere in the room began to match the emptiness in Sheila's heart. Pictures of nameless things rose up in her mind and she realised that her new assurance was not quite enough to fill the gap left by past uneasiness. After a few false starts Paddy began to speak. He proposed that Maggie should be brought to live with herself and Joe now that they had more room. It was clear he said, she was not going to adapt to her present circumstances. Sheila reacted like a snail that had been touched on its horns. When she recovered a little she said she needed time to think over the proposal and to discuss it with her husband before giving an answer.

After the visitors left Sheila went into the garden and sat on a wooden bench. Memories of how she had always been at fault in her mother's eyes every time she tried to make a decision for herself arose in her mind. She could not forget the scorn heaped on her for being a plain girl who would never, according to Maggie, catch a husband. A stupid person who made up things when she was found writing a poem or drawing a picture. Having lived so long in this straitjacket, Sheila had no wish to return to it. Worse, Joe might be persuaded of at least some of her mother's opinions and attitudes. Lately she had begun to see herself in her husband's eyes and the image she found there was tolerable. She knew him well enough to realise he would be willing to consent to Paddy and Elizabeth's proposal. He would not be able to endure the thought of an unhappy old woman living alone and lonely in a damp cottage. She was continually amazed at his generosity and his concern for others. She knew he would not try to influence her but she thought he would be disappointed in her if she did not agree to accommodate her mother. At last very reluctantly she wrote to Paddy and Elizabeth consenting to their wishes.

In spite of her fears Sheila found to her relief that her mother took little time to settle into the regime of their household. Sometimes from an open window in the kitchen she could hear Maggie with Patricia in the garden, chatting cheerfully and arguing which of them could stick the most empty acorn cups on their tongues or make the loudest pop when the flower of a foxglove was burst against an open palm. She found a plank, mounted it on a stone and sitting opposite her granddaughter, they swayed and sang, "See saw Marjorie Daw, Johnnie shall have a new master, He shall have but a penny a day because he won't work any faster."

Sheila was almost fifty-one when all the indications seemed

to point to the fact that she was pregnant again. At first she refused to believe it, it was nine years since she had been in this condition. Joe's delight made up for her anxieties and once again her friend Dorothy was a source of encouragement. When the time came Sheila asked her to be Godmother and named the baby in her honour. In time the little one, unable to say Dorothy, called herself Dodie and the name stuck.

Patricia was less happy with her name. One day she came in from school with an aggrieved look on her face and in a demanding voice asked her mother, "Why didn't you give me a nice safe name?"

"Safe?"

"Yes, like Molly or Susan or Jane…"

"Don't you feel safe?"

"Only sometimes. At school they call me horrible names like Paddy, or Patsy, or Podge, never my proper name Patricia or even Trish."

"Ah well, when you are old enough you can change it to something else."

"Honest?"

"Yes." Patricia brightened up.

"There are lots of other things I will change too."

Sheila was not to learn what those other things might be as Joe came in just then and the subject was not pursued. Most of the time Patricia seemed to her mother a girl who was quiet in her ways and talked little to anyone. She had a habit of staring at people as though she thought that by looking hard enough she could learn what they were thinking. Once Sheila found her with an ear pressed against Dodie's head.

"What on earth are you doing?" Sheila wanted to know.

"I'm listening to what she's thinking."

When Joe's attention was drawn to these peculiarities he just laughed and answered, "Yes, I've often thought she has more eyes than a seed potato."

Two days after Dodie's second birthday, she stumbled on a step leading out of the kitchen. Although she came to no obvious harm, she announced solemnly, "Me not walk," and it was over a year until she was on her feet again. She lay in bed and refused to eat. Nothing Sheila cooked could tempt her. She grew weak and lost weight. The local doctor was baffled and called for another opinion but a satisfactory diagnosis was not forthcoming. Soon the child was refusing not only food but determinedly avoiding liquids. Doctor Lister called each morning and at length told Sheila to prepare herself for the worst any of these days.

She was ironing the lacy christening robe in which she intended to bury her younger daughter when a purposeful Dorothy strode into the kitchen one day. She had been keeping up Joe and Sheila's spirits recently, suggesting various remedies, pouring cod liver oil and other brews into Dodie's mouth and watching with disappointment when it trickled out again. She rubbed her over with various essences and herbal oils, none of which had any effect. Today she had with her a bottle wrapped in soft paper, carried carefully under her arm.

"Buckfast Tonic Wine," read this devoutly Catholic lady, looking at the label. "Made by the monks from a secret recipe, and guaranteed to nourish body and soul."

Sheila was persuaded to leave her ironing and pour some of the liquid into a spoon. She trickled it into Dodie's mouth and, to the astonishment of the women, it was slowly swallowed. A second helping was offered with similar results. They gave her another and soon the alcohol was taking effect on the small, emaciated body, and she was grinning up at them with a wicked look in her eyes. Sheila warmed some milk and put it in a feeder. Supporting the drunken child in a sitting position, she held it to her lips. This too was consumed without fuss. They covered her with a blanket, warmed at the fire. In no time Dodie was fast asleep. She continued to feed and in a few weeks she was running round again. Dorothy never doubted that the cure was the result of the prayers and sacrifices made by the holy monks. She sent them a grateful letter, she confided in Sheila, and a hefty donation. Maggie said she hoped the child would not grow up to be an alcoholic.

CHAPTER THIRTY

There came a time when Patricia and Dodie spent much of their days at school. Sheila noticed that the hours seemed to be long and boring for her mother, who would sit staring into the fire or wander aimlessly around the house. When she drew Joe's attention to it, he suggested that they should find her something that was connected with her earlier life on the farm, something that would keep her happily occupied. With help from Jimmy, he fenced off an area in the orchard and a few days after it was completed arrived home with a dozen geese. These he informed Maggie were for her to look after, and they could see that she was delighted with her new acquisitions. She derived a great deal of satisfaction from nurturing them with tidbits filched from the kitchen cupboard when she thought Sheila was not looking. She spent a lot of time talking to them, coaxing them to lay and when the first egg appeared she insisted on getting up early to cook it for Joe's breakfast. She liked to point out to anyone who would listen that her birds were clever, without being taught they guarded the property with their loud quacking when a stranger approached.

Workmen coming to the house to do repairs, fix a leaking

pipe or mend a fault in the electricity were afraid to get out of their vans and would only do so when Maggie came out of the door flapping her apron to chase them away. In the mornings they gabbled harshly at her approach, only softening their cries when she threw a handful of corn into the air in a golden spray. She laughingly told Patricia that their practice of trampling down the grass with flat iron feet was to enable them to see over it in case an intruder tried to break in. She found a lame duck which followed her everywhere and would have nothing to do with its brothers and sisters who lay peacefully in the grass in the orchard their bills reversed into the long feathers in their backs. Instead it followed Maggie into the house where it settled down beside Pangur on the hearth, its yellow eyes watching her every move.

Sheila regarded her mother with some astonishment and disbelief. Was this mild old woman the same person who had ruled the family so rigidly all through her childhood? Sometimes she thought the change was genuine but mostly kept an open mind while hoping things would continue like this.

CHAPTER THIRTY-ONE

"De Valera had a cat and it sat on the fender, And every time it caught a rat it shouted 'no surrender'."

Sheila straightened up from the sink, her face creased with laughter.

"I think you've got your politics a bit mixed up. Who taught you that?"

"Michael Fearon. The boys in his class know a lot of songs."

"His mother says he would do better to pay attention to his reading than to listen to that sort of rubbish. It's not a nice song."

The kitchen smelled of soap suds and washing soda. Monday was the busiest and the most unpleasant day in the week for Sheila. She always made a great pot of Irish stew in the morning to leave her free to get on with the washing, but it was a dish nobody appreciated, nor did they like the washing odours that permeated the house.

"Come on, Dodie, hold the clothes pegs for me please."

When they had finished and the washing was all attached to the line, Dodie told her mother that the sheets looked like great birds flapping forlornly, pinned down and longing to fly away. They mopped the floor and put the things they had used away, and then Sheila gave Dodie a glass of milk and a slice of treacle bread.

"When I'm grown up and have a house of my own," Dodie announced, "I will never wash clothes, hang them up on a line or bake any bread."

"What will you do for clean clothes then, and what will you eat?"

"I will buy new things when there are holes in the old ones and eat lovely sliced bread wrapped in shiny waxy paper from Bernard Hughes bakery."

"You will have to marry a rich man so that you will have plenty of money for all those things."

"I will never get married."

"Why not? Would you like to live by yourself? Wouldn't you be lonely?"

"No, no," answered Dodie. "When I'm married I'll have two dogs, three white kittens and a baby."

"Well there's plenty of time for that." Sheila turned away to place her own and Dodie's cup on the draining board when her daughter began to sing again.

"De Valera had a cat..."

"Dodie, please." Sheila sighed; in this country, she thought, it is impossible to get away from politics and, worst of all, sectarianism. She often heard the children on their way home from school, taunting each other.

"Splatter, splatter, holy water, we'll bury the papishes every one, If that doesn't do we'll cut them in two and give them a taste of the red, white and blue."

The reply to this might be, "Up a long ladder, down a short rope, To hell with King Billy and God bless the pope."

Antagonisms continued and although the riots in Belfast, Derry and other cities calmed down eventually, there were still sporadic outbursts of violence. It was an uneasy peace with discontent simmering not far below the surface. Sheila hoped nevertheless that the legacy left to them by their ancestors would somehow bypass her children.

Now and then when Dodie and Trish were at school and Maggie resting, Sheila would wander down the garden, maybe as far as the fields that surrounded the village. If something caught her eye, a clump of grass sticking out at an absurd angle, the formation of clouds or a heap of stones, she would sit down and make a sketch. She kept these activities secret, fearing the girls would think she was trying to compete with the pictures they made in school and brandished so proudly in her face. For many years she continued to draw and make sketches which she concealed and no one ever found out or even suspected that she had a secret addiction, even though she was quite unable to prevent herself filling in scraps of paper, old envelopes and the blank side of cardboard cartons with lines and doodles.

When Dodie was four and had not been seen for several hours, Sheila remained calm. She related how the child had come running to her crying and clearly in pain. She told her mother that Vonnie, one of her little friends, had pushed her over when they were playing a game of tig. Dodie fell on her arm which was now she said very sore. Sheila took her to the doctor who informed them, "Well young lady, you have broken your collar bone. We will be able to mend it but for a time you will have to have it in a sling."

Sheila turned towards the doctor to discuss the procedure and had taken her eyes off her daughter. In a flash, Dodie raced out through the surgery door and ran all the way down the street in the direction of home.

After an hour's fruitless search around the house and garden and, having questioned Vonnie to see if she could help them, they decided to look around their next door neighbour's garden which had a shed at the bottom housing bicycles and games equipment. They got no answer to their now frantic calls but on an impulse Jimmy got a ladder and propped it up against the outdoor toilet which adjoined the shed. He reported to those on the ground that Dodie was indeed within, sitting on the toilet seat, Pangur clasped tightly in her arms. She raised her eyes, he said, and looked straight at him but remained mute and defiant when he indicated that she should unlock the door. Sheila had to dissuade her husband against getting permission from their neighbour to break the door down, pleading for time and requesting everyone to leave.

At first she tried with bribes, a whole bar of chocolate, a day off school, but none of these had the desired effect. Knowing that her daughter was afraid in the dark, Sheila told her that she was leaving her as she had to make the evening meal, and waited nearby for several minutes. The light was fading rapidly and at last the door of the toilet was edged open. Pangur streaked out, followed by a tearful Dodie, but not before Sheila promised that there was no question of putting her arm or, as Dodie had understood it, her body in a sling. Not much wonder, Sheila thought, the child was in a panic. She evaded Joe's work place herself, going there only if it was unavoidable. The turkeys, having been killed and plucked, had their feet tied together and were then suspended by a hook attached to a beam in the rafters of the loft. The process was referred to as 'putting the birds in slings'. It was a fearsome sight, rows of turkeys hanging upside down with blood dripping from their beaks. It could unnerve an adult, never mind a child. Once Dodie was persuaded this was not to be her own fate, she seemed to forget her fright and was even persuaded by her father to visit the scene of the slaughter after a few weeks.

Chapter Thirty-two

"hy is Dorothy always late?" Sheila mused as she waited for her friend to join her in a shopping expedition. It was an outing both women enjoyed and she was impatient to be off. Idly she picked up a book that lay on a small table beside her and flicked through the pages. As her mind gradually began to take in the text, she grew absorbed and did not notice Dorothy coming into the room and standing before her, inserting a long pin into her hat.

"Well what do you think of *Pride and Prejudice*?"

Startled, Sheila looked up. "I don't know. I've never read anything since I left school so I can't judge. Reading always irritated my mother, discussing a book was showing off. Maggie always saw education in terms of procuring a way to make a living."

"Perhaps," Dorothy said thoughtfully, "she might also have imagined that it would put a gulf between you; a sort of jealousy."

Suddenly Sheila felt some pity for the old woman, realising the emptiness in her life that could have been filled if pride had not stood in her way.

"You know, Dorothy," she reflected, "she contributes to

magazines every week, religious writings; *The Far East* and *The Messenger of the Sacred Heart*. She reads them from cover to cover so evidently it is not a lack of literary skills that makes her stop short of more ambitious writing. She also reads the daily paper."

"Well," Dorothy pointed out quietly, "you can do better than that. Take this with you," pointing to the volume in Sheila's hand, "and let me know what you think of it when you are finished."

Dorothy was amused by her friend's response to Jane Austen's book.

"I just cannot imagine a woman sitting all day doing nothing except trying to make herself look good or at best working on a bit of embroidery. And I don't hold with plotting and scheming to ensnare some rich man into marrying, so that she can live in luxury for the rest of her life. It's immoral."

Dorothy laughed and took another volume from a shelf.

"Try this one, *Jane Eyre*. It was written by a woman whose father was born just a few miles from here. Not that she had much sympathy for the Irish. I think it might appeal to you more than *Pride and Prejudice*."

Dorothy was right and amused by Sheila's enthusiasm. She suggested that next time they were both in town she would introduce her to the local library.

So began an interest that gave Sheila pleasure for the rest of her life but it was not unmixed with guilt. In addition to stealing time to draw, she felt she was also taking time to read. Shouldn't she be washing or mending or doing something for the children? Was such indulgence not sinful? Soon, however, the delight she took in reading overcame her worst scruples. At first she restricted herself to a period when the girls and Maggie were in bed and Joe engrossed in his music. She would leave the door ajar in case anyone called to her and usually, for a blissful hour or so, lose herself in a book.

CHAPTER THIRTY-THREE

Underpants, socks, nightshirt," Sheila murmured to herself as she neatly packed the case that lay open on the bed beside her. "He won't need much for a day or two, at the most three nights."

"Why don't you go with him?"

Sheila turned round and a handful of linen handkerchiefs fell to the floor. Picking them up she waved them about vaguely enquiring from the figure that stood at the door, "Go where?"

"With him. Where ever he is going."

"You know he is going to Liverpool on business. You were there when we talked about it this morning."

"I did not hear him discuss the business he had with Old Ned on Saturday afternoon."

Sheila paused, closing the case firmly before lifting it from the bed and facing her mother. She was disturbed now and wondered if this was what was intended? It dismayed her to think that in spite of her new found confidence in herself and Maggie's welcome affability she was not wholly convinced that the change was either genuine or enduring. She thought now that Maggie had reverted to her old suspicious ways, assuming that Joe was going on some sort of spree leaving his wife at home. He had been away before, not often; three times in the past five years to be exact. On his return he had not said much about what he had been doing and she had thought nothing worth talking about had occurred. He had been to Manchester, Glasgow and London and always said how glad he was to be back home. In spite of that, he had often seemed depressed but she put it down to fatigue. Impatiently she shook her head; she would not let Maggie see that she would question her husband's affairs.

However the doubts that her mother had managed to implant in her mind persisted. What about Old Ned? Looking back, it now seemed that his visits had always preceded Joe's decision to go on a journey. Three days ago when he came to the back door she invited him in but he declined her offer of a warm drink in spite of the cold November chill and stood, his shoulders bowed, feet shuffling uneasily in shabby boots. She knew little about him, only that he lived alone at the edge of the village and kept himself very much to himself. What business could he have with her husband? He had not been prepared to tell her, that much was clear. In any case, Jimmy had walked up to them and offered to escort him to the packing shed where Joe was supervising some orders.

Later when she was giving the children their after-school bread and honey, these misgivings were driven from her mind by the young ones' chatter but during the evening meal Maggie put to Joe the same question she had asked her daughter earlier in the day. "Why don't you take her with you to Liverpool?" she asked.

Sheila glanced at him and for a moment wondered if there

was alarm in his face? At the bottom of the table Jimmy dropped his knife which fell to the floor with a loud clatter. He picked it up and immediately and asked if someone would please pass the salt? Sheila's instinct was to protect Joe from her mother's intrusiveness and she broke in quickly, "It's impossible for me to get away. The children need me here and on Thursday there is the meeting of the Saint Vincent De Paul Society and..."

"I'm sure Saint Vincent De Paul could do without you for once. And between myself and Dorothy we could see that the children would come to no harm."

Sheila was about to make a sharp retort, but Joe joked quickly that he would take Maggie herself only he knew she would not be parted from her geese. Sheila took a deep breath and turned to her mother, speaking gently, "Thanks for the offer but there is no need for me to be away from home at present."

The somewhat awkward silence that followed was relieved when Patricia spoke up, "Our teacher slapped a boy in school today."

"She did? Why was that?"

"He pulled the wings off a fly and then poked it with a pencil to make it walk across his desk. I told Mrs Mackey on him, so I did."

"Tell tale tit, your tongue will split and all the little doggies shall have a little bit." Dodie chanted.

"No Dodie," Sheila intervened, "it was right that Patricia should try to put a stop to such wickedness. He was making the poor fly suffer. That was wrong."

A discussion on cruelty to insects, birds and animals followed and the subject of Joe's trip was brushed aside.

Sheila hoped her husband would set her mind at rest before they went to bed that night. He helped with the washing up and to settle the children to sleep before disappearing into the sitting room to play his violin as usual. Later, when he joined her, he was carrying the instrument with him. She watched as he placed it in its case and closed the lid firmly before turning to her.

"I'll be taking this with me," he said. "Dorothy's brother and myself will play a few duets before the night sailing goes out."

The fire moved restlessly in the grate. Sheila sat for a long time listening to the quiet tick and tock of the clock, before realising that she would have to be content with this crumb of information. Suddenly the sound of the clock ceased to be soothing and grew into something ominous.

Try as she might, Sheila was unable to dismiss the questions that rose in her mind. John Toland, Dorothy's brother was a teacher; a bachelor who lived in Belfast. It was quite normal that Joe should pay him a visit when he had the opportunity. It did not have any connection with the business trip her husband was about to undertake. All the same...would Dorothy be able to set her mind at rest? At once she dismissed the notion of asking her friend. It might put her in the position of having to be disloyal to one or the other of them. Maybe Joe would tell her in his own good time. But in the sleepless night her curiosity grew and with it more disturbing thoughts. Her husband did not trust her. She began to feel this as a snub to the citadel of the self that she had so painfully built up. During the day she feigned a cheerfulness that she did not feel and at last came to the conclusion that it was imperative for her own peace of mind to find out more. The alternative, she feared, would be a life of waiting, never knowing any certainties which would settle into a grey hopelessness that could destroy her. Already she imagined she and Joe were becoming unreachable to each other. She questioned herself. Had she been remiss in any way? Had there been in their marriage any kind of deception? Did she only see the things she wanted to see? And if so, wasn't that a kind of dishonesty? She now resolved to face up to anything that might lie concealed.

Lily came to see her mother two days later and was easily persuaded to stay for a little longer than she intended. Sheila kept the plans she was making to herself. It was easy to book a passage on the Liverpool steamer for travel on the day after Joe's intended departure. She would take a taxi from the docks and go to Reid and Armour, the company with which he did business in the city. It was straightforward. In the early days of her marriage she had taken over Joe's book-keeping and the address on the accounts was familiar to her. It would not be difficult to find the offices of such a well known firm. Dressed in her good winter coat and Joe's favourite blue dress, Sheila sat in the bus bound for Belfast and for a while she was able to put her anxieties aside and enjoy the scenery. She was filled with a sense of adventure, shivering with anticipation. Having spent the whole of her life attached to earth, she reflected she was now going to part from it and sail on the sea. What would it be like? Joe would be glad to see her, and later they would go out for dinner and she would explain gently to him how his silence was undermining her peace of mind. It would be a new beginning. She thought of how they had started their life together, the flowers he had brought into her flowerless life. She saw them sitting together in the Belfast Opera House and remembered the maroon and gold walls, the glittering chandelier and velvet curtains. She had not loved him then, but had moved mountains so that he would continue to love her. Now she felt she could not live without him.

CHAPTER THIRTY-FOUR

Standing at the rail of the departing ship overlooking Belfast Lough, Sheila wondered for a moment how she must look to the people waving on the quayside, a small solitary figure with no one to send her off. An anxiety had taken hold of her now, tinged with a slight pity for her plight. Soon, however, the boat began to rock as gently as a cradle and lulled her into quietude.

At last she made her way to her cabin and found, to her dismay, that she had to share with another passenger. It had not occurred to her to book a single compartment and she had presumed she would be alone. The other occupant was asleep in the bottom bunk. Without undressing, Sheila climbed aloft and lay listening to the engine. It reminded her of the sound of the threshing machine on the farm which had so fascinated Dodie when she first heard it on a visit to her grandmother. She saw her child's face before her. Was she waking from one of her occasional nightmares, her little fists scrunched up into her eyes and the tears escaping down her flushed cheeks? Was her sister Trish sitting on the edge of the bed telling her a story that would send her gently back to sleep, their differences of the day forgotten? Sensible

Trish, probably assuring her that Mammy would be back in the morning when they woke up. Dodie, she reflected fondly, always open to the sufferings of others; a bird, an animal, a sick person. The boat began to rock and roll, its movements causing her to feel nauseous. Soon she had to get up to be sick. The girl in the bottom bunk groaned and turned her face to the wall. Sheila stumbled out on deck, remaining there until the icy wind drove her in again.

Next morning she washed her face and hands but could not eat breakfast. Making her way down the gangplank feeling listless and insecure, she thought she had been deprived of a great adventure. All about her she saw evidence of frenetic industry, factory sheds, networks of coiled greasy pipes connected to fuel tankers, oil drums, bridges and cranes stretching away up into the air. The smell of oil made her fear she would be sick again. Her fellow passengers chattered cheerfully as they made their way to bus or train. One or two of them glanced curiously at her before hurrying on. Looking down, she saw a bird lying on its side. It seemed to be very sick with ruffled feathers and a yellow beak that kept opening and closing as though it was trying to tell her something. She moved away with the intention of finding food or water and as she turned aside she thought she heard it calling her back. After buying biscuits and a bottle of water, she returned to succour the poor creature but could find no trace of it although she spent at least fifteen minutes searching. A gull sat on an upturned oil drum near where she was searching, watching her with a malevolent eye. She shooed it away and then sat down in the place it had vacated.

Sheila did not know how long she sat on the oil drum

or if she had dozed a little. Behind her she heard the water dashing against the sea wall like an angry bull.

"What am I doing here at all, at all?" she asked herself aloud. "What would Joe think of me if he could see me sitting here like a diltie without a thought in my head for my home or children? He has already handed over everything of himself that he can in order to make me happy, everything I ever wished for. What matter if he keeps a bit of himself to himself? Haven't I too always been quiet about some of the things that are most important to me?"

She heard his voice calling to her as he came in from work.

"Are you there, Sheila?" As if he feared she would have run away. And her unchanging answer, "Sure, where else would I be?"

His return always illuminated her, making her feel needed as the smile on her face transferred itself to his features. She thought of the way he led her into the garden of an evening to look at a beautiful sunset or at the stars glittering high up in the sky on a dark night. He gave her his eyes to see through, so that she could appreciate the wonderful things of this world, to which she had previously been blind. Now she experienced such grief mixed with intense shame that she thought it would never leave her.

She opened her eyes and saw the sun reflected on the sea. It began to vibrate like a soft light within her body, bearing her away to another realm, strange but at the same time familiar. Colours were vibrant and a clearness filled the air and filled her too. She had experienced this bliss before but its recurrence had always managed to elude her. Now she knew it was a gift, unearned, unasked for, something bestowed on her like a blessing. Smiling, she rose, her footsteps making no sound as she walked through the falling snow to the ticket office where she purchased a fare to Belfast on the next sailing.

A bird sang overhead as Sheila stepped off the bus. She stood listening for a moment feeling grateful to be home. She entered the house by the backyard and saw the clothes she had hung on the line the day before. They creaked and swayed in the frosty wind, stiff-legged trousers and jumpers with unyielding arms. She looked through the kitchen window and saw Maggie sitting dozing by the fire. At the long pine table, Trish was bending over her homework. Dodie, with head to one side and tongue sticking out was making a picture with coloured crayons. In the middle of the table sat Pangur, back straight, her tail a ramrod, looking from one to the other of the children as though acting in a supervisory capacity. Sheila lifted the door latch without making a sound. The cat saw her first. With one vertical leap she rose in the air and landed on Sheila's shoulder, draping her soft body round her neck, making a fur collar.

"Where have you been?" Maggie asked crossly. "You look awful. Your eyes are like two holes burnt in a blanket."

She was spared making a reply when Dodie jumped up and hurled herself against her mother's legs, clinging on tightly.

"Gran said you had gone off with the gypsies because we didn't behave ourselves."

Sheila patted the unruly red hair. Between her sobs the child gasped, "I love you Mammy."

"Sure, why wouldn't you, daughter? Now let me take off my coat and hat and we'll have a bit of this nice chocolate cake I bought for you in Belfast."

"Belfast, is it?" Maggie sniffed.

Sheila looked round her. All I need is here, she thought. I have lived through a storm and sailed safely back to port. In time, I hope I will find it difficult to remember I ever made such a foolish journey.

After her abortive trip to Liverpool, Sheila resurrected the invisibility she had practised in her early years. She was content to accept whatever came her way and when she did so found everything simplified, no questions, few problems. This led to a place where peace of mind was once more possible. She made herself indispensable to the family, a protector and caretaker, and ruled her house with cheerful service. Outside and inside the home she was popular, if somewhat withdrawn at times. She was grateful that her mother continued to show no animosity towards her and Joe, who noticed her new found contentment and put it down to the influence of his friend Dorothy. Trish imitated her mother; she too was learning to watch in silence.

CHAPTER THIRTY-FIVE

In early 1939 rumours of war with Germany abounded and there were those who, aware of the horrors of World War One, simply refused to believe that England would not find a way to escape another such obscenity. Around Sheila's kitchen table the talk took on a decidedly political aspect. A few of Joe's workmen supported Hitler, pointing out what he was doing for the impoverished in his country. Old Ned held the extreme view that England's misfortune might be to Ireland's advantage. Others replied angrily that this was merely wanting revenge for past wrongs, and anyway violence only resulted in more violence. Hadn't this always been the case in Ireland? A few of the younger men spoke of joining the forces in the hope of a better way of life when the war, if it came, was over. The air seemed full of menace and anxiety. Sheila, listening to their talk, was filled with memories of her oldest brother Johnnie's fate, but she kept her thoughts to herself.

In spring, Old Ned came to the back door and Joe disappeared again for a few days. He returned from wherever he had been, looking pale and tired, and although it was early afternoon he took himself off to bed for a rest. Next day he did not work, but spent the time restlessly footering about the house, lifting his violin and then putting it down again without playing a note. A few days later he sent for his solicitor and was closeted with him for over an hour. Sheila was somewhat reassured when he told her he was making his will because the times were once again unsettled. She told him she thanked God she had a husband who was too old to be involved in war but he turned away from her and as he did so she noticed there was sadness in his face. To cheer him up she insisted they have a holiday together by the sea. It was the first time since they were married that they had gone away for any length of time, and, although Joe said he enjoyed it, she could sense that he was restless and anxious away from the children. His health did not improve and in a few months he was unable to get out of bed.

Both girls were now at school and one day, when the house was quiet, Joe said to her, "Stay with me for a while. There are some things you and I ought to talk about." He began by telling her the details of the will he had made, then hesitantly, "Maybe I should have spoken to you before about my brother Michael, but I kept hoping he would turn up and explain himself why he disappeared so many years ago."

For some time there was silence until, with what seemed an effort, he began again. Sheila, who knew her husband for a man of few words, held her breath. "Michael is six years younger than me; when our mother died, he was just a little fellow in short trousers. He was completely lost and followed me around like a puppy dog. He wouldn't let me out of his sight. My sister, Noreen, looked after us the best she could until she got married."

He took a sip of water from the glass on the bedside table.

"Michael and I were both musical and learned to play violin and piano. He was more talented than me and was often invited to play at parties and in the drawing rooms of the wealthy."

"Didn't you get invited too?"

"Oh yes. we frequently played duets, but Michael was the popular one. He was handsome and many of the girls in the village fell in love with him, including your friend Dorothy. Then he disappeared."

"Dorothy? She never once mentioned Michael to me in all the years I have known her."

"None of us talked about him, except in private. People felt in the end we should forget about the troubles and get on with our lives."

"How long is it since Michael went away?"

"After the treaty with England was signed; this was followed by partition and then the civil war. As you know, even our small village was in turmoil, and around here there were lots of republican supporters. Anyone in the IRA was sworn to secrecy. A parent, brother, sister, wife, would not know for sure if a relative was engaged in warfare. This, of course, was to protect families and friends from the reprisals that were carried out frequently and often with great cruelty. Old Ned's sister, for instance, was found in a ditch, and it was clear she had been physically tortured."

"Was Ned in the IRA?"

"That I would not swear to, but he was picked up and put in prison after the police barracks was blown up. You know where it stood? The remains are that heap of stones by the school. He probably learned a lot of things when he was inside and anyway he is one of those people who seem to know or have heard of everyone. Well, after my brother disappeared I didn't know who to turn to, until it occurred to me that Ned might be able to find out something about Michael's whereabouts. Although he seems a simple sort of fellow, Old Ned is not as stupid as he seems. It was only after things settled down he began to boast about his escapades while he was on the run from the British army. He claimed to have been head of one of the divisions of the IRA, but most people think now that he was only boasting to make himself some sort of hero. Anyway, if there is any truth in this, might he not be able to find out the fate of my brother I asked myself, because some people would say even to this day that Michael was an insurrectionist?"

"Did you ever get proof that he wasn't?"

"I have been to Morocco, London, Manchester and Liverpool, but all the leads were in vain."

Suddenly she understood why she had found her husband, on more than one occasion, caressing a violin that belonged to his brother, but never attempting to play it. Nor would he allow anyone else to use it. At such times there was an intensity of grief on his face that, although she longed to comfort him, she refrained from doing so, instinctively feeling that such a sorrow could only surface when he was alone. Now, when he mentioned Liverpool, she bent her head and the tears came, and at last, she admitted to herself that there had always remained a suspicion in her mind that Joe might have a lover, perhaps even a second family. Her husband, mistaking her tears for sympathy for himself, reached out for her hand where it lay like a limp flower. After a few minutes he began to talk again.

"There were those in the village who maintained that Michael was involved in the blowing up of the barracks and that this was the reason the government requisitioned this house. I doubt that very much. It seems to me they did not have much choice. This was the most suitable place around. It was central and had lots of rooms. Michael loved the old house and I know he would have come back to it, and to me, if something hadn't happened to prevent it."

"What do you think is the most likely explanation?" Sheila asked, drying her eyes on the corner of a sheet.

"If it was true that he was in the IRA, there is the likelihood that he died in some sort of shoot-out. I don't believe it, as you know, but he should realise how I miss him, and in the passing of the years he must have heard that we now have relative peace. So he would be in no danger were he to return home. I fear something else has happened to him, some other misfortune. Mind you, he was a bit of a wanderer. He once went off to South America on a cargo ship, but he would be, like myself, an old man now and the homing instinct too strong for him to stay away."

"Maybe he learned that you got married and didn't like the idea of sharing you and his home with a wife."

"Ach Sheila, my brother would love you as I do, I have no doubt of that." Her hand still lay in his like a helpless little bird.

"The reason I'm telling you this now, Avic, is because when I'm not here, there is just a chance that he will turn up. I have left everything to you in my will but I want you to understand the situation and take him in if he came back, homeless."

"Joe, you know full well that he would be as welcome

as the flowers in May if he ever showed up on the doorstep."

"No matter what happens to me now, I will die happy in the knowledge that you will not only look after our children but my brother as well, if need be."

"Shush. You're doing rightly. In no time you'll be out and about," she said confidently withdrawing her hand. "Now you must let me go and see to the children who will be back from school any minute…"

CHAPTER THIRTY-SIX

In spite of Sheila's optimism, Joe did not long survive. At his funeral service the local church was packed to overflowing with villagers, friends and relatives. Sheila's sisters with black-clad bodies and sombre voices moved quietly down the aisle with their husbands. Elizabeth, wearing a hat with great swaying plumes was supported on Paddy's arm. Sheila sat with her children in the front row. She looked with dazed eyes at the throng of people as they made their way out, feeling acutely that the village had never belonged to her as it had to Joe. He had been her homeland.

For many months Sheila felt numb. One night, unable to sleep, she rose and wandered around the garden, listening to the night voices all around her; the screech of an owl, the croaking of frogs and the call of a nightjar. In the bright moonlight she saw a dead rabbit where it lay under the hedge with open eyes like the eyes of a child. A sob escaped her throat. Nearby a spider's web caught in a gleam of light had droplets of dew reflecting the tears that came at last to her eyes. It was only then that she felt able to go back to bed, where she fell sound asleep.

At first she attempted to carry on her husband's business

but she lacked the experience of buying and selling. Soon the lorry, carts and other equipment was sold. Jimmy declared his intention of using the small legacy Joe had left him to repair an old cottage bequeathed to him by a hitherto unheard of uncle. He volunteered to come back once a week to do some gardening or running repairs when needed, and if his new job permitted. Sheila tried to persuade him to stay but he was determined to strike out on his own. She suspected he had always been jealous of her place in Joe's affections and although they had always been reserved with each other, she would miss him. So too would Patricia and Dodie who in their early years, had appreciated the piggy-backs he gave them and his quick responses to their entreaties to mend broken toys or bicycles.

Weekly visits to the library had always been a pleasure to Sheila. In the years that followed Joe's death they became central to her life. At first she used books as a means of escape, reading quickly and remembering little of the content. Gradually she perused them more slowly and began to widen the scope of her intake. She found herself interested in art and the lives of artists. She remembered a time when she was young and, when making up stories to amuse her brother and sisters, she had often made sketches of the fairies, ogres and animals she told them about. She brought a sketchbook and it was not long before it was filled with drawings that, although they gave her satisfaction, she kept well hidden from the eyes of the family.

When she saw an advertisement for art classes in the library, she decided to enrol. Here she learned to mix colours and was expected to make copies of arrangements of fruit and flowers. Instead of doing so, Sheila simply messed about, experimenting with colour and shade. At home she continued to sketch with pencil, and, seeing some of these, the teacher suggested she use black oil paint to delineate instead. She kept this piece of advice in the back of her mind but continued to enjoy her own abstract water colours. Soon she was producing work that pleased her teacher, but which still left her unsatisfied. She would look at a thundery, dark sky which threw an oppressive light over the garden. It found an echo inside her, but no matter how hard she tried, she was unable to get it on canvas. She wanted to catch the nuances of light as it fell on Pangur's face when he stretched a paw to swat a butterfly, or the fall of the shadows under the trees at sunset. Sometimes she would sit, narrowing her eyes and looking intently at a scene trying to find a way to reproduce what was in front of her. She believed that a painting should be beautiful and that somehow she was failing in her appreciation of what was around her. All the same, she continued to paint, finding satisfaction in the effort itself. She knew that Maggie was baffled by this new enthusiasm and suggested her lovely white geese would be more worthy of Sheila's time and trouble.

CHAPTER THIRTY-SEVEN

At Joe's graveside on the day of the funeral a vague anxiety, light as thistledown, had blown in Sheila's direction. At the time her heart and mind were too overflowing with grief to pay much attention to anything outside herself. She remembered afterwards, however, that Patricia, always so consistent, had acted peculiarly. She stood with the mourners her face smiling one minute and then rapidly changing to a twisted grin. She had to be persuaded by the aunts to leave the cemetery, pulling away from them as they took her by the arm to lead her home. In the days that followed she was quietly sorrowful but remained tearless. She began to work even harder at school, especially at mathematics, a subject in which she had shown little interest previously as far as her mother knew. She asked Paul Murray, a neighbour and newly qualified teacher, to tutor her in his spare time. None of this application to her studies was unusual for Trish but her mother was vaguely troubled although she found nothing with which she could tax her.

Sheila was aware that her elder daughter was impatient and occasionally ashamed of her family. She was kind and obedient and found it impossible to refuse people's requests, especially those of her grandmother. When Maggie asked her to go shopping with her she seemed to believe it was a duty to obey, but Sheila noticed that she cringed when they were ready to set out, Maggie wearing a long bombazine skirt and ugly buttoned boots which showed up her bunions. Dodie informed her mother that on such occasions Trish tried to avoid her school companions, stopping to stare into a window or dragging Gran down a side street. Some boys made fun of her, Dodie said and when they did she would stop and confront them to Trish's mortification, saying loudly, "Bad scran to the lot of you," which made them laugh even more.

When Sheila questioned Dodie further she learned that the people in the village thought that their family was peculiar, not quite right. The animals they said, were treated as though they were royalty. Maggie's white cat was often seen sitting on the table demanding to be fed before anyone else. The dog was served next and given the same food as the children and they believed the geese walked up to the back door refusing to move until Maggie handed each one a piece of chocolate cake. Sheila knew from the many complaints she received that the goat was a nuisance to several of the villagers. Often it escaped from its tether and roved free in the village, feasting on the tenderest shoots on the rose bushes. Dodie said that the little boy next door told her that Gran's duck, which had taken to sleeping under the kitchen sink, was a witch. When her mother asked if she minded these thing being said about her family she laughed and replied, "Not at all but Trish minds a lot."

Sheila had been vaguely aware before Joe's death that Trish had tried to say some of this to her but at the time she was preoccupied with her husband's illness. She now remembered a conversation they had and thought she had put Trish off by saying, "People should only believe half of what they see and none of what they hear." Perhaps she had failed Trish who was now intent on getting away from home? She had hoped that her daughter would be offered a place at Queen's University but of course, she must make her own decisions. This was her last term at school. She intended to take the Civil Service examination which if she decided on such a career would mean she would leave home and live in London. The prospect filled her mother with sadness.

At the back of the house the sun shone on the ancient stone wall which supported a heavily fruiting plum tree. A bee zigzagged drunkenly across the yard humming lazily after a surfeit of ripe juice. Sheila sat sharing a bench with her mother. She put down her book to listen to Dodie and her friend Maura Murray singing together as they skipped, "Ladybird, ladybird fly away home, your house is on fire, your children will burn."

The tune changed; she listened to the thud of the rope, smiling and admiring the girls' dexterity as they picked up an old duster from the ground and continued evenly with their skipping, never missing a beat.

"Early in the morning before eight o'clock, you will hear the postman knock, Postman, postman, drop your letter, lady, lady, pick it up."

When September came that year Sheila was more upset about Patricia leaving home than by the outbreak of the war. She had passed the Civil Service examination with honours and was undaunted by the knowledge that food shortages and bombings were to be a part of her future. She went about finalising her plans and then slipped away without fuss. The family clothing coupons had been pooled to enable her to buy a new wool suit and a green edge to edge coat. Dodie said she looked so smart that some man would be sure to propose to her before she reached London. Trish wrote home dutifully to Sheila but her letters gave only meagre information about her life in the women's hostel and her job. She made light of the bombings and gave amusing accounts of the periods she spent in the shelters. About her personal life she said nothing at all.

Dodie was now at boarding school leaving time and space for Sheila to concentrate on her art. In the spring she painted bluebells, ferns unfolding, catkins swaying in the breeze. She made pictures of clumps of violets, purple and white, that sheltered beneath the hedgerows. Now and then she created something that pleased her, once a spider's web, its delicate structure sparkling with raindrops. She destroyed most of her work however, feeling it to be of no consequence. Beauty, she thought, was all very well in its way but you didn't need a painting to see what was all around you. She believed that art should make a statement of some sort or tell a truth that might not otherwise come to light. After a time she joined a more advanced class and found there new encouragement as well as new ideas.

On a rare visit after the war was over Trish came to see her family. Sheila could see that she took little notice of the changes that had taken place in her absence. There was now a new white fridge in the kitchen filled with food. In the cupboard tins of pineapple and mandarin oranges were stacked high. The old flat iron that used to be heated on the stove was abandoned and replaced with an electric one that looked like solid silver. There was a gramophone that Sheila bought for Dodie's seventeenth birthday and a radio in a great mahogany case that took up a whole corner of the kitchen. Trish, her mother saw, appeared to ignore all the improvements that had taken place but was quick to note and often disapprove of many of the old routines that still existed. The rosary continued to be said and it was clear that Trish joined in reluctantly. The Messenger of the Sacred Heart' still came through the letterbox, even though, as Trish pointed out, Maggie's eyesight was so poor that she was unable to read it. Sheila admitted to her sceptical daughter that Gran was able to persuade Dodie to pick mayflowers in the spring and rowan berries in the autumn to distribute round the house in order to ward off evil. Seeing disbelief on her daughter's face, she defended herself, "Sure what harm will it do? She would only get upset if we oppose it."

Trish laughed unkindly when she saw Maggie throw salt over her shoulder when anyone left the house to bring them luck. She pointed out to Sheila that the old woman had ignored history all her life in one sense, being ashamed of her past but now she was hanging on to the most useless part of it.

In the evenings Sheila took her out walking by the river. Sometimes the mist did not clear all day and stayed hanging like wisps of muslin on the autumn hedges. Her mother could see that Trish noted the deep colouring of the leaves and the bloom on the sloes but knew the beauty that was all around them did not register in her daughter's mind nor touch her emotionally as it did Dodie. Paul Murray took her to the new cinema where an old film was showing *Gold Diggers of Nineteen Thirty Six*. Trish did not bother to conceal her boredom. After a week she cut her holiday short and returned to London.

CHAPTER THIRTY-EIGHT

A little over a month after Trish's visit, Sheila went upstairs one morning to help her mother to get dressed and found she had died in the night. The news shocked no one, as she had lived to be very old. After the funeral guests had departed and Dodie returned to her boarding school, the house seemed eerily empty. It was several weeks before Sheila could bring herself to enter her mother's room to clear out her belongings. She opened the trunk that sat below a window and propped the lid up against the wall. Immediately, an overpowering smell of mothballs arose. It was not a scent that she associated with Maggie, who had always emitted an aroma of nutmegs and cloves, on which she was accustomed to chew. When her nose grew used to the pungent odour, she looked inside and there lying on the top she saw something that was familiar, a faded orange brown envelope from the Home Office, announcing that her brother Johnnie was missing. It was almost illegible, but although it was many years since she had seen it, Sheila knew the exact wording. She was touched that her mother had kept this memento of her son and suddenly she was back in her childhood, remembering the first time she and Johnnie had been sent to visit Cliona. It was a cold, wet day. A damp mist hung in the air, chilling them through and through. Johnnie was silent most of the way and she guessed that something was troubling him. In spite of her efforts to make him respond, he remained silent. When at last they reached the lane that led to their grandmother's home, Johnnie stopped and, head down, he began to kick at a lump of mud with the toe of his boot.

"You'll ruin your boots," she scolded, and was surprised to hear how like her mother she sounded. "Stop it now and let's run all the way up to warm our feet."

"Witches don't feel the cold."

"Witches?"

"Yes. Don't you know that old woman who lives up there is a witch?"

"She is not so. She is our grandmother."

"She has a hump on her back, and Jimmy Murphy told me she has a black cat."

"Is that the same old woman that the master caned Jimmy Murphy for throwing stones at last week?"

"It is."

"Well you are wrong. That old woman up there," pointing to the top of the lane, "has a white cat like our Pangur, so she has. You're afraid, that's what's wrong with you. Cowardy, cowardy custard."

Sheila did a little jig around him but did not succeed in shaming him into action. "Well I am not afraid of witches," she declared grandly, "I'm going to see for myself. Are you coming with me?"

"No." Suddenly Johnnie was decisive. He set down the can of buttermilk that he was carrying on the ground beside him and wheeled around, heading back the way they had come. Sheila stood for a minute looking after him and then, picking up the buttermilk, she marched resolutely forward. In spite of her brave words she felt nervous. Before she could knock, the old woman's face appeared over the half door. For a minute she stood looking at the girl. In spite of her almost toothless grin, her face had a warmth that was reassuring.

"Failthe. Failthe. Come in and get warm," she said. "I don't need to ask who you are. You're Sheila. Many's the day I watched you and your brothers head off for home after the master had let yous out of school. 'Tis welcome you are surely." Sheila hesitated slightly before stepping into the dimly lit room. Looking around she noticed at once, hanging from a hook on a wooden beam, what she took at first to be a great grey bird, and was relieved when she got used to the gloom to find that it was only a dress. Following her gaze, her grandmother said, "It's my best dress. I take it out now and again for an airing."

She removed a pair of well worn boots from the hearth where they had been drying, and put them under the table. She offered her visitor a mint, popped another into her own mouth and seated herself on a stool, indicating that Sheila should sit on the only chair in the room. The white cat Pangur came out of hiding, placed herself beside Sheila and began to wash her face. With delicate paws she reached up and swatted a fly with great precision. It fell on the floor and she jumped on it and held it up to be admired. Both Sheila and the old woman laughed, breaking the slightly uncomfortable silence between them.

"You are being made welcome. Now tell me all about your brothers and sisters and the rest of the family."

Sheila began to enjoy herself.

When the light began to fade Sheila said 'goodbye' to Cliona, promising to return the following Saturday. Johnnie was waiting for her at the end of the lane and together they set off in silence. Ostentatiously Sheila drew from her pocket a piece of 'Peggy's leg' and after a moment's hesitation popped it in her mouth. At first she chewed warily, picking from her teeth now and then a white hair, which, coming from Pangur, she told herself, would do her no harm at all. She began to crunch noisily relishing the crisp mint flavour. At last Johnnie could bear it no longer, "Give me a piece," he begged.

Sheila ignored his plea munching louder than ever.

"What was it like inside?" No reply. "Did you tell her I wouldn't go up to see her because I was afraid she was a witch?" Still no answer. "Come on tell me what she is like?"

Like a tortoise being tormented out of its shell, Sheila turned to him at last and said slowly, "You could find out for yourself next Saturday. Daddy's not going to be pleased when he hears you went off and left me on my own. You'll have to have a good spiel ready."

"I suppose you'll tell him I went to the lough?"

"I won't need to. Ma will see that your clothes are soaking. She'll be as cross as a weasel about that and won't she be vexed when she hears you called her mother a witch?"

"Oh please don't tell on me," he wailed.

Sheila lapsed into silence again and they walked without speaking for a good ten minutes. "Look, if you don't tell on me I promise I will walk up all the way with you next Saturday."

Then looking at her unrelenting face he pleaded, "And

next week I'll get up early to let the hens out so you can have a lie-in."

"Okay. But if you ever call my gran a witch again I'll go straight to Ma and tell her. Anyway I don't need you and there will be more 'Peggy's leg' for me if I go by myself."

She could taste the sweet flavour of the 'Peggy's leg' that she had refused to share with Johnnie so many years ago. After a few minutes the sweetness mingled with the bitterness of salt tears. Sheila did not know if she was weeping for her brother, her mother or her grandmother; maybe all of them. At last she left the telegram aside and going downstairs poured herself some whiskey.

Next day she went back to the trunk and took out the journals. She could see that the yellowing pages with faint black lines were written recognisably in the same hand in all three exercise books. Over the years it had transformed itself from a tight little script into an almost devil-may-care scrawl. She remembered how her grandmother had occasionally sent her to fetch ink powder and a new quill. Now she was looking at the use they had been put to and it made her feel infinitely close to Cliona and to her own mother who had preserved these writings all though the years. She found a comfortable chair and began to read, starting with the letter 'Dear daughter Margaret,' and continuing to the end of the journals.

SECOND NOTEBOOK

I climbed down from the coach and stepped inside this little cabin with its floor of hardened mud. A square hole in the back wall gave a little light and lots of draughts. On the hearth a fire had been laid. Over it a crook was suspended and nearby sat a black iron pot waiting to be filled with food and hung on the crook. But food was the last thing on my mind just then. When I got a little more used to the gloom I crossed the room, looked out and there he was, not more than a few yards away. At first I thought he was a dolman or some other sort of standing stone. At last curiosity got the better of me and, leaving my possessions where I had dropped them on the floor, I went outside, approaching cautiously until I was right beside him. Night had come down but the darkness gave way to the brightness of a full moon. In its light I could see that he was a poor trashy thing, made of bits of stick with arms outstretched as though appealing for help. His coat flapped forlornly in the mild breeze and one of his boots lay abandoned nearby. It was as if a thief had changed his mind and decided it was not worth carrying off. He was comical too. His hat stuck out at a jaunty angle and the straw dangling from his mouth gave him a nonchalant air in spite of his helpless appearance. I found myself smiling for the first time in many weeks. Looking up at him, I thought as a scarecrow, he couldn't be much good at his job.

When I went back inside I found the moonlight streaming

through my glassless window. I began to inspect my new home more closely and decided someone had prepared the place for my arrival. There was a heap of dry kindling in a corner of the hearth and an old zinc bath with a hole in the bottom, piled high with turf. A line of shelving ran across one wall and it held two tin mugs, a cracked Delph plate and an aluminium saucepan, black and twisted by the application of constant heat. A quart jug of fresh milk and some bread sat on a wooden table, alongside which stretched a narrow bench. The second room was even less well furnished. It had a bed with a lumpy straw mattress but it looked clean enough. There was a cracked mirror on one wall and a woven straw chair that had loose strands dangling down almost to the floor.

I had got used to a degree of comfort working for so long in the 'big house' as we called Harold Foster's home. The work had been constant but not difficult. Now I was at a loss to know how to fill my time. At first I spent many hours cleaning and scrubbing the shelves and their contents, sweeping the hearth and doing little jobs that I thought would improve the place. I picked wild flowers and filled one of the mugs with daisies, poppies, Queen Anne's lace and any brightly coloured blooms that grew in the fields around me. When I had swept and aired I would go outside and sit by the scarecrow. I decided to call him Sammy. At first I talked to myself but more and more I found I was including Sammy in my outpourings.

One day when I thought he looked cold in the chill spring air, I reached up and put my old shawl over his shoulders, tying it in a knot on his chest. I told him that bright red suited him and he seemed to nod his head in agreement. As I stepped away I noticed that, as in an ancient taboo, his feet were raised on a piece of wood to prevent them touching the ground. I dreamed of him that night.

"My name is Sammy. My name is Sammy," he kept repeating. Then there was a loud laugh and Harold Foster appeared from nowhere. He stood in front of me as he had done that first day I had seen him in the workhouse and put his hand on my head. "Don't mind that old amadon," he said, "he is only here to lead the birds astray."

Not only in my dreams, but in all the long days I had plenty of time to consider my situation. My life had taken a wrong turn but did I have to follow this road and where would it lead me?

One day when the weather was kind, I sat beside Sammy to eat my bread and cheese. In my head I had a list of names for the boy who would be born to me and who would take care of me in my old age.

"Shall I call him Seamus or Kevin or Peter?" I asked the scarecrow.

"Dec-lan, Dec-lan," a whisper seemed to answer.

"No," I answered crossly, "I'd rather call him Sammy after you."

March slowly made its way to August and then at last on to September. The corn had grown so high in the field below where I was living that I could just see the top of Sammy's head, my red shawl peeping out beneath it. The wind sometimes caught his face, turning it from me and I would wait until it swung back again and looked at me, so full of compassion and understanding. Night folks plagued my dreams: bats, rats, foxes, badgers, moths and, scarily, fat black slugs that crawled and slithered over the floor. I would then wake up and grow more fearful for the future of my unborn son.

One morning I was awakened by the sound of horses' irons jangling beneath my window and the shouts of workmen as they harvested the corn in the field below. Sammy was nowhere to be seen. I dressed hurriedly and ran outside.

"Where is he? Where is Sammy?" I yelled at one of the farmhands. The man scratched his head and at last reluctantly, followed me as I ran to the place where the scarecrow had been standing. I scrabbled wildly among the fallen sheaves and at last found Sammy lying face down on the ground. I threw myself on top of him sobbing and was dimly aware of the worker murmuring, "Well I'd best be getting on with the job."

He moved away and as he did so I felt the birth pains beginning. Pulling myself upright I made my way back to the cabin.

Later that evening the midwife came. She told me afterwards that the labourers were engaged by Harold Foster. The man I had approached went to the overseer who had been instructed to keep a watch on me. He informed his boss and as a result Annie was sent to help me bring you into the world.

Annie seemed surprised when I asked her to see my baby son.

"I thought," she said, "you would have had enough of men after this. No. It's not a boy. It's a daughter and a beautiful one at that."

Then I looked at you and knew that this was what I wanted all along. Like the shawl I folded round the shoulders of the scarecrow, I had draped the knowledge on the outside of myself and refused to admit it in my mind. Now suddenly the sun blazed in my head and I felt nothing but the purest joy.

You were a child dipped in dew. The tiny mother-of-pearl nails on your fingertips were perfect. They reminded me of a string of pearls in the window of the jeweller's shop that I used to walk past on my way to visit Mrs Moore, evenly matched and tinged with the palest pink. Margaret. A pearl. That's what I would name you. I would make a transition, I told myself from the old Irish names and traditions. My child would make a break from my own unfortunate beginnings. My Margaret, my pearl, I decided would grow up to marry well and make a better life for both of us. You would go to school and with education might become a teacher or a nurse. I would not breed you up to be like me. The thought of my own mother who had died to give me life sustained me. I would trust our future to God.

The day after you were born the midwife called again and gave me good advice about feeding and caring for you. As she was leaving, she handed me a letter. I was so taken up with nursing you that I did not open it for some time and in any case I was afraid of what it might contain. I waited until you were asleep and then at last I found a knife and slit open the envelope and a gold sovereign fell out and rolled over the floor. I had never seen so much money except in the cash box of Harold Foster. I picked it up and polished it with my calico petticoat until it twinkled at me in the firelight. Then I placed it for safety in my underwear where it warmed and comforted me. I was still reluctant to open the letter and sat there until there was not a gleed left in the fire. Were we to be deprived of our shelter? What was in store for us? At last I lighted a candle and forced myself to read.

Dear Miss O'Donnell

Murphy has reported to me that you have been delivered of a girl child and you are both healthy. I am glad of it. You will need to work soon, so I have spoken on your behalf to Mrs Magda Browning. I am sure you will find her a just employer and I hope you will labour diligently at whatever tasks she sets you to, and make yourself useful in any way you can. She is most generous in agreeing to give a home to both yourself and your child. Mrs Browning will expect you to call on her next Wednesday morning at ten o'clock sharp. The address is The Beeches, Dromalane Road, Newry.

The cottage will be retained for your use for as long as you need it. I will not contact you again and you will not acknowledge me if ever we meet in public.

I wish you and your child good fortune.

The letter was unsigned and unaddressed.

To be sure, I was relieved to find we still had a roof over our heads and enough money to be going on with. But after this assurance, I realised a sovereign would not keep us for the rest of our lives. Who would change it for me anyway? A shopkeeper might be forgiven for thinking I had stolen it and call in the guards. What would Harold Foster do to me if there was an investigation? Other problems crowded in on me. The job he was proposing I take with Mrs Browning would make me dependent once more on unknown people and circumstances. If this woman had a husband or grown up sons would I be safe; able to protect myself from getting into trouble again? Worse still what would happen if Harold Foster came to visit? I never wanted to see his face again. Was there no other way I could earn a living? I badly needed someone to advise me but I was living in isolation and had no family or friend that I could call on for help. I was much too ashamed to go to Mrs Moore who, in any case, had been ill the last time I went to see her.

As I sat brooding an angel came to my aid. Yes, Margaret, you may laugh and say it was all my imagination or that I was distracted with worry but I saw her clearly, hovering a few feet above the floor. At first the light she was giving out hurt my eyes and I could not look at her properly. Then in a gentle voice she asked me where my mother would have gone for help in the same circumstances and she suggested I should try the same source. The light dimmed a little as she turned to depart and I raised my head and saw the most beautiful creature I have ever witnessed. I knew without a doubt she came from my mother and I fell on my knees and thanked God, knowing I had help after all. The angel was disappearing and as she turned from me I saw the little mark on her right shoulder which I knew was the mark of a true angel.

Next morning I rose and dressed carefully, putting on my best brogues and the blue bonnet that had been a present from Mrs Moore when I was leaving the workhouse. I wrapped you tightly in my shawl and we set off for the nearest priest's house.

It was a bright morning and in record time we reached our destination. I knocked for some time before the door was opened by the housekeeper who kept me outside waiting on the doorstep. She left the door slightly ajar and I looked in and saw, there in the kitchen, the priest bathing his feet in a basin from which the steam was rising into the air in spirals.

As it rose he signed contentedly, breathing deeply. This was a parish adjacent to the one in which I lived, and it was half way up the Mourne Mountains. It had not the rich fertile soil that covered Harold Foster's land. The parishioners were scattered over a wide area and this meant the priest had to walk many miles each day over hard rocky ground to visit the old and the sick. He told me later that they were saving their pennies to buy a donkey for him.

"But where in God's name would I get the money to pay for grazing for an animal?"

"There's someone to see you Father McManus," the housekeeper called out to him. "I told her to go away because you were busy, but she will not leave."

Lizzie Pullen's features were as grey as the hair she scraped from her face and wore hanging down her back in a long plait that looked like a serpent. She was about to close the door on me when I heard the priest say, "Find out who she is, Lizzie."

Without asking my name, the woman went on, "Never set eyes on her before in my life. She has a wean strapped up in a shawl and no ring on her finger."

Father McManus sighed loudly. He had guessed the cause of Lizzie's disapproval. "Show her into the other room and tell her I will be with her shortly."

I stood before him clutching the letter.

"Sit down, child."

I could see that he was taking in my appearance, my best shawl, my good brogues, and, above all, my bonnet, as in those days only ladies wore bonnets. Quickly, I let him know that I had not come for charity, but advice. I handed him the letter.

"Can you not read?"

"Yes, Father, but if you will be so good as to read it you will then understand the kind of help I need."

"Very well," he looked at the envelope, "Miss Cliona O'Donnell? That's you, I take it?"

Before drawing out the letter he lifted a small hand bell and shook it briskly.

"Tea please Lizzie," he requested when she reappeared, "for two please, if you would."

"Are you from these parts?"

"Newry, Father."

"Newry, is it? I know it well, I was at school there. Any family?"

"No, Father."

Lizzie bustled in again with a forbidding look. She placed the tray on a corner of the table in front of me. I couldn't help eyeing the plate of bread and butter that she also provided and I felt glad and ashamed when Father McManus said, "Couldn't eat a bite of that myself. Lizzie is so proud and she will be offended if I send it back to the kitchen. You will do me a kindness by eating it."

He handed me the plate and while I was enjoying what to me was a feast, he read the letter.

Such a relief came over me that after all the months of loneliness I seemed to melt and tears came streeling down my cheeks.

"What ails you, child?" he asked. "There's nothing to cry about. This trouble is behind you. Things could be a lot worse. You have a roof over your head and money for food. And if that's not enough what about that beautiful baby I see peeping out at me from under your shawl?"

I dried my tears in no time and was soon telling him the story of my early life and my misfortune with Harold Foster.

"Father," I said, "I knew it was wrong but he said if I didn't do what he wanted he would send me away and I would never get another job."

"Well, he can't have been all that bad or he would have washed his hands of you and denied that he was the father of your child. He has some conscience but not that much."

I heard the last four words although he had spoken them under his breath.

"Do you think, Father, that I should go to this Mrs Browning?"

"Maybe. First though you should consider carefully before you make a decision. In the meantime I'll get some enquiries under way and if she is not a responsible person we will have to make some other plan." He thought for a while before saying, "Would you be able to take in washing?"

Then and there I decided to embrace this suggestion. Father McManus promised he would visit me tomorrow with change for the sovereign. I would need to buy a zinc bath, a copper and a clothes mangle, I told him. Then hesitantly, I asked if he would hear my confession. The priest kissed his stole and placed it round his neck.

"Bless me, Father, for I have sinned ..." A great wave of serenity descended on me as he said softly, "Go in peace my child, your sins are forgiven you." A pause and then, "Now what about baptising the baby?"

"I've given her a name already, Father," I answered. "You see I didn't know anyone who would be a godparent."

"We'll soon fix that. We have two here ready made. Tim McConville out there," pointing to the stooping figure which was weeding a vegetable plot, "will make a grand godfather. He will keep the matter to himself and so will Lizzie."

"Lizzie?"

"Just you leave her to me."

The priest went out of the room and while I was waiting you made little cooing sounds which I took to be approval for the plans we were making.

The door had been left open and I could hear what was being said in the kitchen. "Lizzie, I have something important to ask of you. It is a very serious matter and I would only entrust it to someone like yourself who can keep a secret and will show charity and understanding when it is called for."

I smiled at his flattery and at the same time realised that these words of appreciation would fall like balm on the heart of a lonely spinster. She didn't speak as Father McManus laid stress on the spiritual duties she would have as a godmother, hinting that the Lord himself had chosen her for such a great honour. I heard her reply. "This will be the first time I've undertaken such a thing and if you instruct me in my duties I will do my best."

"I knew I could rely on you, Lizzie. Now go and find Tim McConville and we will ask him to be the other godparent."

"Is it Tim McConville? Sure that oul eejit would be no good looking after a child. He can't even look after the few turnips I planted in the spring." I could hear the housekeeper's indignant gasp.

The priest silenced her, saying there was a soul to be saved and quickly, in case anything happened to the poor wee thing. He reminded her again there was a need to keep the matter from prying eyes. Tim had seen the visitors coming up to the house and taking part in the baptism would be a means of keeping him quiet.

"Both you and I will be able to remind him of his duties."

Lizzie was mollified and when she came back with Tim she took you from my arms and held you out to him gingerly as though you were a little bit of the most delicate china. With a smile she tried to coax Tim to touch you as if she was your owner but he backed away, blushing furiously.

The baptism took place in the small church next door. You howled loudly when the holy water was poured on your head and when I looked anxious Lizzie informed me it was a good sign, your lungs were strong. Afterwards she suggested we should have a small celebration.

"Nothing much," turning to Father McManus. "A drink of tea and a few slices of currant bread, that won't cause us to starve for the rest of the week.

He nodded his permission and asked Tim to lend a hand. Meanwhile when I got the opportunity and, out of the men's hearing, I explained to Lizzie that I needed to feed you. She marched into the sitting room and ordered the priest outside, saying we had women's business to attend to; she made me comfortable in his deep armchair and I put you to my breast. Lizzie stood by me, fascinated. Maybe she had never seen a child being fed before or maybe she was making sure I was doing it right. I could hear poor Father McManus walking up and down outside the sitting room in the rain saying his office.

I had to smile, listening to Lizzie scolding away at Tim in the kitchen.

"Not those old mugs you galoot, the good china cups."

"I thought those were kept especially for when the bishop visits?"

"And what harm will it do the bishop if we drink out of them for once? Are we not helping to bring a new soul into his diocese? Have we not the right to be proud of ourselves? You and I, Tim McConville are assisting that wee dote in there to get to heaven. Put the good cups out, lad, and see if you can find a few blossoms to brighten up the table.

The books were cleared away and a spotless damask cloth was spread. Sitting at the top, Lizzie presided like a queen. Later, when we parted, we were laden with vegetables, apples, a jar of honey and our new friends promised they would come and visit as indeed they did. Tim walked home with us at Lizzie's suggestion and on the way he talked of his family and of his hopes for the future and the telling made the going shorter than the coming. As he left, Tim laid a finger on your soft cheek and you smiled up at him. I'm sure you remember these three good people with pleasure; they were almost the only visitors we saw during your early childhood.

A few days later a farm cart rattled up to our door. Tim jumped out and hauled an old chest of drawers into the cabin. Then he handed me a brand new, bright blue blanket and some other bedclothes from Lizzie. She said I was to remove the bottom drawer and put you to sleep in it.

"And mind," Lizzie told him, "before you leave, see to

it that it is well lined and cosy for my godchild to sleep in."

One day, when the last of the autumn sun was breaking through the clouds, I took you in my arms and we went in search of the scarecrow. I found him at last where he had been thrown by the workmen. It was my old red shawl that revealed his whereabouts. I raised him, and when he was upright I saw that, though he was broken and in tatters, from his feet and legs new green shoots were beginning to sprout.

End of Second Notebook

CHAPTER THIRTY-NINE

On a quiet evening Sheila sat down to re-read the three journals in their faded blue covers, the pages yellow and brittle. Over time the writing had transformed itself from an uncertain scrawl to a more devil-may-care hand with frequent crossings out and a blot here and there. She had not guessed that her mother was Cliona's illegitimate daughter. Maggie, of course, had been too proud to reveal something she considered a disgrace to the family. She had always been aware of her mother's reluctance to talk about the past and presumed she hid her shame, thinking that by refusing to admit to events they could be exorcised. She remembered her oft repeated phrase, "What's the good of talking? Sure talking won't mend anything."

Perhaps for Maggie and her mother before her, this was a strategy for survival, the only one open to them at a time when the past had become too difficult to contemplate. Then she thought that she herself had not been very communicative with her own daughters. She realised now that the less spoken about events might be the best course for some people, but for her what remained unsaid stayed longer and more vividly in the mind.

Although the journals brought Cliona sharply into focus, Sheila found herself more preoccupied with thoughts of her own mother. She had never considered her in terms of love, only in terms of strength. Maggie had made something of her life in a materialistic way but until near the end of it she seemed to wait for the world to apologise for what it had done to her. Sheila could understand now that early hardships had left her with a stony inability to reach out to others. What she had accomplished had been made by turning herself into a steely single-minded individual. A slight breeze ruffled the branches of the plum tree under which she sat and a leaf floated down, landing at her feet like a large green tear. For a while she stared at it motionless, her mind filled with deep regret that she would now never have the chance to be fully reconciled with her mother. All the same, she reminded herself, Maggie had found at least a measure of peace in her later years.

For several nights she was unable to sleep. Through the undrawn curtains she watched the moon travel over a cloudy sky. She wished she could talk to Joe about what she had read, remembering how he had pointed out to her names and places in the nearby towns and villages through which they often passed. There was 'Hungry Lane' at Magheragall near Lisburn, the 'Porridge House' in Monaghan Road, Armagh and 'Pot Stick Row' in Scarva, just a few miles from where she sat. These were all reminders of a starving people, of which only a few found enough charity to keep them alive after the nettles, sorrel and cresses were stripped from the fields.

Winter came and went and snow arrived, covering the ground with a soft blanket. The trees with their few remaining leaves shone with frost and it seemed to Sheila the world slept waiting for spring to appear. However, there were dandelions and daisies here and there and a few snowdrops for her to catch their likeness in subtle colours.

Her paintings now took on a new dimension. Restless, she roamed the fields surrounding the village with her sketchbook but she was no longer content with the pretty scenes she had produced earlier and looked with disinterest at some of the fleecy clouds or yellow whins that had seemed to satisfy the eye and her brush once upon a time. One day she came across a newly fallen tree and sat by it for at least an hour absorbing what was before her. Back home, she mounted a large canvas and began to paint feverishly. Using blacks, purples and angry reds, she succeeded after many weeks in creating a picture of hurt and havoc. The fallen tree showed the unsettling of nature at its source. Insect and bird life was disturbed, stumps, loose briars and ferns all gave evidence of life that had been obliterated with great brutality. The natural order was overcome with violence. She did not know whether to be pleased or horrified with the result of her many months of work but it was with a sense of relief she finished the picture.

When Dodie came home on visits, she described a different Belfast from the one Sheila remembered Tommy describing so many years ago. Dodie told her mother that on Sundays she had been amazed to find girls of her own age promenading after lunch, discreetly eyeing the boys of their own religious persuasion. Occasionally they would stop to talk, all the time keeping watch on younger sisters and brothers who were, she was convinced, only taken along to deflect the suspicion of their parents. They could be heard admonishing the little ones to take care not to dirty their white ankle socks or scuff their shiny patent shoes. Most of the children looked bored and sulky, often too hot in wool coats trimmed with velvet. Their hair, which had been wrapped in rags the previous night to make it curly, came undone in the damp Irish air and returned to its former stringy wisps.

"Poor kids," Dodie said. "There are no cinemas open on the Sabbath and the parks are all locked on Saturday nights and not opened again until Monday morning." She informed her mother that she had found nowhere to relax in the city at weekends. Theatres too were closed and the only game played was Gaelic football. A few Catholic parishes had dance halls but these were supervised vigilantly by the clergy. It was very claustrophobic, she complained. Sheila guessed that it would not be long until her younger daughter would move on. She hoped it might not be too far away; perhaps she would find Dublin an attractive place to live?

Sheila's painting classes were becoming more and more absorbing. She had shed most of her earlier inhibitions and regularly asked for advice and comment. She now learned how to apply paint in order to make her work look like sculptures, using light to indicate weight and density, putting several applications of brushwork, one on top of the other. She found how to create dramatic effects by using a knife to scrape across the thick layers. At home she would sit for hours, eyes narrowed, trying to empty her mind, letting nothing in except what she could see before her. It took a long time for her to feel she was making any progress. Her work now centred on old historic places and objects near the village. She painted 'The Three Sisters of Greenan', large stones that had once, she supposed, been part of an alignment. At this particular site she found the atmosphere threatening and at the same time magnetic. To express this on paper, she made a vague circle, broken here and there with shadowy figures emerging from the background. She tried to suggest rituals and ceremonials not now understood but for her still suggestive, giving her a feeling that she belonged to a shared past with primitive beings. Although she painted many of the local historic monuments, this was her favourite and, unlike so much of her work, she did not destroy it.

Dodie was neither forbidden nor encouraged to visit the upstairs bedroom that Sheila had turned into a studio. The girl showed no wish to do so and her mother concluded that she had little interest in art but was pleased her mother was so happily absorbed for much of the time.

CHAPTER FORTY

At last the spring rain died away. Sheila stood in the orchard looking at the blossom on the apple trees that would in time give way to Beauty of Baths, Russets, Blenheims, Golden Wonders and Bramleys. A sharp breeze came up, making her fear for the delicate blooms. Suddenly Dodie appeared before her, the wind arranging and rearranging her tousle of red hair. Sheila put an arm round her waist.

"Why didn't you tell me you were coming? I thought you had no time off this week."

"I have as much or more time than you have now. Let's go into the house. I could smell seed cake as I passed the back door. You must have guessed I was just round the corner."

Sitting in the kitchen with mugs of tea in front of them, Dodie informed her mother that she had given up her job and secured another in the famous Guy's Hospital in London. Sheila was aware that her face was being scrutinised for any sign of distress and kept her expression bland.

"I've written to Trish," Dodie continued, "who has told me I can stay in her flat until I get a place of my own. I hardly know my big sister and I am looking forward to getting close to her again."

Sheila had to admit that it would be nice, but had to stop herself pleading that it would be even nicer if Dodie would remain with her in Ireland.

"Of course I'll miss my friends and colleagues but I want to get a wider experience in nursing."

Her mother nodded. "Indeed, you must do what's right for you," she answered, pouring more tea.

After Dodie's departure to London, Sheila found herself thinking even more intently about Cliona's journals. It was as though her grandmother was stretching a hand out to her over the years. She thought about how much Dodie resembled her; so full of imagination, seeing the form of a bird or an animal in a puddle of water. When she was little she believed the clouds contained fairies, sometimes chased by grey monsters. She had the same surge of delight in nature and could lose herself in any stretch of water as Cliona had in the bogs of Donegal.

For a time, left alone in a large rambling house, Sheila expressed her loneliness in work. She at last found another class, this time in Belfast, where she learned how to paint more accurately the human face and figure. Several times she thought she might give up. She was getting no younger and the journey to the city once a week was taxing. But she enjoyed the camaraderie and the encouragement she was given by colleagues and the tutor, so she continued to attend. After a lot of hard work she finished two large canvases in oils. One depicted a crowd of the most pitiful wretches who jostled against each other, their faces livid, arms outstretched all in the same direction as though in mute supplication. Their gaunt features and staring eyes were beyond hope. In the foreground, the legs were twisted round each other as in some hell. She used sombre colours throughout. It was a picture of unrelieved gloom. The second canvas was quite different. In it the plum tree at the back of the house was in full bloom. Delicate pinks and subtle shades of green predominated. The impression was one of simple beauty until, almost hidden by the blossom, a long serpent-like figure could be detected twisted over and under a main branch. These two paintings took well over a year to complete and when they were finished Sheila took a rest, feeling she had exhausted all her ideas and energies.

Sheila sat looking at a photograph Dodie had sent her from London that morning. She stared at the familiar face, noting the smiling eyes and the deepening shadows around them. Her daughter, she decided, looked happy enough but there was something unresolved in the face under the nurse's cap. It gave her mother an unsettled feeling, and, drawing a piece of blank paper towards her, she began to sketch an outline in charcoal. She screwed the page up and threw it away. A second attempt met with the same fate. Soon the wastepaper basket was filled to overflowing and in the end she gave up and went out shopping. That night she woke, got out of bed, and began again. The first try satisfied her and after breakfast the next morning she mixed paints with great care and started on a portrait of her daughter Dodie. Several times she scraped the canvas clean and began all over again. Working all day with only minimal breaks for food, at night she fell into bed and slept soundly. When she woke her mind was already filled with the ways she would attempt to portray the various aspects of her subject. To draw attention away from superficial parts of her work, for instance, the uninteresting view of the hospital garden where Dodie had posed for the photographer, Sheila put on the paint smoothly. But, on forehead and chin she piled it on thickly and drew a palette knife across them almost at random. She made delicate pinks appear on arms and cheek bones and at last she felt she had created something that pleased her so much she had it framed – the only one of her works she had so honoured – and hung it over the mantelpiece in the living room.

Sheila had found a talent for self-expression late in life. It was a gift that appeared unexpectedly and had now disappeared just as suddenly. Sitting alone in the garden, she found that the silence around her was not a silence at all; she could hear her heart beat, a rustle in the hedge and the sighing of the wind in the leaves of the trees. At last 'the vision', as she had come to call it in her own mind, that she had tried to explain to a disbelieving Michael Morgan, returned to her and she was found some hours later, motionless, her face full of joy. She died a week later.

Dodie

CHAPTER FORTY-ONE

Dodie watched as the tug manoeuvred the Heysham steamer right round and led it into the deeper waters of Belfast Lough. The waving crowds on the quayside were now irrevocably lost. Paul Murray's face disappeared from her view. A great sigh seemed to rise from the passengers, a mixture of sadness and relief. Some headed for the bar, others continued to stand gazing out at the fast receding shoreline. Seagulls plunged and dipped in the wake of the ship, looking for scraps of food. One landed on the rail on which Dodie was leaning and stared into her face with a glass bead eye.

"Luggedly goo. Who are you?" it asked before flying away.

She smiled and allowed a small feeling of excitement to rise in her. She is off to new places, new faces at last. She is hungry for them. Already she has escaped from grey uniform days and is on her way to something she could not find amid the circumscribed lives she knows so well. Their certainty of her future appalled her. Now in London she will become a new person. She will bury her past as deep as the bog bodies that had been found in the damp peat in her native land, where they had lain for centuries. When she first saw them in the Belfast museum, anchored with stones on top of birch saplings, she wondered then as now had they been sacrificed? Perhaps they were willing victims? They looked so serene as though they had fallen asleep. Well, neither self-sacrifice nor sleeping her way through life were for her. The boat began to rock, and she straightened up and remained looking out at the tumbling waves for a time before making her way to her cabin.

It was difficult to sleep in such a small space. Her mind dwelt on her sister Patricia. She was sure Trish felt as strongly as she did about the numbing trivialities of the life she was leaving behind. She too must have disliked the idle chatter that surrounded them where neighbours and friends could talk for hours and hours without communicating anything of value. Hadn't they both been bored by the enthusiasm with which people exchanged inconsequential information and viewed with displeasure those who declined to join in? Her own lack of participation had made her unpopular, she suspected. When she said so to Paul Murray he laughed and said this was rubbish, they were not that intolerant, and in any case she had a right to be different. He had looked at her gravely for a minute before adding, "All the same it really makes for lovely listening."

Paul was a good listener, both he and his sister Maura always seemed at ease with their way of life and able to resist their surroundings, while she herself felt she was defined by them.

Unable to sleep, she thought of her own sister and wondered what her boyfriend was like? For a while she speculated on his appearance and manner. What kind of man would please her fastidious sister? He wouldn't be like Paul who was chunky and solid. More sophisticated perhaps, but would he love her as much? The ship was now rocking and rolling from side to side and she heard the engine chant softly, "Lovely listening, lovely listening," until well into the small hours of the morning before she at last dozed off.

She was awakened by the scrape of the anchor dropping down the side of the ship. There were excited voices on deck and she hastily washed and made her way up the steps and over the railway lines to the London train. The sea air was invigorating and she felt wide awake in spite of her lack of sleep. Sitting in the corner of a carriage, she speculated on what her mother might be doing at this moment? An early riser, she was likely kneeling at the bedside saying her prayers before beginning her day's routine. Without thinking, Dodie began to mouth the 'morning offering' wondering at herself and how easily she had slipped back into a childhood habit. She used to pray a lot for God to make her a good child, to let her get slim, but remained plump as a plum until she decided to take things into her own hands and eat less food. Once she had a quarrel with Trish who teased her about it, and she retaliated unkindly saying that she could get thin any time she wished but that her sister would always stay stupid no matter what she did. She squirmed a little uncomfortably in her seat. They had made it up after rows, and now she could admit to herself that she had always been more than a little jealous of her older sister. Trish, dark eyed and slender while she, awkward and unprepossessing, managed to appear clumsy no matter what the circumstances. She was surrounded by Ulster accents. People were drawing food and drink from hand luggage. Determinedly, she fended off the passionate social involvement into which these total strangers tried to draw her, offering sandwiches along with unwanted information about themselves; train journeys of the past, possible arrival times and how difficult it might be to get a taxi in the rain. She attempted to take refuge in a book but an elderly man beside her kept trying to draw her into conversation.

"Where are you from?"

She knew instinctively he was the kind of person she was so familiar with, who would, if she answered his questions, continue with something like, "Ah, I know a fellow from there. He has a two-storey house on the edge of the village, a garden, a wife, x children and an elderly mother living with him ..." If she admitted to the slightest recognition of that person it would be taken as a sign of a sort of common ancestry and the beginning of an authorised friendship. She gave him a distant smile, turned away and feigned sleep.

Had she missed her? The crowds were beginning to thin out and she could not see anyone who looked like Trish. She walked the whole length of the platform, gazing around sleepily. Someone stood a little way off staring at her. Could this person, her hair cut in a trendy bob, wearing the shortest of mini skirts and flaunting an enormous purple boa, be her sister? Was this the girl who had to be persuaded to try even the merest trace of Tangee lipstick or the tiniest squirt of Evening in Paris perfume not all that many years ago? Yes it was Trish, standing quite still, who told her afterwards that she had been mesmerised by the sight of Dodie's red hair flickering flames on the dismal windy platform. They stared at each other for several seconds before rushing over to hug and kiss delightedly.

On the way to the bus stop, Dodie regaled her sister with

news of home. Ma was painting away furiously, keeping her efforts out of sight in the bedroom. Paul Murray had been offered the post of deputy head of his academy and Maura is expecting her second baby any day now. The bus came and Trish took Dodie's case exclaiming, "What on earth have you got in this? It feels as though it's full of stones."

"Ma insisted on packing some home-made jam and soda bread for you and she says I'm to find out if you have plenty of warm underwear for the winter? If not I am to let her know and she will send you some 'Smedleys'." Both girls were laughing as the conductor came up to them for fares. Soon however, Dodie's face sobered, "Ma hasn't been too well lately and that made it hard for me to leave."

Seeing the look of concern on her sister's face, she added quickly, "But Paul's mother has promised to look in on her every day and will let me know how things are and the neighbours are all very helpful and will rally round if she needs anything."

After a brief silence they moved on to more light-hearted matters and the chime of their chatter rang out, raising both their spirits again. Dodie looked at her sister and the slight feeling of unfamiliarity that had been between them seemed to have disappeared.

CHAPTER FORTY-TWO

Dodie had never liked showers. Her aversion to them stemmed from the time she was in boarding school. She never managed to get the pressure or the temperature right, no matter how much she fiddled with the taps. Then she had to hunker down to avoid being blinded by the gushing water. Now as she washed she remembered Sister Francis, the nun in charge of the dormitory, warning the girls, "Always say your aspirations in the bath or the shower and wash your naughty parts without looking."

A grin spread over Dodie's face as she reached for a towel and rubbed her wet hair. Still smiling absently, she put on a nightdress, the way Sister Francis taught them to do without exposing any part of their bodies. Men, the nun said, were interested in one thing only and it was the duty of a good woman to stop them. She supposed they would be horrified at the thought of the contraceptive pill? Presumably her sister used it, she had come a long way.

The flat was a revelation to her. Things could be turned into something else with a little sleight of hand; the couch into a bed, the coffee table expanded into a dining table, and another couch into a folding stool. The walls were painted white and the furniture was a shining chrome. She lay in bed thinking of her first impressions. James, late in the evening came bounding up the stairs whistling as though he had a bird in his throat and carrying himself confidently in an expensive cashmere coat.

"Well my dear, I'm so glad to see you at last," was his friendly greeting and he held on to her hand as though reluctant to let it go. He was courteous throughout the evening and, as they sipped champagne, he encouraged her to talk about herself, her early life and the way they lived in Ireland. Now and then he interjected laughingly, "Why didn't you tell me all this?" or "You kept that a close secret from me, my darling."

Yes, Dodie thought, he has a lot of charm although she found herself thinking that his washed-out denim blue eyes were a little cold. She chided herself for making quick criticisms, Trish evidently adored him. She had said little, content to sit on the floor, her back supported by his knees. All the same she could sense tension in her sister that had not been there before he came into the flat. At around midnight he rose. "Why don't you two girls stay up for a while and talk? I'm, sure you must have plenty of news to exchange. I'm all in and have another hard day in front of me tomorrow." Dodie liked the suggestion and was taken aback when Trish also got up and murmured something about having lots of time to chat in the next few days. Strange, Dodie thought, remembering the nights they had spent at home when Trish returned for a holiday from London. Then they had talked well into what their grandmother called the 'scriak of dawn'.

She could understand why her sister would regard James

as the perfect partner. His knowledge of the arts, his comments on her perfume, his frequent use of French phrases and his knowledge of wines or at least champagnes, all indicated to her that he was well informed in the 'art of living'. He was the perfect companion for the life which she supposed, Trish proposed to lead. All the same Dodie was uneasy about the relationship. During their conversation she had a puzzled feeling, not knowing what was making her uncomfortable. Now she realised that although Trish had not exactly told lies; it would seem she had permitted certain assumptions to be made about the family and its status in the village; its way of life added up to a picture at once more important and more exciting than it really was. Her sister, she felt, had laundered her past to suit her present. Before sleep at last overcame her, Dodie remembered a little heap of notes which she had knocked to the floor when placing her glass on a side table. As she picked them up she could not help noticing that one was headed 'Freshwater Fish' and underneath a list: perch, eel, roach... . When they were children she would tease Trish about her habit of counting things: rails, steps, paving stones. Perhaps it was persisting in this slightly different form?

Next morning Dodie sat on the couch in the living room pretending to read while James prepared to go out. His shirt she noticed, was ironed meticulously, the crease in his dark trousers flawless. She wondered if her sister did his laundering? He reached for a clothes brush and began to flick it over his lapels.

"Here, let me do that," and Trish took the brush from his hand and began to give the coat a thorough if unnecessary brushing.

"You remind me of my mother," he protested. "And the way she used to fuss when I was getting ready to go to school," and, snatching the brush, he threw it aside and made a half-hearted flick at his trouser legs with one hand.

There was a slightly embarrassed pause: "What about this evening? Shall I cook for us?" Trish asked.

"No, no," he answered impatiently, "you two go ahead and eat without me. I will have to stay in the studio until that American I told you about," turning to Trish, "makes up his mind about buying the watercolour. He will stand in front of it for hours cogitating and then go off for lunch. In the afternoon he will come back, stand gazing at it some more and then say he will make his decision tomorrow. If by any chance he decides on a purchase he might take me out to dinner, if not I'll just grab a sandwich somewhere."

James sighed as he looked at Trish's crestfallen face. "You two go out and have a nice meal somewhere and there is plenty of champagne in the fridge left over from the exhibition, so you can live it up when you get back here."

When Edward, James partner came to the flat with some colleagues the following evening, Dodie learned more about the exhibition. Trish had taken a few days off work to help. It was mounted in a small alley off Cork Street and they had worried that the venue was not in a more prominent position in order to attract viewers. Edward told Dodie laughingly that in the end the place had not mattered, crowds had flocked to them, not to see the pictures but to look at her sister's pretty face. Trish blushed and said not to talk rubbish but her sister could see that she was pleased by the compliment. The clothes that James persuaded her to buy in Biba's in Kensington High Street gave her an elegant sophisticated air, while her hair in a dark bob framed an oval face and made the whole of her appearance slightly mysterious – a mixture of innocence and knowingness.

Dodie enjoyed hearing something of James and Edward's work but did not feel very comfortable in their friends' company. The talk was all about buying and selling art and the difficulty of budding hopefuls getting any recognition. They spoke of artists whose names were unknown to her and after a few polite overtures they left her alone. She didn't blame them, realising they were bored by her lack of knowledge and genuine interest. Trish, the perfect hostess, was too busy to notice her discomfort, passing round plates of strange-looking nibbles and filling up glasses. Her black skirt almost reached the floor and was so tight that her steps were mincing and abbreviated. She looked, Dodie thought, like some tall, stalking animal, albeit an elegant one. At last she was rescued by Edward who could see she was not enjoying herself. He came and sat by her and in the course of their conversation she said she was looking for a flat. Edward promised to join in the search and he said he would arrange to get her invited to a party one of these days. She smiled up at him, noting the warmth in his soft brown eyes.

CHAPTER FORTY-THREE

When three days had passed and the sisters had not managed to talk in private, Dodie wondered was Trish avoiding doing so? She pushed the suspicion away quickly, and pulled a piece of paper from her handbag on which she had written a number of addresses taken from newspapers. It was imperative, she felt, to find a place of her own. Trish's face was beginning to haunt her, beautiful Trish, always well liked at school and in the village but who could never be persuaded of her popularity. Dodie loved her for her humility but something had gone wrong. Her sister was now an insecure woman who was ignoring her intelligence, pushing it down like rubbish in a trashcan. How could she settle for a life with James in these cramped quarters? They did not seem to be thinking of moving. The suggestion, she supposed, would have to come from James. Trish gave the impression that it was her duty to fit in with everything he decided. Worse, Dodie could see how her sister irritated him by being too effusive, praising him for the smallest thing with sentimental overstatements. Now and then after being impatient with her, he would indulge in spurts of tenderness and, like a withering flower, Trish soaked up every drop as though it was a liquid to sustain her in the next dry period. She was a little like their mother, Dodie decided, whose whole life she considered was one of self abnegation, always doing things in the interests of others.

She pulled on a jacket and was about to leave the flat when she heard the key being turned in the lock. Trish came rushing in exclaiming, "We shall have the place to ourselves at the weekend. James and Edward are going to Paris this afternoon to see some pictures which they hope to borrow for next year's exhibition. We will have lots of time to talk and we can please ourselves how we spend the time...but now I have to run off again. I've only dashed over in my lunch hour to tell you."

She grabbed a knife and cut herself a hunk of cheese and a piece of a loaf and was gone before Dodie could properly comment.

None of the flats Dodie looked at were remotely suitable. Some were filthy, others so bohemian that she could guess she would have difficulty in fitting in with the occupants. Several had the sweet tell-tale smell that indicated the use of drugs. Anything promising was far too expensive. At last she gave up and made her way to an appointment at the hospital where she hoped to start work in another week. On the way she passed a convent and was surprised to see excited children running around like drunken rabbits in the playground attached to the school. At first she supposed they were using the premises without permission as it was holiday time. Then she noticed a young nun with skirts pinned up kicking a ball in their midst. She stood watching until the ball flew over the gate and landed at her feet. Picking it up, she handed it to the sister who approached with a smiling face, murmuring her thanks. The nun paused to wipe the perspiration from her forehead and, recognising Dodie's look of curiosity, she explained that the convent encouraged the youngsters to use the playground during the holidays hoping it would keep them off the streets and out of mischief. They were all, she said, from materially deprived homes, and they were also provided with bread and cheese in the recreation room; she pointed to a large building adjoining the convent. In answer to a question from Dodie, she replied that she had volunteered to teach the children to play football. Recognising Dodie's Irish accent, she informed her that she too came from Northern Ireland. It became clear that she enjoyed talking to a fellow countrywoman and she invited Dodie to join her in the football any day. Laughingly, the invitation was refused but before they parted Dodie promised to call at the convent during visiting hours to see Sister Carmel again.

Some hours later, making her way to the train, Dodie took shelter in a doorway from a sudden shower of rain. Looking around, she found that she was at the entrance to a church and impulsively she walked in. The sweet sharp smell of incense hung in the air as she walked up the aisle and settled herself in a pew. Memories came back to her of when she was a child. She would sit as near as she could get to the swinging thurible, hoping the smoke would be absorbed by her hair and clothing. Now, she smiled at her younger self who would conjure up pictures of holy hermits, communing only with animals, and adventurous monks who sailed the seas in leather boats to bring the gospel to foreign lands. After a while, feeling remarkably refreshed, she left, and with a sense of elation, quoting to herself, "I'm the Miller of Dee, I care for nobody, no not I". Of course, if Trish had problems she would do all she could to help her, but she was not going to let herself be swamped by them. She was starting a new life, wasn't she?

CHAPTER FORTY-FOUR

When she got back to the flat she found Trish sitting, listlessly turning over the pages of a fashion magazine, staring at impossibly thin girls who smiled at lovers or stepped daintily around in exotic locations. They wore elegant clothes and some had no shoes on their flawless feet.

"Dodie, where on earth have you been? I'm so glad you are back. Let me take your jacket. Shall I make you some coffee?"

As she removed her damp outer clothing, Dodie could see that there were more lists on the table, the top one naming fragrant flowers; sweet peas, roses, lilies of the valley. A photograph of the two sisters stood on the mantelpiece. It had been taken some years ago when Trish had been working for several years and was home on holiday. The background showed the walls of the convent where they had both been educated. Dodie's eyes followed her sister's to the likeness and noticed that she had written underneath 'united we stand, divided we fall'.

"Is there anything the matter?" she asked quietly.

"Yes," was the answer, "I hope you'll stand by me now." There was a pause. "Dodie, I'm pregnant."

"Well, that's good news. Congratulations."

"You don't understand. James doesn't want the baby. Doesn't want me either, I suppose. Oh Dodie, what am I to do?"

The sob in her voice brought Dodie swiftly to her side. She slipped an arm round her shoulders.

"We'll do what we have always done, remember. 'United we stand.' Think of our old motto and how it served us through bad times before. Like the time I thought I was going to be expelled from school for drinking the altar wine, and when I put the frog in Mother Gerard's desk and you wrote a letter explaining that I loved animals, and frogs especially. She believed you when you said I meant the frog as a gift. But Trish refused to be comforted by reminders of childhood pranks and began to weep silently.

"Don't cry. Lots of women nowadays have a baby outside marriage. You and I will decide between us what's the best thing to do." She led her sister to a seat, handed her a tissue to wipe her eyes and kissed her softly on the cheek. Then she announced briskly, "Since we have the place to ourselves we can do as we please. I suggest we dress up and I'll take you out to dinner. Between soup and coffee we'll have everything sorted out."

They dined at a little Italian restaurant. Trish left most of the melon and Parma ham on her plate and only toyed with her pasta. She was silent until coffee was set before them, and then suddenly words began to flow from her as though they had been dammed up tightly and now a sluice had been released. At first she explained, she thought James might be pleased to know he was going to become a father but instead he was angry.

"Yes," she answered to Dodie's query about contraception. "I was on the pill but one night after a party when I suppose I had too much to drink, I missed out – about three months ago." She sipped her coffee. "When I realised I was pregnant and I told James he said quite abruptly I must have an abortion. I protested and he said he didn't want to discuss it, picked up *The Times* and started to read. I got mad and snatched the paper from his hands, threw it on the floor, stamped on it and told him he was a monster who had no feelings for his child." She took a long drink from her cup and continued more slowly. "It's not a child," he said, "it's just a foetus and how do you think," he asked, "we could bring a baby up in this small flat?"

"I suggested we move," Trish said, "but he refused to consider it." He informed her that he had had endless trouble getting the one they were in so near the gallery. She offered to leave but he asked where would she go? Becoming tearful again, she said he sounded as though she was behaving like some irresponsible teenager. Since then it had not been mentioned between them except once when he offered to provide money or whatever she would need for the termination of the pregnancy.

They ordered more coffee. Dodie said little but encouraged her sister to talk. Trish grew more calm.

"I suppose I was unfair," she said. "I told him I had given myself to him and that he hadn't even loved me, just made use of me and that's not really true."

"What did he say to that?"

" 'We can't give ourselves away, Patricia.' Those were his words. We belong only to ourselves." There was silence for a little while and then Trish began again.

"He keeps telling me I should take life as it comes and I have tried to do that but then I began to realise that that's just a way of refusing to think or act. His favourite expression is 'be yourself'. Well," she told Dodie, "at this moment in time I want to be anyone but the person I am: a girl brought up to exist only as somebody's wife and to believe it was actually a duty to find a man to love me. Look how miserably I have failed, Dodie."

Dodie took her sister's hand and held it tightly.

"Everything is wrong and I feel so guilty. Here you are out of things if you are not laid back, cool. Nobody is ashamed of anything. I hate my own lack of confidence and being so dependant on James emotionally. He says it is the way I was brought up and I should forget it and get on with living, get right into the 'swinging sixties' as he puts it."

"But Trish," Dodie protested, "how can you be yourself if you don't relate to what went on before? Surely you must have something to build on? And anyway it's not possible to forget completely, no matter how hard we try." Dodie remembered the tranquillity she had experienced earlier in the church as she sheltered from the rain.

"I don't know about that. I was glad to leave home because there was so little freedom but here freedom seems compulsory. You are meant to reject all the values you have, what your parents, teachers, the church have taught you."

"Does James really expect this? After all he must have liked you the way you were before you went to live with him?"

"I thought so. Now I'm not so sure but I admire him. I like the way he cares for nobody and does not mind if people notice or disapprove of him. I'm not like that. I need somebody to love me. I'd be devastated if he ceased to care for me." She paused and then resumed, "I thought I had found a person who would share his life with me, in a place I could feel I belonged. Now I know what belonging means. It means fitting in whether you like it or not. It means giving up any independence you might have had. I suppose I was disarmed by his kindness and tried to be what I thought he imagined I was."

For a time they sat in silence. It was only much later that Dodie would appreciate how these things could come about: how a kiss could lead to a desire to be touched all over her skin and make her feel beautiful, so worthwhile. Until it happened, how could she be aware how easy it was to lose control of her own actions? She did not yet know such stings of pleasure lay asleep and unimagined in her own body, great waves of feeling that could swamp the brain and leave her heedless of anything else. They had never been warned. The nuns had said, "Girls, your bodies are the temples of the Holy Ghost. If you go astray it will be your own fault. A man cannot control his passions."

But neither could Trish, Dodie speculated, although neither of the sisters could articulate such intimacies just then.

CHAPTER FORTY-FIVE

The clang of the outer door woke Dodie and she heard her sister's footsteps grow more and more faint on the pavement outside the flat. Then she remembered that Trish had mentioned an appointment with the hairdresser this morning. She lay looking up at the ceiling. Its many cracks hardly outnumbered the wrinkles she remembered on her grandmother Maggie's face. There was only one grandparent left when she was born, a wisp of a woman with legs and arms like chicken bones. Her fine silver hair was parted in the middle and drawn back to lie like two cosy little ammonites, one on each ear. A sharp spicy smell emanated from the supply of cloves she kept in her apron pocket. Her eyes were mild; at odds with her character. She was shrewd, bossy, staunch, upright and determined. Dodie's own mother Sheila, became a child again in her presence, striving to avoid arguments at all costs. Gran talked of witches and fairies with great familiarity. She was superstitious, believing that to break a mirror would bring bad luck and that the banshees always came to warn you of approaching death.

"You have to believe in magic," she used to say, "else it won't happen." Dodie had loved her and believed all she told her. Now she wondered what Gran would have made of Trish and her situation?

She ate some cornflakes and drank a mug of coffee and then decided to take a little time to herself – after all, Trish had not told her when she would be back. Maybe during a walk, a few solutions would present themselves. One or two things had been established the previous evening. Trish intended to keep the baby. Other things were less clear. It was by no means certain that Trish would leave James in the foreseeable future. When Dodie had suggested she should look for a flat for both herself and Trish, she had got an evasive answer.

This morning Dodie was less patient with her sister's vagaries. Last night it would have been cruel she felt to insist on further clarifications. She could have cancelled her appointment with the hairdresser, all the same, to give them time to settle a few more issues when they had the opportunity. A little resentful she left a note, walked out of the flat and headed for Trafalgar Square.

This she presumed was the heart of London. For a time she stood watching people feeding the pigeons and then walked on to consider England's imperial past. There was Nelson's pillar with four bronze lions whose faces she thought looked more human than the man they guarded. A bas relief informed her that 'England expects every man to do his duty'. Would James do his duty by Trish and if he didn't marry her would he contribute financially to the upkeep of the child? Grandmother Maggie would have expected that much at least. And what about their own mother? She looked at Sir Charles Napier who stood with his head thrown back, gripping in one hand a sword, in the other a scroll. Next to him, Sir Havelock Nelson bareheaded, his desertion of his wife once a scandal, now forgotten. King Charles the First looked down on the Palace of Westminster to the place of his execution. Behind Nelson, near the National Gallery, she saw King George the Fourth who had secretly married Mrs Fitzherbert, denied it and later got rid of his queen, Caroline, in a sensational divorce. Looking at these men, it seemed to Dodie that fame and neglect of their women had gone hand in hand except perhaps in the case of King Charles. A pigeon on the head of King George nodded in the direction of the National Gallery and her eyes, obeying its instruction, paused in delight at the beauty of the nearby church of Saint Martin in the Fields. Its elegant architecture banished her troubled thoughts, and, more tranquil now, she made her way back to the flat.

She was stricken when she saw her sister's face with all the joy wrung out of it. She looked, Dodie thought, just like the pictures one saw now and then of a prisoner without hope, condemned, and suddenly she thought that a marriage with James would only entrap her more firmly. She looked up from the list she was once again occupied in compiling, and Dodie suspected that this was a device she used to try to control her life, but instead it seemed to be controlling her.

"Shall I make us some lunch?" she asked gently.

As they ate a cheese omelette a fly skittered around the surface of the table looking for crumbs. It rose and landed on the rim of the milk jug where it walked unsteadily around the perimeter. Suddenly it slipped over the edge and began to struggle wildly in the milk. After several seconds Trish fished it out with a spoon and they watched the insect crawl wetly away.

"I think," said Trish, "you have come just in time to rescue me."

"I can't rescue you until I know what you want to be rescued from. If you like, I will look out for a place for us to live in together, but meantime I am going to ask if there is a vacancy in the nurses' hostel. I feel I've overstayed my welcome here."

"No, no. James doesn't mind."

"Yes, Trish, he does and who could blame him? And I mind too. I don't like to see you like this, always on the alert and anxious to please everybody. I think it's time you decided what you want for yourself and your baby, for a change."

"You don't understand. It's not the real James you see. I know him. Everyone has faults and after all any half decent man is better than none."

Dodie, who was clearing away the plates, sat down again abruptly. Was it possible that her sister, like their grandmother held the unquestioning assumption that a woman only existed to find a husband? Was she playing a role that forced her into the mould of another person's expectations? Surely she did not think this was an acceptable way to live? Suddenly Dodie saw that she did not know her sister at all. Her hopes and expectations of life were in complete contrast to hers despite the fact that they came from the same parents, the same place and had a similar education. She felt an unaccustomed weight of depression descend on her.

"Look Trish, I think we should leave discussions until you have talked to James and made up your mind what you wish to do. I don't suppose we would get into a theatre this evening without a booking but what about a film? What do you say?

"Okay," Trish answered listlessly.

Next day James phoned from the airport to say that he and Edward had managed to get away early and should be home in time for tea. Immediately Trish began to fuss, tidy the flat and worry about what she could produce for them to eat. At first Dodie joined in but after a few minutes she decided she did not want to be involved. She told her puzzled sister that she was going out for a while and would have a meal in town. When she got back, in answer to a question from James she simply stated that she felt she should leave them together as they probably had things to talk about. Neither of them gave any indication that they grasped her meaning.

CHAPTER FORTY-SIX

A letter from Paul Murray dropped into her indecision the next morning.

"Dear Dodie," she read. "Hope you and your sister are having a fabulous time together painting the town bright scarlet. Glad the new job (according to your mother) sounds so promising. Sheila is relieved you write to her so frequently, she says she is lucky if she gets a letter from Trish every six months. Your news is of course passed on and eagerly awaited in our house.

It won't be long now until half term is upon us. I had thought of slipping over the pond to spend a few days in London. I would like to visit the National Gallery and take in a few theatres. Could you two take some time out to accompany me? I could do with someone to show me about and I expect you both know your way around quite well by this time.

Your mother's health, while it has not greatly improved has not got any worse as far as I know. We do all we can for her.

Let me know if there is a decent B and B near to where

you live, or better still book me in for the second week in October.

Looking forward to hearing from you, Paul."

Dodie stared at the letter. By half term it would be obvious that Trish was pregnant; already she was wearing the loosest clothes in her wardrobe. She was adamant that Sheila was not to be informed of her condition. Perhaps Paul could persuade her that their mother had a right to know she would be a grandmother in the near future. Sheila was not the kind of person who would be judgmental and Paul was tactful. Dodie's spirits rose as she thought about it.

"Oh well," Trish said that evening when both girls were preparing a meal in the flat. "There is an obvious way to get around it. You simply write to Paul and tell him that you ought to go home to see mother in a couple of weeks time as she has not been well."

Dodie stared at her. "But I have no intention of going to Ireland in the near future."

"Why not?"

"Well, first of all, I don't think I could get enough time off so soon after starting a new job. Secondly, I can't afford the fare."

"I'll be happy to give you as much as you need. You can pay me back at any old time."

"Trish, I simply do not want to go to Ireland right now."

"Now Dodie, remember. United we stand, divided we fall."

Dodie turned away from her. What has happened to her, she asked herself? Could her sister have changed so much over the years away from home? She had wrongly assumed that their early life would still be the blueprint for Trish's behaviour.

★

Dodie's first day at work was satisfying, even exciting and for a while she was able to forget her personal problems. And she had a stroke of luck. The nurse who was supervising the ward to which she was assigned accompanied her to lunch. In a friendly way she enquired how she was fixed for accommodation. Dodie explained her predicament and said she supposed there was nothing else for it but to apply for a vacancy in the nurses' home.

"You will probably have a fairly long wait," she was informed, "but if you are desperate, I know of someone who wants to share her house. She is a friend of my mother, a retired teacher. I've known her for many years and find her very friendly and she has a great sense of humour. Her own mother died two years ago and she's now finding the place too big for one person. Yesterday evening she came over to our house and asked if I knew anyone suitable. I promised to ask around and of course it goes without saying if you don't like living there you can always leave."

"It sounds like a God send," Dodie replied as she wrote down the telephone number.

Veronica Wright was a sprightly sixty-seven-years-old with softly waving hair and gentle eyes. She showed Dodie into a room filled with heavy Victorian furniture.

"I haven't changed anything much since my mother died," she informed Dodie, sounding almost apologetic. "Couldn't be bothered really, but you must move things around to suit yourself – that is if you decide to live here."

The large airy bedroom had a small annexe off that had once been a dressing room. It could be used for a study if Dodie wished, Veronica said. She could have the breakfast room downstairs as a private sitting room. All this space at a peppercorn rent astonished Dodie, she couldn't believe her luck.

"Let's have some tea," Veronica offered, leading the way into the kitchen. As she moved around setting out cups, saucers, biscuits she continued to talk. "I must warn you I do go out a lot; having lived all my life in this area, I'm roped into committee meetings and various associations. I also visit a lot and occasionally with friends go bird watching. So if you are nervous about being alone in the house you should think twice."

Dodie laughed and assured her it wouldn't be a problem.

"And of course you can have friends to visit any time you please."

As they sipped tea, Veronica skilfully extracted from Dodie what were her interests and if she had a boyfriend in London. She too exchanged confidences with such openness and warmth that Dodie found herself liking the woman already. They agreed she could move in the day after tomorrow.

"I'll make up the bed for you," Veronica said as they were parting. "You can let me know if there is anything else you will need."

It didn't take long to put her belongings together, most of which had not been unpacked in any case. She looked at Trish's white crestfallen face and felt almost guilty.

"We can see each other as often as you wish," she offered, "and when I'm settled in I know that Veronica will not mind if I have you and James over for a meal now and then."

Next day as she was taking her leave, Dodie glanced at her sister's face and was shocked by her anguished look.

"I'll stand by you whatever you decide, don't forget that," she promised.

CHAPTER FORTY-SEVEN

Dodie had been living in Veronica Wright's house for a week when Edward knocked on the door. She greeted him warmly, invited him in, and over cups of coffee he told her that Trish was concerned how she was getting on.

"Why can't she come over herself?"

"She will in a few days. At the moment she is busy helping James to prepare a design for in-between exhibition posters. She wants to know if there is anything you need in the meantime?"

Her annoyance at her sister's silence or neglect as she thought of it was allayed by Edward's friendliness. It was pleasant to see him again. She had filled her larder, moved things around to her satisfaction, and was now beginning to feel in need of company. The nurses were sociable but it stopped at the hospital gates. She had been taken aback that no one had yet invited her out for a cup of coffee, never mind a visit to their homes. It was so different to what she was used to.

Edward looked around and pronounced the place a find. She was lucky, he said, to have so much space.

"It would be just the right place for a party," he exclaimed and then, "Tell you what, Cynthia, a friend of mine, is having a shindig next Saturday night, it's just down the road from here. Why don't you come along?"

"What kind of shindig? What shall I wear? Do I bring anything with me?"

Edward laughed at her evident excitement. "Wear any old thing, nobody dresses up at Cynthia's. I suppose a bottle of something wouldn't go amiss," and he rose to go.

After Edward left it occurred to her that he had not arranged to pick her up. It wouldn't matter, she told herself, I know the address, it's just a few steps away and he said that the party would start around nine o'clock. This, she told herself, is going to be my entry into the swinging sixties and, whatever Edward's opinion is, I am going to dress up to look as attractive as possible. And she admitted to herself she was looking forward to seeing him again. She was already deeply taken by the warmth of his smile and the obvious sensitivity with which he had divined her need for friends in a strange city.

What to wear? She wandered around Kensington High Street gazing into windows which were stocked with crystal beads, joss sticks and amber ornaments, wondering if it was the done thing to buy some of these for the party? She did not want to spend much money on a new dress and anyway what did people wear to parties here? She thought woefully of the expensive Donegal tweed suit and wool skirt she had splashed out on before leaving Ireland, which were hanging in her wardrobe. Would the time ever come when they could be worn with impunity? Truth to tell she had never been interested in clothes and was at a loss to know what really suited her. After an hour or two she came back home empty-handed except for a bottle of wine. She had, all the same, made up her mind to telephone a good hairdresser for an appointment. A new hairstyle would lift her morale.

Well pleased with the 'beehive' which the young man in the salon has persuaded her to have, she made her way to the party the following Saturday evening, her new hairdo lending confidence to her image of herself. She walked up the steps of the semi-detached Victorian house and found the party had started, people spilling out into the garden. No one answered her knock and, as the door was open, she pushed her way in and found herself in a crowded hallway. She had to fight her way to the kitchen and stood wondering where she could find her hostess to introduce herself? She looked about her. The walls were a surprising purple colour, great swathes of branches dangling from the ceiling and light fittings. The floor tiles shone with what seemed to be black boot polish. She had never seen a kitchen like this before. In the middle was a table laden with food, most of it unfamiliar, and numerous bottles of drink. Dodie placed her sherry alongside these, and made her way towards the sound of music which came from a room where people jigged and jived and took no notice of her at all. Further down a corridor she heard boogie woogie being played on a piano, and for a while she stood watching the pianist before going upstairs, picking her way between knees and feet. Through an open door she could see a couple on a bed having sex. The bathroom door was closed and alarming sounds could be heard from behind it. Dodie finished her exploration of the upper part of the house and stood looking over the banisters. The voice of Van Morrison arose from a downstairs room: "Here comes the night".

"How's your sex life?" A great lanky galoot of a fellow who had been lounging against a wall straightened up and placed himself much too close behind her.

"Let me pass please." She spoke politely but he lurched nearer and tried to grasp her by the arm. She pushed him away and he toppled over some of the recumbent figures stretched out on the landing. Dodie fled.

At last she saw him. He was talking to a handsome older man who was making what she took to be negative gestures with one hand while trying to free himself from Edward's grasp on his sleeve with the other. The exchange between the two seemed hostile. Then the man pulled away and walked off. For a minute Edward stood looking after him indecisively before turning in the opposite direction and heading for the garden. Dodie followed and found him sitting on a stone bench in a corner. Uninvited, she sat down beside him.

"Hello," she chirped brightly and for a moment she thought he did not recognise her.

"What on earth have you done to your lovely hair?"

Dismayed, she sat silent. She watched as he took a tin from his pocket, extracted some papers and a few curls of tobacco. He laid these along a paper, fidgeting them into a crease he had already made in the middle. Then he heated a small lump of dope at one end with a lighted match making it smoulder, giving out a smell that was not unlike incense. He crumbled it along the edge of the tobacco and twirled the whole thing up into a neat cylinder. Then he slid in a piece of cardboard, making what he said was a roach, twisted it and set it alight. He inhaled deeply before passing it on to his companion. She shook her head.

"Go on. Don't you want to try something new?"

Gingerly she took a puff and emboldened by the lack of instant effect she took another. For a while they sat in silence passing it between them.

"Are you enjoying the party?"

"Not really, but it's probably because I haven't put myself out to make friends with anyone. I should have made more effort to approach people..."

He cut in before she could finish. "Why do you Irish think that everything is your fault? I suppose you are just like your sister; a beautiful intelligent girl who has turned herself into a doormat for James." He paused. "She won't leave him, you know."

Dodie was taken aback at this outburst. While realising that he was only expressing what she herself thought, it was more than she could bear to hear her sister criticised by someone she perceived to be a friend. Abruptly she rose and made her way to the house, walking unsteadily through the hall, picking her steps carefully to avoid bits of scorched foil and broken glass. She found her coat, and Edward waiting for her by the door.

"Come on. I'll see you safely home," he offered. "Are you sure you're all right? It was only a spliff and shouldn't have any after-effects."

Dodie wasn't sure she was all right. Her gait was unsteady. Nothing seemed to be solid any more, not the pavements they trod nor the walls of the buildings they passed. Everything was made of liquid, all was in motion. She lurched forward and Edward put an arm around her waist. When they reached her door she did not invite him in, went straight upstairs and threw herself on her bed. Her sleep was haunted by faces leering at her from all directions. Hands clawed at her. She tried to scream but no sound came. She sat up in the bed and began to cry for help in the dummy language she had learned to use at school in the refectory when they were forbidden to talk during meals. Then, as now, her hands became her mouth but in her nightmare no one noticed, or if they did, they merely laughed nastily. At last a face that could have been Edward's appeared. She woke with tears streaming from her eyes. Next day a dozen yellow roses were delivered to her with a note bearing only Edward's name.

CHAPTER FORTY-EIGHT

Trish had not answered the phone for three days and, frustrated by the inability to speak to her sister, Dodie got in touch with her office. Trish started making vague excuses about not visiting her until Dodie threatened to go and see James and tell him what she thought of the situation. Two evenings after this conversation, she stood in the underground watching the caterpillar faces of two trains, which arrived and departed without dropping off the expected passenger. Her sister had always had the habit of being late and, as she waited, Dodie thought of the times when they were young – how she did as she pleased, accepting or dismissing things at will. She had regarded her as someone who was complete in herself and found it difficult now to accept that she had grown into a woman who needed to see herself in others' eyes to be sure that her own life had meaning. Dodie wondered how she was coping with her present uncertainties? Did she imagine that things would come right by some sleight of hand? Her strong reliable sister had disappeared and in her stead was a damaged young woman, too perfect, too rigid, always blaming herself when things went wrong. Dodie's recent understanding of this did not take away her annoyance at Trish's reluctance to act in her own interests, or indeed to keep to time but it helped her to exhibit more sympathy than she would otherwise have been capable of in the circumstances. When Trish at last stepped on to the platform, Dodie gave her a smile and arm in arm they walked out into the street.

Veronica Wright played bridge on Wednesdays in the house of one of her friends. When Dodie proposed having her sister over for a meal she had suggested that her evening out would give them privacy. Trish seemed in no hurry to talk about intimate things and Dodie thought it expedient not to rush her. For a while the conversation was trivial. Dodie served soup and compared working in a busy London hospital to the more easy-going ways of the Royal in Belfast. Trish nibbled her fish and picked at her vegetables, and Dodie wondered if she ever intended to open up and begin to talk about herself. After coffee she murmured something about having to go soon, but Dodie was determined to have her say.

"Please don't think of going until we sort out a few things."

She indicated that her sister should make herself comfortable in an armchair and said, "Trish, I have been thinking over your proposal to write to Paul asking him to put off his visit."

"Ah I hoped you would come round to agreeing with me."

"But I haven't. I have made up my mind firmly against it. First of all I would like to see him again myself, and I would enjoy going to the shows he proposes we attend. Also, it will be an opportunity for me to see more of London. It will be better than exploring on my own. It is up to you whether you see him or not. Let me know before he arrives."

"Dodie, you are making this harder for me."

"I don't want to, but you must not involve me in dishonesty."

Dodie got up to place the milk and cream in the fridge and when she returned she expressed herself even more forcibly to her sister.

"Now, about his baby. Let me repeat that I will do everything I can to help. But you must see that it is not possible to make any plans until you make up your mind when you are going to leave James and find another place to live."

"Leave James? Another place to live?" Trish looked at her in astonishment.

"Well since he doesn't want the baby and you do, the only course of action, as I see it, is to cut your losses and find a place for yourself and the child," Dodie said with some exasperation in her voice. Then seeing the blank look on her sister's face she added hastily, "With my help of course."

"But you don't understand. James might change his mind. After all, he is not denying paternity. We must wait and see what happens."

"How long will you wait? Suppose you go into labour prematurely? It occurs quite frequently. And what if it happens when James is away from home? Trish, you must make some plans for the baby's sake if not your own. It seems to me you can't just go sailing on hoping that a miracle will come along when you need it."

"Maybe it will," Trish answered dreamily. "We will call

it James if it is a boy and either Dodie or Sheila if it is a girl."

Dodie stared at her. Had she escaped into a world of fantasy rather than face up to reality, she wondered?

Suddenly Trish stood up and declared firmly, "James will wonder where I am. He does not like being left on his own for too long."

Dodie swallowed hard and made no further protests or suggestions as she accompanied her sister to the underground. When she returned she washed up and tidied things away. Then slowly she climbed the stairs, sat down at her desk and began to write.

Dear Paul,

Forgive the delay in answering your letter. As Mammy told you I am liking my new job and am comfortably ensconced in a very pretty house owned by a delightful and interesting lady called Veronica. She plays cards, climbs hills to watch birds and looks after me in a most caring way. She goes out often when I have the place to myself. She came in just five minutes ago and I asked her as you suggested, did she know of any decent B and Bs around here and she immediately suggested you must stay here with us as there is lots of room. I think she has the mistaken notion that you are my boyfriend. We'll soon disabuse her of that idea.

Trish, as you know, works full time and is also heavily engaged in helping to run an art gallery with the man she hopes to marry. She hardly takes time out to bless herself.

Let me know when and where you arrive and if it is at all possible I will meet you. I've led a fairly quiet life since coming here and look forward to painting the town, if not red, then at least a pale shade of pink.

Love to my Ma, your Ma and of course Maura.

As ever,

Dodie.

CHAPTER FORTY-NINE

Although Trish telephoned Paul the day after he arrived she did not propose meeting him. She was, she said, up to the eyes helping James but would make a big effort to see him before he went back home. Dodie suspected she was making excuses because she was not willing to expose her pregnancy. In a way Dodie was relieved. What would Paul have thought of her, with her lists and her mania for tidiness and order, her impeccable make-up? Would he have been impressed by her elegance or would he see it as a way of attempting to keep up her values in the marriage market? Probably not, she decided; it was not a man's way of looking at things. Nor would he appreciate the fearful tyranny that such an attitude imposed on a woman.

She was amazed at how knowledgeable he was about her life in London. He asked her questions about its counter-culture, the philosophy of Timothy O'Leary who advocated 'make love not war' and what did she understand about 'flower power'? Had she written off the fifties as conformist and complacent? They talked long into the night and she enjoyed his ability to make her think where she stood in all this. He was not the least intrusive even when he enquired if she had ever considered marriage? Laughingly, she replied that when she was in Ireland the men who were interested in her were dull types. They saw only the sober side of her and imagined she would make a dutiful wife. She knew she was not the person they wished her to be. In any case she wanted more out of life – excitement perhaps. "I suppose," she said thoughtfully, "I have always thought myself to be different, maybe the word I should use is – odd."

"To be different, Dodie," he suggested, "is not a failure on your part but in the expectations of others. Have you never met anyone who would even come up halfway to those standards you hold?"

They were walking home after supper in an Indian restaurant on the evening the conversation took place, and she found herself blushing and hoped if it showed he would put it down to the spicy food. She had no intention of telling him about Edward.

"I don't think so," she replied changing the subject hastily. "Going back to what we were talking about yesterday, you remember, the old strictures and rules of behaviour, well it seems to me it was much easier for our mothers and fathers when they were young. Their unquestioning morality made things straightforward. Their view of life is simple and it is one of the things I love about them."

"Yes," Paul agreed, "but you know their lives in some ways are stunted and out of joint with the times."

On his last evening in London Paul took Veronica and Dodie out to dinner. Afterwards Veronica told Dodie that she couldn't imagine why or how she had been able to leave such an interesting young man behind in Ireland. When he had gone, Dodie remembered the visit with pleasure and thought how much she had enjoyed sharing her thoughts with him. She was sorry she had not had the opportunity to introduce him to Edward and wondered how they would have got on together? Edward was occupying her mind a lot these days. She wondered if she was in love with him? How could she find out if he was attracted to her? Could she be the one to make the first move? She would prefer it to be the other way round of course. On the other hand could she endure meeting with him without pretending to accidentally touch him or let him see how passionate she was feeling? She thought the dilemma might be solved when Trish rang to invite her for drinks. She had some news to impart she said. Edward was going to be there with a friend. Having extracted the information that the friend was male, she promised to go over but warned she might be a little late as she was on duty until ten o'clock.

Before leaving the hospital, she changed out of her uniform, put on a pair of high-heeled shoes, brushed her hair and sprayed a little perfume behind her ears and on her wrists. In a mood of extravagance she hailed a taxi and when she got out gave the driver a broad smile and an even broader tip. She walked towards the entrance to the flat and entered the hallway. In the dim light she could see two figures clinging together in a passionate embrace of love. The lift clattered down and they stepped inside, arms still entwined. When they turned to face her she could see that one of the men was Edward and the other the person with whom he had been arguing at the party. Dodie turned and ran outside. She saw the taxi she had just left turning on the other side of the road and waved wildly to the driver.

"Did you leave something behind, love?" he enquired,

winding down a window. Dodie shook her head and searched inside herself for a steady voice. Finding it, she climbed into the cab, gave Veronica's address and sank back into the seat.

That night she lay awake listening to the downstairs clock, which ticked and tocked with despairing regularity. When it was six she rose, dressed and set off for the hospital. In the evening, too tired to cook, she ate a slice of bread and jam and decided to go straight to bed. She had reached the top of the staircase when the doorbell rang. Veronica was not at home. Perhaps she had lost her key? After a moment's hesitation she made her way wearily down again. James and Trish stood on the doorstep, smiling up at her.

"We were worried because you didn't turn up last night. Why did you not phone?"

Searching for an acceptable explanation, Dodie ushered them inside and busied herself taking their coats and offering to make tea. James shook his head and said they had come to take her out for a meal but she explained she had a bad migraine and needed to sleep. In spite of her extreme tiredness she could see that Trish was quietly elated.

"Well if you're quite sure you won't come out we will tell you our news and then leave you in peace." She smiled at James who continued, "Yesterday, we were celebrating Edward and Bill's decision to go to New Zealand, which means that we can have their flat."

"Much bigger than ours," Trish broke in, grinning. "It will be more suitable for a pram as it's on the ground floor."

James nodded and smiled. Dodie stared from one to another. This was not news she was expecting to hear. At first she wondered if it was part of the little routine dance they did around one another. Then she remembered Trish said she didn't really know the real James. Dodie imagined she had said this at a time when she meant to do all in her power to persuade him to marry her, a sort of overblown wishful thinking. But she was glad for both of them. Even if it was, on their part, an avoidance of truth, it seemed to have landed them in a sort of safety zone. She shook her head and thought she had probably got it all wrong. She should have remembered her sister had a will of iron under her meek exterior, and she had more experience of life. After all she was her senior by nine years.

CHAPTER FIFTY

In the weeks that followed Dodie threw herself into anything in the way of entertainment that came her way. It did not take her long to see that it was not really entertainment but a means of passing away hours that were empty and meaningless to her. Sex was everywhere and nowhere. She joined clubs and was introduced into a world of colour and loud music. After work she dressed in mini skirts and see-through blouses. She wore white lipstick and pencilled around her eyes. She spent a week in Hampshire in a commune listening to acquaintances expound theories on life, smoke hash and, as far as she could tell, sleep together indiscriminately. Nothing in what she saw or heard gave her satisfaction, not even the company of pleasant enough young people of her own age. They were able to embrace what they believed in with an exhilarating fervour as though they were in the process of making a better world. But on the way to work on the same train each morning, she saw careworn travellers who looked sad and disillusioned. Sometimes she sat behind one young man who endlessly watched his reflection in the glass of the window. She could see his mouth working, telling somebody off ceaselessly, his face contorted with rage. Others looked merely bored, burying themselves behind their newspapers. She found herself thinking of her own unsatisfying way of life and her inability to find a means of escape. There were times she felt like an insect trapped in a piece of amber.

She woke one morning still stunned by the deafening, night-long cacophony of sound on maximum amplification that she had experienced the previous evening. It was as if she had been flogged round the ears. She watched the net curtains on her windows move gently in the soft breeze, like a bridal veil. For a time she lay still and later, in her bath, she realised she had abandoned a way of life and the precepts she had once lived by but had nothing with which to replace them. She dressed, drank a cup of coffee and, without eating breakfast, started off for the hospital. It was a dull November morning and as usual she took the short cut through the nuns' garden which Sister Carmel had made available to her. Apart from Veronica Wright, she reflected, this nun was the only real friend she had made since coming to London. When she visited they sat together in the convent parlour where Dodie was served tea in delicate china cups by this sister who herself always obeyed the rule of the order which forbade them to eat or drink with anyone who was not of the community. She was a good listener and Dodie found herself confiding in her; she never criticised or found fault with any of her revelations.

This morning Dodie was early and she met several of the sisters coming from the chapel where they had been attending mass. They hurried to start the day's duties and seemed so cheerful and purposeful that she too wished she could be more motivated to begin her work. Others remained in the chapel for benediction. Dodie slipped in and sat down in a back pew. She listened to the 'litany of saints' and afterwards to the pure voices singing 'O Salutaris'. A sense of peace came to her and with it the notion that she too might be able to acquire this serenity if she became a nun. There was nothing much in life that she had not experienced she told herself, and her choices were dwindling fast. She resolved to think this over and discuss it with Sister Carmel. Then at Christmas she would go home and talk to her mother. She stepped out into the chill November air and surprised herself by wondering what Paul Murray would think about it? She had not heard from him since his visit to London. What had he made of it? Had she inadvertently indicated her interest in Edward? It would be nice to be able to discuss her recent thinking with him when she saw him at Christmas.

CHAPTER FIFTY-ONE

Sheila and Dodie emerged from midnight mass to find snow whirling gently downwards. They watched the flakes move faster, grow bigger, brush against each other until they lay in undistinguished piles on the ground. Neighbours and friends stopped briefly in greeting before hurrying away from the cold. Paul Murray appeared at Dodie's elbow and walked a little way with herself and her mother before saying that he too must rush off, he was anxious to overtake his mother who had started off without him.

"She's not so good on her feet these days and I'm afraid she will slip on the ice."

"Tell her we look forward to having you both for supper on Boxing Day."

Paul shook his head. "Mother will come of course but you will have to do without me. I have to be off very early next morning to catch my plane to Vancouver."

"Vancouver?"

"Billy Maguire is settled out there now as you probably know. He and Mary have asked me to go out and spend the rest of the holiday with them and meet the baby."

"Well I hope you have a lovely time," Dodie answered more cheerfully than she felt, only then realising how much she had been looking forward to his company. He waved and was gone, his footsteps hardly audible in the snow.

The visit was pleasant enough. She knew Sheila was delighted to have her home again. In spite of this, Dodie felt uncomfortable at having to keep a promise to Trish not to let their mother know she was pregnant. At times she experienced a divided loyalty and she was tempted to let the secret out. One day in a shady corner of the garden she found a spent dandelion and thoughtlessly began to blow on its down.

"I will. I won't, I will. I won't, I will. I won't."

Decisions should never be a matter of chance, she told herself severely as she threw the stalk away, and anyway it's not my responsibility.

Every night Sheila took her rosary beads from the knob of the bed and together she and Dodie kneeled down to pray. It was the same bed with the brass fittings in which Dodie had slept as a child. She smiled now, remembering how she used to unscrew the knobs and fill the hollows with her small treasures to keep them from prying eyes; a pretty marble, a few Dolly Mixtures or a brightly coloured autumn leaf. She looked at her mother praying fervently, her eyes closed, her face calm. It was time she decided she should confide in her that she was thinking of becoming a nun. She would do so tomorrow when they were relaxing after supper.

Sheila's reaction surprised her. She didn't object outright but mustered arguments to dissuade her from such a course of action.

"If you go into a convent, your life, in my opinion, will

be unlived. At best you would spend it in a safe shell instead of going out to challenge what comes." A pause and then, "What would Trish do without you in London? You know I worry about your sister. She is very secretive and I always believed I could depend on you to keep an eye on her. You were always close in spite of the difference in your ages. If you go into a convent you will become just as remote as she is. And anyway," she concluded, "I think you should wait a year at least before taking such a big step."

Dodie was taken aback that her mother, such an unquestioningly religious woman was not delighted at the prospect of having a daughter a nun. Yet she knew she was only thinking of what was best for her. She was the most unselfish person she knew. The subject was not raised again but Dodie, not happy with her life in London, now found she was less comfortable in her childhood home than she had been.

At night she lay tossing things over in her mind and listening to the scratching and mewing of her mother's new kitten in the confines of its cardboard box. She borrowed a car and drove with Sheila all over her native county. Then they visited neighbouring Antrim, stopping in the small seaside towns of Cushenall and Cushendun. They climbed down the side of the waterfalls now in full flood, and after lunch set off for home. The beauty of this area never failed to touch them, the purples and reds of the winter fuchsia in the hedges, the 'white lady' in the limestone rocks and the 'red arch' through which they passed on their journey.

That night in bed she continued to hear the sound of the waves breaking on Murlough Bay and saw again the outline of Rathlin Island. She found herself repeating over and over the names of the glens of Antrim as in a litany; Glenanne, Glenshesk, Glenarriffe, Glendun, Glenshane, Glenarm, Glenballyemon as though she was trying to hold on to some sense of tenure in her own country.

When it was time to return to London, Dodie hugged Sheila to her and felt her small bones close to her own, like twigs on the same branch. She looked at her and thought she saw in her mother's eyes a hunger for the things they had not been able to say to one and other. She wished she could put into words the notion that she was trying to find a place where she could disappear in order to discover she was another person. Indeed she was not fully aware of this herself.

CHAPTER FIFTY-TWO

Dodie learned to her surprise that James wished his son to be called David, after his father who had deserted him and his mother when he was four years old and had not been heard of since. His mother, with whom he was not on good terms, lived quite near and Trish told Dodie that James blamed her for the failure of the marriage. She had managed to persuade him to let her know that she now had a grandchild. Mrs Richmond promptly invited them to lunch and made much of the baby. Soon there were regular visits and, although she was included, Dodie felt slightly out of things when Trish, ignoring her sister's nursing experience, referred all questions about the welfare and training of the baby to Mrs Richmond. After six weeks Trish returned to work in the Civil Service leaving little David in the care of his delighted grandmother. Trish had now written to Sheila who, when she heard the news, seemed to take it for granted that James and her daughter were married. She begged them to visit her soon. Dodie was pleased when James told her quite casually one day that he was looking forward to visiting Ireland and meeting her mother. They had decided that an unmarried couple with a child might prove an embarrassment to her so they would remedy the situation. Trish added that having parents with different surnames could cause confusion when David started school.

It was a quiet wedding in a register office. The guests were James' mother and two of his friends, two of Trish's colleagues from work and Veronica Wright. Edward flew over from New Zealand, and Dodie and he were the principal witnesses. Afterwards the little party lunched at the Gay Hussar, drank champagne and then dispersed fairly quickly. Edward suggested that he and Dodie might take in a film. She declined the offer but not before Veronica, who was standing within earshot, invited them to tea in her house. Edward accepted with pleasure and Dodie felt it would be churlish of her to refuse. She was surprised to find herself still affected by his physicality and longed for his departure.

After the wedding she lost no time in making plans for her reception into the convent. She talked to Sister Carmel and had lengthy discussions with Reverend Mother who noticed her pale cheeks and the rings under here eyes. She was advised to take a holiday before beginning religious life.

"The first year in a convent will be strenuous," she was told. "It requires the postulant to give of herself spiritually and physically. Your hours of sleep and relaxation will be curtailed and this can be taxing until you get used to it, so before you begin it is imperative you are refreshed and ready to give yourself to God."

"But Mother, I have thought well about this and am longing to take my place with the other sisters in the convent."

"The other sisters will make demands on you for which you may not be prepared." Dodie could not imagine what these demands might be and when she discussed it with Trish, her sister guessed that it might be taking care of the sick or elderly nuns as she was trained in that sort of work. Then, in a puzzled tone, she reminded Dodie how much she had disliked them when she was at school and asked why she had changed her way of thinking.

"This is different," Dodie said. "What is chosen is not the same as what is forced on you."

That night in her bed she prayed, asking God to make her a good nun. The invocation seemed familiar and then she remembered how she had prayed when she was a young child. "God make me a good girl." She wrote to Paul Murray, confiding her plans to him, and after a long silence he wrote back wishing her well.

In obedience to Reverend Mother's suggestion, Dodie took a short holiday, which she spent with her mother. She found her reading the obituaries in the local paper just as Grandmother Maggie used to do. She said goodbye to friends and neighbours in the village and spent an evening with Maura and her mother. Paul, they told her, was in Donegal taking a Gaelic language class. He would be sorry to miss her. As she hugged her mother to her for the last time, Sheila said, "Remember, Dodie, if you take a wrong turn in life never be too frightened to turn back. Faith is in the search for understanding."

Dodie checked back a sob and stood motionless until a small pool of quiet began to spread inside her. Then she bent and kissed her mother's pale face.

CHAPTER FIFTY-THREE

Surely there was more of Mother De Sales than God intended? Dodie pushed the unworthy thought away as the nun, overflowing her armchair, sat and listened to the two postulants make suggestions about which names they would take in religion. Dodie smiled, remembering how many years ago, she had asked her mother why she had not been given a safe name when she was baptised. She thought then that one grew into the person the name implied and when she was nicknamed Dodie or Dopey or Dodo she felt she was each of these in turn. She was surprised that the Mistress of Novices seemed to be confirming that she had been right. It was recommended that they pray to the saint whose name they had chosen so that they would grow in virtue like their namesakes. Mother De Sales turned down her proposal as inappropriate. Genevieve was a name Sheila had wished to call her younger daughter, but was deterred by the Dean of the parish, who insisted there was no such name in the 'litany of the Irish Saints'. It seemed it was not appropriate now either. Agnes was suggested more than once. She was advised to read up all she could about the life of the saint. Obediently she learned all she could about the thirteen-year-old Agnes, saint and martyr, but none of the biographies brought her to any genuine admiration or made her feel she would like to imitate her life. It seemed to her that any teenage girl faced with a rapist would resist as violently as she could; screaming, biting, kicking. Perhaps she was just unlucky that her assailant lost his head and murdered her? She thrust these thoughts away and was suddenly compliant, knowing that her reluctance to accept Mother De Sales' choice might be interpreted as disobedience. Bowing her head meekly, she reminded herself that she was a postulant, which meant 'begging to be let in'. She was here to become someone else anyway. To impose a new name was not all there was to defining a new life. The habit she would eventually wear was calculated to make her look different from those outside the convent. In six months time she would be clad in black from head to toe, a leather belt at her waist, from which dangled an outsize rosary beads. She told herself she would have no difficulty leaving the world. Soon she would take her vows for a year and later renew them for life.

The day began with the ringing of the bell. Each sister would rise and murmur, "Deo gratias," as if in answer to the voice of God. They washed and dressed and turned out their beds before going to the chapel to pray for an hour. All meals were taken in the refectory, a long room with a scrubbed wooden table which had a bench at each side. On an otherwise empty wall a huge crucifix was hanging where everyone could see it. Talking was not permitted at meal times. One of their number was designated to read from the New Testament or other holy book. New entrants were served last and often the food was cold when it reached the two postulants. During the day, time was taken up with the study of approved literature or the menial tasks of the convent. After lunch which invariably consisted of bread and cheese they were allowed a half hour break in the garden or if it rained in the recreation room. Speaking was allowed during this time and also in emergencies. Otherwise custody of the lips was observed, together with custody of the eyes which were trained downwards and inwards. Custody of the hands was achieved by tucking them into the wide sleeves of the habit. Nuns were forbidden to touch each other and must give up the right to express personal opinions, always submitting to the judgements of senior sisters. Humility, chastity, obedience, poverty were the aims of everyone. All property was held in common. Families and the past were not talked about; only the necessary present and the future in heaven were subjects to be discussed.

Dodie found her time was governed by minutiae and filled with detail every second of the day. It was imperative to be continually occupied in doing something for God. At first a sense of purpose and certainty beguiled her and she felt she had come to a place where she could at last find peace. However, in a short time she discovered this way of life left her physically tired and lack of sleep befuddled her brain, removing any energy for thinking of the meaning of the life she was leading. Gradually she got used to the physical toll taken on her body and her mind began to function again. Soon she was struggling with doubts. Was she giving up the freedom she had fought and thought her way towards? Was it right that spirituality was only achieved by unquestioning obedience? At last she shared her doubts with the Mistress of Novices who informed her that all new entrants had similar misgivings. She advised patience, extra prayers and more penance. Dodie wished fervently that her friend Carmel had not been moved to another convent. It would have been comforting to have someone she felt would understand her anxieties.

In the sixties, the dogma of the Catholic church that constricted nuns was eased and they were given more choices regarding the running of their lives. Much was now left to the individual, including how they should dress. Reform came late to the convent in which Dodie was commencing her religious life. The older sisters were dismayed, refusing the new innovations. Most would not give up or even modify the cumbersome garments in which they had been clothed for so long. Some refused to accept the small amount of pocket money which was allocated to each nun. Many rules became obsolete. Confusion reigned. Changes were made in the hierarchical structure. Mother De Sales retained her position as Mistress of Novices and refused to vary her training one whit. She insisted the postulants must conform as before until they were properly received into the order. Then, she conceded, they would decide for themselves which innovations they would adopt.

CHAPTER FIFTY-FOUR

Usually alert at Mass, Dodie found herself preoccupied one morning as she looked at Mother De Sales' face that resembled a tightly shut door. Swallowing, she found her throat as raw as if she had swallowed a hedgehog. A message had been sent to her before she entered the chapel. She was to report to Reverend Mother's office after breakfast. It could mean only one thing. Yesterday she and her fellow postulant Una were walking sedately and silently through the recreation room on their way to the garden. Suddenly her companion, a young girl of seventeen, looked around and seeing no one about hitched up her skirts and jumped on to the polished banister of the staircase. With a loud whoop, she slid to the bottom in a heap of swirling skirts. They stood laughing until a noise behind made them hurry outside, still suffused with laughter. Dodie thought of the angelic face suddenly full of mischief and smiled at the memory. Her companion's openness and sense of fun had endeared her to Dodie in spite of the frequent admonitions that nuns should have no attachments to each other. Dodie guessed now that Una's antics had been reported and presumed that this was the reason she had been summoned by her superior.

She knocked on the heavy oak door and a voice called out bidding her to come in. It was the first time since she entered the convent that she had been inside this room with its dark panelling on the walls and heavy brocade curtains, so contrasting to the austerity of the other parts of the building. Reverend Mother sat behind a huge mahogany desk and gazed at Dodie over her spectacles.

"Are you aware, Sister Agnes, that when a member of the community does wrong, the matter – if known – must be reported to the appropriate person who is appointed to deal with it?"

Dodie nodded and shifted her feet, aware that she had not been invited to sit.

"Well then, why did you not as a responsible member of this community, report your companion's behaviour of yesterday, at once…?"

"But Mother," Dodie broke in impulsively, "she didn't do anything wrong, she only…"

"Indeed. And how would you describe her actions?"

"She acted lightheartedly and impulsively, I suppose." Suddenly Dodie had a memory of the swinging skirts and the look of impish glee on the face of her fellow postulant and a smile came over her face. "In fact, I thought it was quite funny."

"Are you contradicting my opinion?" Reverend Mother asked with eyes like frozen frogspawn.

"No, Mother," she replied.

"Then go and think the incident over, and when you have realised how erroneous your judgement is we will talk about it again. Meanwhile, this evening you will apologise to all the sisters during recreation, explaining as best you can, your defiance to my authority and your inability to be obedient to the rules of the convent."

"I don't think I can do that, Mother. It would be dishonest on my part."

"Go to your cell now and think well before you get yourself into worse trouble."

The flowering period was over, only duty remained. Dodie refused to comply with her superior's wishes and remained in her cell for the next twenty-four hours. She was aware that voting was taking place to appoint a new Reverend Mother and Mistress of Novices, but she gave this little thought as she was not yet formally received into the community and was without a say in the matter. However, she was surprised when she received the news that decisions that had far-reaching effects on herself were reached, and she rejoiced to learn the names of the new appointees who were more liberal-minded than their predecessors. She could not help feeling that God was on her side that evening as she and her fellow novice smiled at each other across the silence of the refectory table. She had been given a chance to start afresh. Now she would make greater efforts to obtain sanctity and strive to ignore her not quite vanquished doubts.

The pure high voices of the nuns greeted Dodie and Una as they entered the convent chapel and the sharp, sweet smell of incense, wax and the fragrant perfume of the blooms that had been picked in the garden that morning drifted towards them. Slowly the two girls walked up the aisle in bridal attire reminiscent of their first communion day when too they had worn white dresses, satin shoes and a veil covering their hair. They reached the altar and prostrated themselves in front of the steps, the bishop in a mitre of cream silk and gold thread began to say mass.

"I will go unto the alter of God. To God who hath given joy to my youth."

Throughout the ceremony the proposed 'brides of Christ' lay prone on the floor silently making the responses until it was time to rise and partake in the sacrament of communion.

Afterwards the two newly received nuns were congratulated warmly. Sheila was too unwell to travel but Veronica Wright, Trish, James, his mother and baby David were there, the latter delighting the whole community. Lunch was served to the visitors, Dodie and Una, now Sisters Agnes and Gabriel, looked on, doing their best to keep their eyes away from the smoked salmon and chocolate mousse as they talked to their friends and families.

CHAPTER FIFTY-FIVE

For a time Dodie's doubts lay dormant until she became uneasily aware that it was taken for granted in the convent she accepted all the tenets of the church without question. Slowly it dawned on her that she was trampling conscience underfoot in the name of blind obedience and allowing a certain laziness of mind to lull her into quiescence. With a new Spiritual Director they found knitting and sewing optional at recreation and literature was not so stringently censored. Dodie was now able to read some of the books of her own choice often late into the night. However she was disappointed to find that none of the sisters shared her interest in even the simplest of theological questions. One evening during a discussion about faith, Dodie expressed the opinion that she could not be certain of anything since it was impossible to know God. The silence that followed was one of shock followed by a rush of attempts to change the conversation. Next day she received a stern rebuke from Reverend Mother and was advised to guard against her tongue so as to avoid any further scandal. But she was on a road where she was convinced progress could only be made by facing doubts in order to arrive at the truth. In confession when she voiced her thoughts to the priest, he suggested that as everyone had a cross to bear in this world, perhaps hers was this state of mind which precluded the comfort of certainty? She found herself envying and at the same time despising the other nuns who seemed untroubled; it was such an easy way to live.

Into her perplexity a letter dropped. It was Easter Sunday and the end of a six-day silent retreat. Dodie had given the periods of meditation and the lectures her whole attention and was looking forward to the festive meal that evening which would end Lent and signal the beginning of the joyful season of the Resurrection. The writing was unfamiliar and the sight of both her secular and religious names on the envelope made her smile. It was as if the writer was unsure to which world she belonged. She turned it over and noted that it had been opened and not too neatly gummed together again. During retreats they were not allowed correspondence but presumably she thought, letters had to be opened by someone in case the contents were of an urgent nature. The news she found inside was indeed urgent. It was from James who wrote to say her mother was gravely ill. Trish was already on her way to her. She had asked him to contact Dodie on the telephone but he was not permitted to speak to her. When he had settled the baby with his mother, he wrote, he would follow Trish to Ireland. Looking at the date stamp, she noticed it was posted almost a week ago. She ran to Mother Superior's office and was told Mother was busy and she would see her after supper. Dodie insisted on an interview there and then and after a wait of ten minutes or so the door opened. She was given permission to go to Ireland but was warned that it might take time to get tickets as it was Easter weekend and flights would possibly be booked out. Having given her consent, Mother Superior turned to face her: "Have you considered that this is the most important time in the whole of the religious year? Would it not be more appropriate to consider putting off this journey for a week?"

Dodie shook her head decisively.

"Well then, we will do our best to make travelling arrangements. Meanwhile we will all pray for your mother."

Dodie rose to leave the room. The older nun got up and, moving towards Dodie, laid a hand on her shoulder. "My dear child, I know how you must feel but there is more important pain in this world than that which you are now experiencing."

Her companion with a distraught face asked, "Does that mean I should ignore it? My mother is dying. Nothing matters to me more than that."

She spoke spontaneously without considering the impact her words might have.

"Go." The voice was the hiss of a snake. "Go now and quickly."

It was as though a great weight was pressing down hard on her shoulders, preventing her from breathing. She wondered if the demoted Mother De Sales, now in charge of the post, had deliberately held up James' letter? Were they all conspiring against her? In an agony she prayed that her mother would not die before she could reach her. She was unable to eat and wept all through supper.

For the next two nights Dodie moved about in her cell waiting for the dawn. On Easter Monday as she walked in the garden she heard her mother's voice each time she answered one of the sister's greetings. As she looked about her unseeingly, an early bee flitted about in the bushes and then hopped on to the ticket that was at last put into her hand. Dodie stared at it hard as she gently shook the bee on to the grass and she felt a stillness rise in her which she thought nothing could violate. The sea, in which she had almost drowned, became shallow again.

The sulphurous smell of hard-boiled eggs came to her as she passed the kitchen door on her way to the basement. There Mother De Sales was waiting for her, sitting quietly reading her office. On a long table in front of her lay an open suitcase which contained the clothes in which Dodie had arrived at the convent.

"Remove your holy habit and hand it to me."

Dodie looked at this woman who had tried to mould her into her own idea of piety and held out her hand in farewell. Mother De Sales held it briefly.

"You know, don't you, that the sin of pride always blinded you to your failings?"

CHAPTER FIFTY-SIX

Dodie woke from an uneasy sleep. High up in the plane she was suddenly paralysed with terror. Looking down between the gaps in the clouds she considered the awful distance of the empty miles between herself and the earth. Her stomach churned like a cement mixer. Below her the sea came into view and she grew a little more calm. The surface of the water undulated gently and she tried to imagine what might be beneath it. There would be dead creatures, bones of fish, shells, pearls, the glint of treasure, perhaps gold coins from the ships of the Spanish Armada many of which had perished here in these very waters. But there would be living creatures too, swimming ceaselessly with the tides. Suddenly the flanked rib of Cave Hill appeared looking like a recumbent figure, breathing and alive. The gantries of the Belfast shipyard reared up beneath her as the plane toiled downwards. Unused to noise, the roar of the engines made her head ache. Finding it unbearable, she put her hands over her ears but she could not blot out the yelp of the wheels hitting the runway followed by the screech of brakes. Unsteadily she climbed down the steps of the aircraft into the lounge where Trish and James were waiting.

A glance at her sister's face told her the news. Speechless they clung together for some minutes before following James to the car park. On the way home she learned that Sheila had died two days ago. Her health had gradually declined but imperceptibly. She had not complained and went on working in her studio. She had been found sitting near her easel, a smile on her face, dying, Dodie thought, as quietly as she had lived.

Standing between them at the graveside, Dodie was aware of James' smart dark suit and her sister's well cut black dress. She had never been fashion-conscious and this, she told herself, was not an appropriate time to be thinking about appearance. Nevertheless, she could not help noticing that her own clothes must have gone out of fashion in the two years she had spent in the convent. Even then, she had worn her worst things on the day she entered, having given the best away to charity in the expectation that she would not need them again. Still, the blouse she was wearing today, without a doubt could have been improved by the application of a hot iron. At her reception, a small piece of her hair had been cut off to symbolise her humility and, later, in a bid for comfort, she had chopped off great swathes of it as it was hot and uncomfortable under her coif. How different it was now from Trish's shining locks. Dragging her thoughts away from herself, she looked at the coffin. Her mother if not fashionable was always neat and fastidious in her dress. She tried to concentrate on the service; the priest was referring to everlasting life. The contrast between the living and the dead she mused, should be made more explicit. She felt herself to be almost lifeless. Although she had been going through the rituals of eating, sleeping and taking part in making arrangements for the funeral, she felt that her mind and heart were untenanted, while her body, like a well oiled machine, carried out all the correct movements. The subdued sobs of her sister and aunts hardly impinged on her consciousness and it was not until Aunt Elizabeth came over and kissed her through the black veil hanging from her hat that Dodie became aware of her present situation.

At night she was constantly aware of her mother's face before her. When she closed here eyes she was again a child, leaning against Sheila's body in church or when she read to her; not wanting to move, hoping the closeness would go on forever. At such times she had been able to convince herself there were only the two of them in the whole world. Yesterday as she stood in the hallway of her mother's house, she caught sight of Sheila's old Donegal tweed coat hanging on a peg by the door where it had always been. Rubbing her face against its rough texture she imagined her mother's warmth flooding through her again but all too soon the feeling ebbed, leaving her with a sense of emptiness.

Sheila's will contained no surprises. She had she left everything to her daughters equally. Three days after the funeral, they sat down with James to decide how best to dispose of her possessions, especially the paintings. Trish asked Dodie if she would like her share of the inheritance to be given to the convent and it was only then she informed them that she did not intend to continue in the life of a nun.

They pulled out stacked canvasses, propped them up against the walls of Sheila's studio and began an inspection by first looking at what James guessed had been her earlier works. Some of the watercolours he said, were quite good; he might be able to sell a few if they agreed. Later pictures consisted of a series of crowd scenes. Some had backgrounds showing tumbled-down shacks with flames coming out of the thatches. People sat around in hopeless despondency holding onto pathetic bundles, babies or small children. The figures in four other pictures depicted human beings naked from the waist up. Their faces were gaunt and emaciated, eyes staring in the same direction. The arms, bony and elongated were stretched out as though trying to grasp at something unseen. The effect was one of despair and desolation. The sisters were aghast.

"But these are so unlike our gentle mother," Dodie gasped. "She must have been suffering greatly without any of us being aware of it."

They stared in silence for a time.

"If you will forgive me for venturing an opinion about the work of someone I only met once," James said, "my guess is that they are representations conjured up by thoughts of the Irish famine. The people in them are wasting away from hunger."

"Yes of course," Trish broke in, "you are quite right, now it all fits into place with the journals."

"Journals?"

"Yes Dodie. Last night I couldn't sleep and I got up and started to look through some of mother's things that were kept in a drawer in the bottom of her wardrobe. I came across these journals by our great-grandmother. They were written just at the end of the famine and described how her mother died as a result of the great hardship she suffered. They have been carefully preserved and placed where we would find them. I will pass them on to you this afternoon."

James managed to lift some of the gloom when he drew

their attention to paintings that did not seem to relate to anything that had gone before. These he thought, were executed fairly recently.

"They tell me," he said, "that Sheila managed to work her way through what might have been some sort of depression to arrive at a wonderful sense of serenity and probably an understanding or resolution of what was troubling her. Look," he went on holding one up to the light, "if you screw your eyes up you will be able to make out in the background just a faint outline of a figure emerging from the shadows. Contrast the colour here with the drab greys, dark purples and blacks used in the earlier ones and you will see what I mean."

The hitherto unnoticed sun shone through the studio window, lighting up the warmth of the pinks, yellows and greens that Sheila had used in great swirling whorls and curlicues.

"They are much more abstract and to me more interesting, indicating a now optimistic artist."

They stood before a picture in which an elongated snakelike creature curled itself round and round the main branch of a tree, blending in with the knotty wood. It was not immediately discernible but once seen could not be obliterated from the vision. The eye was encouraged to follow its curves from the benign face to the top of the tail which thrust jauntily in the air. Trish said she thought it was reminiscent of the *Book of Kells*, remembering that she had once treated Sheila to a visit to Dublin and Trinity College. Sheila, she informed them, had been much impressed with the old Celtic art forms and maybe she was here trying to imitate those artists who painted in this convoluted manner.

But Dodie laughed uncontrollably and at last, recovering, led them to her mother's bedroom where she pointed to the ceiling. A damp stain wriggled across the plaster, shaped like a reptile, its body tapering to a tail that stuck up in the air. Light-hearted now, they tripped downstairs and stood in front of Dodie's portrait in the dining room.

"That grim face can't be mine."

"Oh I don't know," Trish responded. "It's one of the few paintings she has had framed so she must have liked it a lot."

"It's not really grim, Dodie." James turned to her: "A bit solemn perhaps and admittedly there is a little sadness round the eyes, but it is the mouth that takes the attention. Those lips curl up into a decided smile."

"How little we knew her," Trish murmured, beginning to weep. James put an arm round each of them.

"Pictures won't unlock her mind completely but they allow us to get a glimpse of what we would not otherwise have seen, maybe even something that is beyond what is painted."

They stood in their own thoughts, until James said hesitantly, "Often we do not throw away what is the most significant part of our lives."

"She was so confined in this small village. I don't think my mother was ever outside Ireland in her whole life."

"Well they say too much freedom can suffocate art," James remarked. "Think of all the writing and paintings that are produced in hospitals and prisons which otherwise would not have seen the light of day, not that it is all good, of course."

Later Dodie thought over what had been said and realised that her mother's life, although governed by strict religious beliefs was not limited by them; nor indeed by her children as most mothers are. No, she was defined by her own creativity.

CHAPTER FIFTY-SEVEN

What Dodie liked best about her old home was its spaciousness and its silence. It was unlike the quiet of the convent, more easeful and without a feeling that she was being watched all the time. But she had no regrets about selling it. It was time she felt, to make drastic changes in her life. There was a good deal of work to do before putting it on the market. While she was tackling the many jobs that she felt were necessary before the sale, she learned to like her own company. From the day when she had stood before her mother's paintings and laughed out loud, she felt for the first time in many months quite optimistic about her future. Like phantom pain, she used the house to find parts of herself. She wondered why she had been so attracted to the religious life? She had thought her vocation was a gift from God but if so it was something she could not keep. She was now able to admit to herself that she had no talent for renunciation but had been looking for what was self-serving. Faith, she decided, was more difficult than sacrifice. She had wanted a miracle to give her a motive for living but miracles she now knew, came from faith; not faith from miracles. All her life she had wanted to be elsewhere, despising the present, waiting for the next thing to happen. Life had been mostly what others did. Gradually as she got to know herself better, the guilt she had expected to overtake her for leaving the convent failed to reach her and was slowly replaced by the wisdom of uncertainty. Meantime she took pleasure in clearing away the weeds in her mother's overgrown garden, and by tending its wounds she was mending her own.

After Trish and James returned to London, Dodie opened the packet containing her great-grandmother's writings. She smoothed out the yellowing pages and noted the handwriting was recognisably by the same person. At first it was neat and careful and then over time it changed to devil-may-care illegibility. She began by reading the letter beginning, "Dear daughter Margaret," and then continued through to the end of the three notebooks.

THIRD NOTEBOOK

You were always careful at night to leave room in your little bed for your guardian Angel. When I looked at your sleeping face and knelt down to say my own prayers I often felt blasphemous. At such times I would ask God to forgive me for loving you more than I loved him.

Sometime in the summer when I had finished the washing and ironing, we would go to town to deliver it. The journey was always slow. You talked to everything that moved, your hands were birds' wings fluttering in the air. When you spied an ant or a spider in the grass: "What's its name? Where does it live? What does it eat?" A wren hopping down a branch would send you off on a hunt for grains or seeds and then it would take a long time to find the most convenient spot to place your offerings. Everything had to be eaten in pairs. You explained to me that if you left a small piece of bread or a single potato on your plate it would be lonely. You had to know how things smelled and what the birds talked to each other about. Evenings when I would have no more energy left to work, I might sit down for a few minutes to take my ease before making the supper. Sometimes when I had my eyes closed and my legs crossed, "Unwobble your legs," was your command and having climbed on my knee and made yourself comfortable a little finger was pushed under my eyelids to make me look at you. Then you'd plague me with more questions.

"Where do we go when we die?" And when I said I would

be first, "Will you come back and tell me what it's like in heaven?" A pause. "If you die before me then I'll be nobody's child."

You saw fairies in the clouds and like most children I suppose, dreamed of monsters. When you were afraid, which wasn't often, and wanted God to grant you some special favour, you would bargain with him, promising to hold the clothes pegs for me or search for more food for the birds. At times your questions were serious enough but I think you lived mostly in a fantasy world and sometimes I thought you had no more sense than a scaldie bird. Ah Margaret, you were my share of the world.

You had no companions before you started school although you did not make strange with people. Any passing tramp was welcomed as though he or she was a dear friend. The parish priest called on us every two months or so and sat for an hour smoking a clay pipe. Later you would imitate him with a twig from the hedge outside. Once you told him you were going to do a pooley and you made for the door, calmly pulling your skirt up over your behind as you went. It was difficult for the priest not to let you hear him laugh.

"There's more flesh," he said to me one day, "on the legs of a wren. I'll have to ask Lizzie to send her some more soda bread."

★

"God be with all here."

"God and Mary be with you," we would answer as Tim McConville called out his greeting in a loud voice so as not to startle us. He always appeared at the edge of dark after finishing his jobs for Lizzie and Father McManus. One winter evening he told us he heard strange sounds in the hedge just beyond our door. As usual you asked questions, "Were they the chirpings of a bird? An animal squeaking? Are they sad or happy sounds?" Dissatisfied with his answers, you asked to be taken to the place where the mystery could be solved. I said it was too cold, too wet, too dark and it might be a witch or a ghost. I had supposed Tim would be reluctant to go out again into the rain but he rose and put on his wet jacket. He could refuse you nothing. At last I said, "Yes," and in next to no time the pair of you arrived back carrying the totiest wee kitten I had ever clapped an eye on. It was drenched and mewing piteously, its ribs stuck out and its breathing was laboured. Before I had time to say anything you announced, "I'm going to keep it so I am. So I am. So I am."

My protests, that we could not afford extra milk or bread to feed it, were met with the assurance that you would give it half of your supper every night. Tim took your side.

"Sure, won't it go out and find its own food when we get it on its feet again?" I was still looking doubtful and you threatened me, "If you don't let me keep it, me run away and get another Mammy."

This was the first sign of defiance I saw in you. Maybe I should have been warned. In any case, that evening I was sure the poor creature wouldn't last long, but I was wrong. Tim tucked it up in a wisp of hay and laid it beside the hearth. You coaxed it to lick a little milk from your fingertips and it made a faint attempt to purr. I looked at your face. It was a round of perfect joy, your eyes two slits of delight.

"We'll call her Pangur," I said, remembering a poem I learned at school about a monk and his white cat. At the top of the page in the verse book was printed: 'This poem was written in Gaelic by an Irish student in the monastery of Carinthia in the eighth century. It was found in a copy of a translation of Saint Paul's epistles on the margins of a page.' Here it is.

Pangur Ban

I and Pangur Ban my cat, 'tis a like task we are at
Hunting mice is his delight, hunting words I sit all night.

Better far than praise of men, 'tis to sit with book and
    pen
Pangur bears me no ill will, he too plies his simple skill.

'Tis a merry thing to see at our tasks how glad are we
When at home we sit and find entertainment in our
    mind.

Oftentimes a mouse will stray in the hero Pangur's way
Oftentimes my keen thought set takes a meaning in
    its net.

'Gainst the wall he sets his eye, full and fierce and sharp
    and sly
'Gainst the wall of knowledge I, all my little wisdom
    try.

When a mouse darts from its den, oh how glad is
    Pangur then

Oh what gladness do I prove when I solve the doubts
    I love.

So in peace our tasks we ply, Pangur Ban my cat and
    I
In our arts we find our bliss, I have mine and he has
    his.

Practice every day has made Pangur perfect in his trade
I get wisdom day and night turning darkness into light.

The little cat was so dirty when you found it that it was
hard to know what colour she would be. As she grew
stronger she cleaned her coat, licking and scratching until
at last she was whiter than the snow that fell outside our
door. Lizzie agreed with you that Pangur was the nicest cat
in the world and sometimes brought you scraps of fish skin
to feed her as a treat. Your treat was slim bread which she
made with potatoes, milk and flour. Lizzie never ceased to
marvel at your capacity for leisure and surmised that for a
child life had no beginnings and no endings. She wondered
how such a small body could contain so much joy. Poor
Lizzie. She was a good friend who left this world far too
early. May God rest her kindly soul.

When it was time for you to go to school, I washed and
sewed together some flour bags that Lizzie had begged from
the grocer. Although I scrubbed and rubbed, some of the
lettering remained, words like 'Ranks flour' and 'best oatmeal'
could be made out on parts of your dress but you looked
quite fetching in your new finery. On your first day I walked
with you into town. I knew you were frightened but you

held your head high and your little body straight as a daffodil.

Soon your questions were of a different order. "Am I pretty?"

"Pretty enough," I would answer, "but beauty is not everything." In truth you were a plain child. I always thought it best to be straightforward but never knew if this was the right way to answer. Would the truth make you less confident? On the other hand I did not want you to be conceited. At school you learned to knit and made me a scarf that would have fitted Pangur. I tucked it into the neck of my blouse and left one end sticking out, proud to display it.

I was glad when you made friends of your own age, although it took some time for you to do so. Now and then in the summer one or two small girls walked out from town to play with you after school. While I scrubbed and boiled and pushed whites around with a stick in a separate pot, I listened to the sing song of small feet melding into the ritual thud of the skipping rope and the sound of the old rhymes, "One potato, two potato, three potato, four; five potato, six potato, seven potato, more." And "Early in the morning before eight o'clock, you will hear the postman knock. Postman, postman drop your letter, lady, lady pick it up."

A game called Piggy Wiggy was played with a bit of wood that had been sharpened at both ends, one of which was hit with a stick. The person who could drive the 'Piggy' farthest won, but often not before many arguments took place. Being the boss here, you often fell out with your companions but soon made it up again. When you were on your own you kept finding things; oddly shaped pebbles or coloured leaves which you would place around Pangur's bed like offerings to a God. I suppose I did not pay enough attention to you as I was often tired out with work – there was always some job or other to be done – but at last I began to notice that you talked to yourself or crooned verses to an old rag doll I had made for you.

"Polly had a dolly that was sick, sick, sick. Send for a doctor, quick, quick, quick. Doctor, doctor shall I die? Yes my dear and so will I."

You were getting tall. Lizzie said you were outgrowing your strength. You became pale and listless and there came a time when you would not let bite nor sup pass your lips. After two days had gone by I wrapped you up in a shawl and we set off for town to visit Doctor Fitzsimmons. It was the longest journey of my life. Sheep bleated with uncomprehending woe as we passed them in the fields. Your eyes were closed to everything around you, even the black crows which seemed to follow us, supervising our journey. The doctor could find no reason for your malady and advised warmth, rest and a bottle of medicine for which I had no money. Back at home I kept you in bed, gathered rose hips and made a syrup to ease your throat. I mashed potatoes for champ and prepared other soft foods which in the end you swallowed reluctantly. At last death decided he would not have you. Emerging into the sunlight, pale as a grub from an apple, you wandered around on mouse feet, speaking in a whisper as though you were afraid death would hear and come back to claim you.

After your illness you remained quiet and uncommunicative and I began to wonder if secrets could be passed on without words. I always said that your father was a sailor who drowned at sea. I meant well for I was afraid that when you went to school and began to mix with more fortunate children they might look down on you. This had been my own fate even though my parents were married. Daddy, you said, often came to you in the dark. You could see him smiling at you but were afraid to speak in case he went away. Now you stopped talking about him and so did I.

One day when I was in town to collect washing you did not wait for me so that, as was usual, we could walk home together. I began to realise you were ashamed of me, mostly I suspect, because of my appearance and, truth to tell, my clothes were ragged and threadbare. We didn't mention this change in our routine which continued until you left school. Another day when I got home from collecting bits of wood for the fire there was a notice stuck to the door.

ANYONE WHO COMES IN HERE WILL BE SHOOTED

Writing was never your best subject and I did not draw your attention to the grammar. I called out, "You don't mean that message for me I suppose," and slipped inside. Hastily, you opened a schoolbook and pretended to read but not before I saw you slip a sheet of paper between the pages. I must confess I searched for it later but without success. Anyway I thought afterwards you were entitled to some privacy.

Tim McConville was the one you told your secrets to, sometimes I was almost jealous of him. Maybe I could have made more effort to understand you but at the end of the day I was drained with hard work, which did not get any easier as the years passed. It was a relief just to get into bed where I fell asleep almost at once. It took a long time for me to realise that with mutual consent we were walking down long avenues of silence, things of importance left unsaid.

Children grow fast without parents noticing sometimes. You with your black curly hair and serious eyes seemed more mature than most of your friends. Near the end of the school year when you were almost fourteen, you came home one evening and announced that you had finished with books and had signed up for an apprenticeship in millinery. At first I couldn't believe you had taken such a step without talking it over with me. I begged you to reconsider but I might as well have been whistling jigs to a milestone. I went to see your teacher who was just as disappointed as I was. You were she said, her brightest pupil and she had taken such pride in your achievements. She had great hopes for your future.

The milliner, Mrs Moffatt your new employer, listened to me but took no part in persuading you to think differently. Tim was sympathetic and understood my concern when he found me weeping one evening but I think he was secretly pleased as, in his eyes, further education would put you above his station. Maybe I am wrong about that. Father McManus had been moved to a different parish many miles away and Lizzie, God be good to her, was dead this three years. I had no one to turn to and it was hard for me not to feel angry.

We made the best of things after that and although you did well with Mrs Moffatt and rose to be a charge hand, I think you were disappointed that you could not get any more promotion. In time I could see that you were disappointed too in your way of life. You would sit with a faraway look in your eyes; silent, morose. Once I came in and saw that

Pangur was using his paws to scoop up and eat some of the bramble jam I had made and set to cool on the table. Although you were sitting right beside him you noticed nothing. I would have liked to have had enough money to start you up in your own business but I could scarcely make ends meet. What's the good of talking? In any case you were hedgehog tight and, try as I might, I could not manage to share anything with you but polite conversation.

The new parish priest made changes and stricter economies. He decided he could no longer pay Tim who now hung about our place unemployed and without hope of finding a job. I suspect you knew he was in love with you?

"The farmer wants a wife, the farmer wants a wife, hey ho the dearie oh, the farmer wants a wife." Tim kept repeating this silly ditty and another, "Blackberry, strawberry, gooseberry jam, tell me the name of your young man." I was ready to throw the wet washing at him. At first you merely smiled and the two of you would exchange sly glances. But after a while you too got annoyed and often told him very rudely to shut up. It was clear there was something from which I was excluded, but I was not prepared for the shock when it came. A few months after the teasing began Paddy O'Neill came to call and told me he wanted to marry you. I asked him to wait as you were young yet, just some months before your eighteenth birthday. Paddy, I think, would have been very happy to agree but I knew it was no good going against you. You wanted lots of children you said and it was better to start early. Nothing I said could make the slightest difference.

Later when Paddy was gone, I pointed out that his mother

used to hawk vegetables round the doors at the edge of the town. She had a reputation for being a bit of a nearbegone and when it came to paying she wouldn't give credit to even the poorest of the poor. You just sniffed at this and there was a more uncomfortable silence between us than there had been earlier. Then you rose one morning before I was awake, slipped out and married with only two witnesses, Tim McConville and Mary Conlon. The fine dress you made for me still hangs on the back of the door in the bedroom till this day.

Ah Margaret. How am I to describe the grief into which I fell when you left me? I have no words for it. But after a few years, one winter's evening I looked up at a pale moon and remembered that this same moon had once looked beautiful to me. The memory brought with it a sense of gratitude and I felt a small bright hope that things atween us would once again be well.

It seemed to me you were always pregnant and too busy to visit. However, at last you sent little Sheila to me once a week with a can of buttermilk and a few vegetables. It did not pass my notice that you called your first child after your Donegal grandmother. It is one of the reasons that I am encouraged to write in these notebooks. Sheila played with Pangur as you used to do. I told her stories and she was a good listener. Unlike you, she was a being made of stillness. One day our quiet was shattered when there was a loud thump and a brown moiley cow looked in at us over the half door with an expression of dumb curiosity. I got such a fright that I nearly left this world. It continued to stand there chewing its cud until Sheila offered it a few of the tops of the carrots she had brought for me. She was delighted with the creature and asked me if it could come inside. I pointed out that there would not be enough room, and she reached up a hand and rubbed its nose until it had swallowed her offerings, mooed loudly and sauntered away, its tail switching.

"Wasn't that a friendly cow to pay us a call?" she said. "I hope it will come again."

Tim McConville went away to Belfast where he at last got work, but he came to see me now and then at weekends when he returned to visit his family. He too fell in love with Sheila and often smiled at me across the hearth as she sat stroking Pangur. You will never guess how glad I was that you left the old cat with me after you married. She was the only constant companion I had until Sheila was old enough to visit me. When the creature died, Tim brought another white kitten, but I never managed to tame it. For days it would disappear and return to me with a torn ear or limping badly. It would sleep for days and at last waken to eat some food. In no time it was off again. Nevertheless it was constant in a way that the first Pangur was not. When I went into town it would stalk me until I knocked on a door to deliver the washing, then it would hide until I was ready to return, bouncing out at me from behind a wall or bush, or springing up like a tiger from the long grass. This Pangur seemed to think I needed someone to see me home safely.

I have told you little of your father. Even after all these years I find it hard to speak of him. You may, if you wish, find out more about the Foster family by looking up the church records. I believe the eldest son and his children are now living in Kilcreggan, the big house where I once worked.

I started filling in these notebooks a bit reluctantly but

began, without noticing, to enjoy the writing for its own sake. Then I realised it was making a big difference to my life. I began to look forward to my sessions with the pen. In fact, I have had great pleasure in reliving the past and it is only now that I can see that the happy times outweigh the sad ones. How can I thank you enough for that and for the gift of my grandchild Sheila?

Yesterday I asked her to buy me a packet of ink powder. This, I fear, will be the last one I will mix with water to start my scribbles again. My fingers ache and my quill sometimes falls from my hands. I write slowly and as you will see, not too clearly. I do not sleep much and sometimes in the early hours of the morning I rise out of bed, open the door and look over the field where the scarecrow once stood. Beyond this I can dimly make out the bog on my right. There at the scriach of dawn I occasionally see the luminous glow of the will-o-the-wisps. Some say they are the spirits of the dead drawing near. If so I am ready to meet them.

I leave this record mostly for you, my Margaret, but also for your children. If you care to indulge me a little, like a bairn on its birthday, then read it but do remember you have no need to take heed of the foolish ramblings of an old woman. Like the blackbird, I do not compel anyone to listen to my song.

End of Third Notebook

CHAPTER FIFTY-EIGHT

While reading the journals, Dodie experienced a strong sense of her great-grandmother's presence. It was as if Cliona had just walked into the room and was now sitting comfortably beside her, talking gently, softly, radiating a warmth that banished the cold spring air. She had sheltered Margaret and Sheila and was continuing to exert a benign influence on herself and Trish. Would she have understood her decision to leave the convent, Dodie wondered? Suddenly a wave of exquisite perfume wafted in through the open door that led to the garden. Dodie took this as a sign of approval. She sat for some time thinking, and at last decided she would try to find out more about this great-grandmother with whom she was beginning to feel such an affinity.

She was sitting on the garden bench under the cherry tree enjoying the gritty skin of a pear. The simple pleasures of seeing things grow; grass, honeysuckle, roses and cherry blossom – to which she had blinded herself of late – came back to her here in the garden. The gate creaked and, looking up, she saw Paul Murray smiling at her over the top bar.

"I'm glad to see you're relaxing a bit. My mother says

you are working yourself to the bone. She is quite worried about you."

"Don't you believe it. I've been footering about for days getting nowhere, and now as you see I'm sitting here idling my time away. Come into the house and have a cup of tea if you have some time to spare."

He followed her up the path and as they sat at the pine table in the kitchen he told her he was going to take a holiday in a few weeks, starting with a visit to Donegal. It would be his last chance to see his favourite county before going to Canada after the summer term.

"I'm planning to settle out there for good."

"My goodness, Paul, I thought nothing could coax you out of Ireland."

"Are you doing anything in the next few weeks?" he asked her hesitantly. "Would you ever think of coming with me? It would be nice to have company on my last trip before leaving the country."

"I would love to," she answered without hesitation. "I have been reading some old journals written by my great-grandmother who came from that part of Ireland. It would be interesting to see some of the places she was familiar with."

"That's settled then. We can start when you like after school closes."

She had never been a woman to make the best of herself. Now, in the mirror she could see that the last year had taken a bigger toll on her looks than she at first realised. She looked much older, although she thought that was no bad thing as she had always resented being told she appeared to be younger than she really was. It would not be fair to Paul, she decided, to appear like this in his company or in front of his friends. She told Maura she was joining her brother on this holiday and asked her to help in shopping for new clothes. Glad of an excuse to have a day away from the children, Maura whisked her off to Belfast where they found shoes and clothes that, to Dodie's surprise, although practical also made her look quite elegant. This visit, however, was not without its more grim moments. The streets were filled with soldiers in open trucks who carried guns which were trained on the pedestrians. Dodie voiced her alarm to Maura who told her almost nonchalantly that this was a feature of everyday life now in Northern Ireland and to live in at least a degree of comfort much had simply to be ignored.

It was a bright morning when they began the journey to Donegal. Paul, relaxed in jeans and sweater and Dodie in well cut trousers and a blue linen blouse.

"Is there anywhere special you want to visit?" he asked as they left the checkpoint outside Derry and headed further North.

"No place in particular but I would like to spend a little time in Dunfanaghy."

"Fine. As my mother says any road will do when you don't know where you are going. I'd like to get in a bit of fishing before we go home."

They spent the first night in a small family-run hotel where Paul was already well known, and were warmly welcomed. After a meal of local freshly caught fish they slept soundly, the waves of the Atlantic lulling them to rest. Next day was bright and the sea invited them in, but the sun had not yet had time to warm up the water. Laughing, they dressed quickly, turned on the heater in the car and drove until they found a clear patch on the side of the hill which was sheltered by rowans. Here they stopped to eat a packed lunch.

"My grandmother used to say that fairies roost in rowans," Dodie remarked idly. "When I was little I used to imagine them flying across from branch to branch in their games, sometimes playing tricks on each other and laughing, whingeing or chattering like a group of monkeys."

"The Celts, our ancestors, believed in a lot of interesting possibilities. They thought that our world and the domain of the spirits were so close in certain places that it was quite easy to stray from one to the other."

"I can understand that. When you look at the roofless houses where the dead once lived, their spirits might well return to haunt such places where they loved and brought up their children. And what about the standing stones? Do you think they house invisible fairies or maybe ghosts?"

Paul laughed. "I thought you believed implicitly in the church's teaching and were immune to such superstition."

"I am, but the past doesn't change. What changes is the way we understand things."

Dodie looked at her companion. His deep chestnut eyes were alive with interest. This encouraged her to speak of herself and her unhappiness in the convent. "For a long time I could not get it into my head that many of the nuns were immature and sometimes childish and spiteful, like youngsters. Their sacrifices, which were many, did not help them to know what the love of God was about, not that I do myself either."

"As I understand it," Paul said gravely, "the highest degree of love is love of oneself – for God's sake."

It was a relief and a delight to her to find someone she

could at last confide in and they sat in companionable silence for some minutes.

"You know," she began again, "I did really want to be one of them, singing in the choir and ceaselessly praying for all the people in the world. But I found I was not happy to be ruled by such a pitiful subjection to sometimes ignorant and deforming opinions. All the same, I did long for the certainties that were held out to me." She paused.

"As far as I am concerned," Paul said, "morality is about what is real, the truth in so far as we can recognise it. Most religions believe that they are born into a certainty that is absolute. I can't subscribe to that at all."

"I know what you mean. Viewpoints forged in a doctrinaire Catholicism."

She watched a cow steadily munching grass in a nearby field with a crow hopping familiarly down its spine.

"I was often told I thought too much, wanting to analyse everything."

"Well, if God gave us an intellect, surely he intended us to use it." Paul's eyes followed Dodie's to the grazing animal with its back passenger. "We are not like the cow or the crow who have no conscience, no self awareness. I think that self knowledge is the basis of all knowledge."

For a time they sat silent, following their own thoughts and enjoying the unexpected heat of the sun after the rain.

"Tomorrow," Paul said, "I would like to go fishing. We could head towards Dunfanaghy and while I catch a fish for our supper you might like to go and search for your ancestors."

CHAPTER FIFTY-NINE

There were many tantalising glimpses of earlier O'Donnells in the parish records of three churches in the area where she guessed her great-grandmother was born. There were seven Sheilas who had lived in the vicinity, born prior to the worst years of famine. Three had died in infancy but, in spite of narrowing down the number, she was unable to determine with any conviction which of them might have been her relative. She visited a reconstruction of the workhouse, rebuilt on the site of the old one which had been destroyed and with it the records, if indeed they ever existed. The place, although it had a forlorn air, did not bring home to her the reality of the suffering of the past, so she lost no more time in the town, and headed for the sea, found the beach and went for a walk. The head of a seal appeared close to the shore, looking at her with curious watery eyes. Moving inland she began to climb, and after an hour or so she sat down to rest. The spot she picked had a tiny stream running below a low wall. She noticed it was made of dressed stone. Large and thin slabs were held together without mortar. Instead, small stones were packed tightly between rows to hold the structure together. The remains of another similar wall ran up against the one on which she sat, making a rough rectangle. She realised it must have once been a stone cabin occupying the lee of the hill. How old it was she could not guess. Pulling away some of the grass from the lower part of one wall, she saw exposed a paved floor with hazel bushes pushing their way here and there through the cracks. In the nearby stream she watched a bird dipping its wings in the water and shaking its feathers to dry, before flying on to one of the hazels and beginning to sing. The countryside was beautiful in its desolation. There had been much hardship here even before the famine. Cliona, and indeed Margaret, had never expected life to be easy, simply that it had to be lived. Something which she herself was not very good at, she thought wryly. A slight mist came up from the sea. In a nearby field three or four donkeys stood wispily together; silent, patient. Gradually she became aware of the power of the place. She was part of it. Here for a time she could feel free from her own limitations. This must be one of those places that Paul had talked about where the spirits are most alive and accessible.

Next day they went fishing. Paul had warned her that it was a silent occupation so she set off with a book under her arm. She watched him expertly fit the bait to the hook on his line and sat by him relaxing prior to the business of casting out in search of a fish.

"The sea air is doing you good. Those ancestors of yours must be pleased that you have taken the trouble to look them up. When I catch a fish or two you must tell me how you got on."

She thought how handsome he was and wondered she had never noticed it before. Then she blushed a little, remembering how much time and trouble she had taken that morning with her hair and make-up. All the same she was not as completely at ease with him as she had been yesterday. When she brushed accidentally against his arm, did she imagine he pulled away quickly? She opened her book and tried to read but was soon caught up in the struggle to land a salmon. It was strong and resisted Paul's efforts but at last it floundered and soon lay thrashing wildly at their feet.

"By the hokey, I've caught a beauty for you, Dodie," Paul crowed. "I'm starving. Let's drive around until we find a quiet spot to eat out of doors. I have brought a bottle of white wine and all the gear necessary for cooking it is in the boot of the car." A pause. "Don't look so disbelieving, woman. I even slipped out this morning before you were up to get us some strawberries and cream."

The found a little sandy cove which extended for about a quarter of a mile before petering out into cliffs. The tantalising smell of cooking fish on Paul's portable brazier came to them as they sat sipping wine. At first he tried to persuade her to talk about her search for her ancestors but she preferred to remain quiet. After their meal they cleared away the remains and stored the utensils in the boot of the car again. Then they stretched out in the warmth of the early evening sun. It was a sheltered place and beneath them the sound of the waves, soothing and eternal, came up from below. Paul broke a long silence.

"What did you say your great-grandmother was called?"
"Cliona."
"Do you know the meaning of the name and its legend?"
She shook her head.
"Well like all good fairytales I'll start with once upon a

time…there was a king who had a beautiful daughter. She fell in love with the son of her father's greatest enemy and they were forbidden to meet. Secretly they sent messages to each other and at last decided to run away. They managed to provision a boat and off they sailed into the rough waters of the Atlantic. For many days they journeyed and at last came to anchor in a sheltered cove where they hoped to be safe from the king's men sent to pursue them. For three days they rested and, having kept a strict lookout, they could see no sign of danger. So the prince decided to go hunting, leaving the princess to take care of the boat. As she sat looking over the ocean waves, dreaming of her lover, her father's men crept up to where their craft was moored. Suddenly a noise alerted her to danger and she pushed the boat out to sea. A great storm arose, the waves so high and threatening that her pursuers were afraid to follow. One wave stronger than the rest, engulfed the little boat and overturning it, cast her into the depths. But the sea gods heard her cries, took pity on her and turned her into a wave. Every day they allowed her to rise from the deep and swim to the shore in search of her lover.

The sea was calm when the prince returned and his enemies departed. He searched in vain for his lost love day after day until at last out of the waters a wave arose and pushed its way to the shore. A voice came from within it explaining what had happened and that it was the princess in disguise and that she would come to him in the form of a wave each day, but only when he walked on the shore alone." Paul looked over the ocean.

"Of course there are several places in Ireland that claim to be the cove where the couple anchored, but I think it was right here. The name Cliona, by the way, means a wave."

"What a lovely story," Dodie cried, turning towards him. Suddenly she saw in his eyes a hunger for something that was beyond speech.

CHAPTER SIXTY

Dodie had longed for physical love before but had only been satisfied if it guaranteed a place to rest her spirit, a guarantee of gentleness. She had never wanted to be told she was beautiful, just that she was loved. A pigeon rose in the air and gave a single handclap. She reached up and touched Paul's face. He opened her blouse and tasted her skin with his tongue, then nestled his face in her hair. Cautiously at first, he kissed her mouth, then more urgently. Her arms came up round his neck and she trembled against him. He kissed her harder, indicating how much he wanted her. His mouth moved over all the parts of her body and she gasped with pleasure. Below the Atlantic continued its ceaseless labours unnoticed by either of them. After a time the waves began to groan and she felt she was being invaded by the ocean itself which was pounding her to pieces, its rhythms becoming the rhythms of their bodies. Afterwards like a tune unsung in her head she felt the separate strands of her life had come together in one harmonious whole.

She woke next morning to the sound of wheels crunching on the gravel below her window. Stretching out a hand, she was dismayed to find the place beside her empty. It was already nine-thirty; no doubt Paul had got tired of waiting for her and gone off somewhere while she had breakfast. Hadn't she heard him say he needed to fill the tank of the car with petrol? She dressed leisurely and went downstairs to the dining room. There was a note on her plate in his handwriting. Smiling she opened it and read that he had gone to say farewell to a friend in Donegal town. He didn't say when he would be back but she should go ahead and eat supper without him in case he was late. She left the note on the table while the waitress took her order. It was not until she picked up the sheet of paper again that she saw the PS at the bottom of the page. "I hope you won't mind but I think we should head for home early tomorrow as I have realised there is so much to do before leaving home. More than I appreciated before we set out."

She passed the rest of the day in a daze feeling more and more perplexed as time went slowly by and her longing for him grew greater. Was he disappointed in her? He was old-fashioned in some ways, maybe he thought she was just another young woman out for sexual adventure? She found it impossible to believe that; their lovemaking had meant something to him too, she was sure of it. She walked up and down the strand restlessly until it began to grow dark and at last returned to the hotel. She checked in at reception hoping for a message from him and turned away quickly from the look of sympathy on the girl's face as she delivered her negative answer. Without eating, she went upstairs and packed her things; then she climbed on top of the bed where she lay without undressing and without sleep through the whole of the night. The grandfather clock in the hall chimed the news that it was ten o'clock the next morning before

Paul put in an appearance. He greeted her casually and asked if she was ready to start the journey home?

All the way he was attentive but seemed to have developed a capacity for unexplained silences. It was raining and the wipers of the car came on intermittently, releasing a beam of light through the gloom that at first seemed to her to promise a gleam of hope. He made trivial remarks about the places they passed through and after a silence more prolonged than usual he began a litany of the things he had to do before leaving home. It was clear that she had no part in his plans. Twice, with great apprehension, she broached the subject of their love-making but he would not be drawn. She turned her head away from him as attempts at conversation petered out completely and the distress between them grew palpable. As they approached the outskirts of Omagh, she asked him to stop the car and put her down somewhere near the railway station, informing him she would make her own way home. He did not protest, but asked if she would not wait and have lunch with him first? She did not even reply. He lifted her bag from the car boot and as he handed it to her gripped her by the arm.

"Dodie please, let me…"

Roughly she pulled away from him and, ignoring the misery in his voice, climbed the steps to the train station.

CHAPTER SIXTY-ONE

July came and with it an unexpected heat wave, making it difficult to sleep at night. Dodie lay listening to the beating of the lambeg drums practising for the twelfth of July parades, the noise primitive, threatening. On the day itself, she watched through the window as the banner of each Orange Lodge was carried past by strongly built men. Four small boys held the gilt tasselled stays firmly in place to prevent the wind from whipping the messages from view. One scene depicted the Dutch King William wearing a plumed hat, wresting the crown from his unpopular father-in-law, James the Second. Another showed a small black boy in a turban handing a casket of jewels to Queen Victoria and underneath the words within a golden scroll 'This we will maintain'.

Later a drum major gave a performance that had delighted Dodie as a child. He threw his baton in the air, twirled it round his back, now round his head, always moving, whirling, rising, falling, never for a moment slowing down or stopping. His feet were all the time dancing as though they contained a magic which only allowed them to glance the ground before taking off again. When she was four or five years old she had tried to imitate him and was peeved to find the Protestant magic was not granted to her. The music of the pipe bands with their silver flutes came then, and was wonderfully soothing after the previous excitement. The marchers followed, mostly men but with a good sprinkling of women and children, some as young as four or five. The boys, like their fathers, wore bright orange sashes across their chests. Apart from this brilliant slash of colour the men were dressed in sober dark suits and bowler hats. They looked straight ahead without smiling, some carrying black umbrellas, as they processed through the main village street and into a field with their followers where their wives and sisters served them tea and party food, after which came lengthy speeches.

These scenes, so colourful and so seductive in childhood, now filled Dodie with depression. Past grievances have no sell-by dates. In another month Catholics too would hold commemorative marches to celebrate rebellions and martyrdoms. They were remembering ancestors who had maimed and killed each other for land or in the name of religion. Yet we come from the same brown earth, speak the same language, with the same accent, have the same sense of humour and are alike in skin colouring. But we find it impossible to take a more responsible attitude towards those who hold different opinions. We know that man landed on the moon ten years ago but what difference does that make to our thinking? Dodie had felt that somehow common sense had come to the country when the flag flew at half-mast over the city hall when Pope John Paul died in 1963 but it now seemed to her old hatreds were being stirred up more violently than ever.

A few days after she had watched the Orange marches, she overheard a conversation between two neighbours.

"When the policeman insisted I would have to get out of the car to be breathalysed, I kept him waiting as long as I could without making him suspicious. All the time I was taking deep breaths and letting them out ever so slowly. And do you know it worked. The old lungs filled up with oxygen and that did the trick. He had to let me go and I can't tell you how many I had before he stopped me."

This was a man who considered himself law-abiding, yet he and his neighbours never failed to avail themselves of a chance to get round the law. People are articulate, Dodie reflected, but mostly of a mindset that seems to believe if A is right, then B must necessarily be wrong. Was it a sort of inability to tolerate the relativity of all things human? She had encountered it in the convent too. Yet these were her own people, charming and kindly. But now she felt herself alien among them. A wide gap had opened up between the person she was and the person she had left behind. Returning had not been any kind of homecoming. She was finding it difficult to connect to the place where she was born. The village itself was familiar, in outline if not in particular. Nevertheless, she felt as though she had betrayed the place in some way. She could no longer live comfortably here, where one eye was always on the past, where people would not forget even for their own sakes; the future always based on what had gone before. The certainties of life here appalled her, yet she too had sought such certainties in the convent. She must get away for a while to think. She would go on a visit to Trish.

CHAPTER SIXTY-TWO

Trish told Dodie of her lonely years in London during the war. She spoke of how she feared the nights in the shelters listening to enemy planes droning overhead. She had met with a lot of friendliness in those days she said but also antagonism. At first she had failed to understand the reason until she heard someone say the Irish were traitors who refused to give up their ports for England's defences. It was no good trying to explain that those in the North of the country were used by the Royal Navy and that there were several military training camps. No one seemed interested in the fact that there was a division between North and South, that in effect there were two countries. She admitted to Dodie she had been too proud to go home as their mother had wanted her to. It would have been an admission of failure, she thought. Instead she continued to endure the misery and danger of the Doodle Bugs and the VIs. Dodie began to look at her sister in a new light and wondered if she would have had as much courage and perseverance in the face of such adversity.

They listened entranced as James talked at length of art in general and of early Irish art in particular.

"There is the intellectual level of course but mostly it hints of things not seen, only imagined; for instance the intertwining of circles and spirals represent eternity." He rose and fetched an illustrated volume. "Now look at this Anglo-Saxon painting of roughly the same period with its straight line thinking. It's quite different."

He introduced them to galleries and suggested books which would give them greater knowledge and was pleased they were both taking an interest in his favourite subject. One evening he said he thought the Irish were, in general, more facile in their use of the written word than in art; they were a hearing rather a seeing people. He found this difficult to understand as centuries ago their art was prolific. What had changed them? Dodie thought about it for a minute and then pointed out that their own language had been suppressed, could that have made them determined to excel in English? Anyhow she pointed out that their most famous exponent of literature, Joyce, really painted pictures in words of the inner mind.

"Yes I do think this has something to do with the loss of our language and the imposition of a foreign one," Trish said thoughtfully.

Dodie grimaced. "I don't know about that but I do know we are trying to keep our past in our present and most of us are pretty garrulous about it."

These exchanges brought the three of them closer and the sisters appreciated how James shared his knowledge about art, giving them a deeper understanding of their mother.

When they talked about their early years, Dodie was amazed at the different memories they had of the same event. When she spoke of her father's death, she commented on how Aunt Lily had made her kiss the face of the corpse and she was horrified to feel a cold sculpture against her lips. Trish insisted that this could not have been the case as she had been sent to stay with Maura's parents and did not come home until after the funeral. Dodie disagreed, saying the memory was so vivid it must be true. Trish said her memory was more likely to be genuine as she was a teenager at the time and Dodie just a child. In the end they agreed to differ and Dodie did not try to bring any other reminiscences to the fore; nor remind her sister that she had been a strait-laced young lady at one time. In her mind she had a picture of the day she had tried to persuade Trish to buy some Evening in Paris perfume or Tangee lipstick. It was the sort of thing that the older sisters of her friends allowed them to try out, but Trish's answers to such pleas were always, "Do you think I can do a better job on myself than God?"

Well it was clear that James had done a good job on her sister's looks. Nearing thirty, she appeared much younger and after the birth of the baby her figure had regained its former elegance with help from the exercises which James had suggested she undertake. As Dodie came to know him better, he confided in her that he guessed Trish had been a shy girl and had unfortunately grown into a very reticent woman, beautiful but lacking in self-confidence. He thought she was unfortunate. Life which he himself was able to take in his stride he said, seemed unnecessarily difficult for her. He found it hard to love someone who did not love herself. It required constant reassurance on his part to make her feel of any worth and he found that a little wearing at times. Dodie agreed with most of what he was saying and let him know that she was appreciative of what he was doing for her sister. She watched fascinated, as Trish learned to fight back and began to understand the struggle her sister had been through. She could see how she had battled with her timidity and dependence and realised that at last she was emerging with an ability to express a belief in herself. Occasionally after an argument with James, she would resort again to making lists but the need was diminishing and anyway Dodie thought, a need is not so great as a compulsion.

She had been critical of the relationship, thinking that there had been a whittling away of the truth until they had found themselves somehow in a sort of safety zone. Was this true of all marriages? She could not believe her sister had married for love. Her mother's marriage, she reckoned, was also one of convenience, otherwise why would Sheila have married a man so much older than herself? But it had turned out well and anyway what did she know of love or marriage?

Little David and she became firm friends. He wanted to share everything with her including the biscuit he would remove from his mouth and offer with a dribbling smile. She paid a visit to Veronica Wright who received her warmly and offered a place to stay should she decide to return to London. The day before she left she spoke to Trish of the reasons she felt that would prevent her from staying in Ireland.

"I'm sure they are what is causing Paul Murray to take himself off to Canada. Maybe you are both seeking the same things but in different ways."

"I didn't know you were in touch with him." Dodie's tone was suspicious.

"Oh we send each other scraps of information now and again written on Christmas or birthday cards. By the way did you enjoy your holiday with him in Donegal? I forgot to ask about it."

Dodie had deliberately avoided the episode, feeling unable to confess the disaster it had been. Now she was uncomfortable not knowing what he had told Trish about it.

"What had he to say?"

"Only that he went fishing and you spent time searching for your ancestors in the remote regions of the mountains. He also mentioned that the holiday was cut short for some reason."

Dodie could hear the curiosity in her voice and again in spite of their new closeness she could not bring herself to talk about the depressing effect it had on her.

When they were saying goodbye, James astonished them. "May you cross the threshold of heaven before you know you are dead." Dodie asked when he had made that one up but he assured them he had heard it in a pub one night. Trish informed him he was like the early Irish invaders who were said to have become more Irish than the Irish themselves. They kissed and she was still smiling as she entered the departure lounge in Heathrow Airport.

CHAPTER SIXTY-THREE

Dodie stood at a window overlooking the main village street. She watched some children skipping and heard their chant.

"Silk, satin, velvet, cotton, taffeta, muslin, rags." and "Jump to the East, jump to the West, tell me the name of the one you love best."

Wryly she remembered the days when she had skipped with Paul's sister, Maura. Some things had remained the same. Much of what she loved was still here but now she was impatient for new horizons. There was no reason to chain herself to the landscape into which she had been born. Nevertheless her life, she felt, was like a knitted garment that had unravelled, and could easily spring back into its original grooves. She remembered Paul's mother had said, "When you don't know where you're going, any road will do."

But that was not enough. Already she had taken too many wrong turnings. She wished she could be more like her mother and put her trust in something she did not see or feel. Sheila believed in her religion as profoundly as the facts of birth and death. Was it because of this she had enjoyed such peace in her lifetime, always taking as much pleasure in the small things as in the greater miracles?

The garden to which she had attended before her trip to Donegal needed more work to be done to it if it was to be shown to advantage to prospective buyers. Now she tackled the undergrowth, ripping up handfuls of grass and weeds, hacking at brambles and clearing paths. At night, physically tired, she slept soundly until some sort of healing took place within her and at last the silence of her old home matched the silence inside her. She heaped up a pile of rubbish and set it alight, and as she watched it burn she blew on a spent dandelion. "Asia, Africa, America, Australia," she murmured. The dandelion down was a judgement of chance. She would not float aimlessly like the tiny little parachutes seeking random resting places, she decided. She had changed. Once, she felt she had been a root underground but was now a branch fighting its way upward into the light.

Often her thoughts returned to her great-grandmother's journal. Cliona perhaps had few choices in her life but she did make one important decision. Her grandmother Maggie had spurned the past, rejecting her mother's sacrifices but she too had built a life of her own. Sheila, unlike both of them, had refused to be defined by her children. Standing before her own portrait, she saw the blue and purple colours under the eyes that were deep and questioning. How well her mother had known her restless mind. She thought of her trip to Donegal. She had gone in search of her family but had used the occasion to exploit personal feelings instead. She felt now she had come to terms with Paul's rejection of her and she told herself a woman at the end of love is not at the end of her tether. She would go back to London, study, get a degree and take up a new life.

One evening she took a walk through the fields where the sheep were tugging at the grass, their teeth making a ripping sound as it parted from the ground. She reached the river. Willows dipped their tresses in the water, swans surrounded by ducks sailed serenely on the surface and a dark-feathered moorhen chugged fussily upstream. After the rain blackberries were beginning to mould and the birds had now abandoned them in favour of hips and haws. On wires overhead, swallows congregated chattering furiously, impatient to be off on their migration. Their chirping was joined occasionally by the chuckle of the waterfowl.

It was here Paul found her. He spoke inconsequently at first and she could see how hard he was trying to overcome the awkwardness that lay heavily between them. She was determined to be gracious to him. She had conquered her disappointment, was in charge of her feelings. She wished to show him that she was willing to forget. After all he was a family friend and he had listened to her when she needed someone to help her clarify her muddled thinking. And she might never see him again after his departure in a few weeks time.

The damp had tempted a snail out from its hiding place. It crawled about waving two horns in the air. A thrush swooped down and grabbed it in its beak and then began to tap the shell smartly on a stone. The clear sound drew their eyes in its direction and they watched as the bird ate greedily, its feathers ruffling slightly in the breeze.

"Dodie," Paul began, "I need to tell you how grateful I am for what we shared in Donegal and I hope you will some day be able to forgive me for taking advantage of you when you were so miserable after leaving the convent, and the death of your mother."

It all came out in a rush and she could see that he was making a tremendous effort to remain calm but he was shaking violently and his voice was a croak. There was a painful silence and then he almost whispered, "Come with me to Canada."

The thrush having dined, flew to the top of a tree and began to sing.